HAVANA HIGHWIRE

Also by John Keyse-Walker

The Teddy Creque mysteries

SUN, SAND, MURDER
BEACH, BREEZE, BLOODSHED
PALMS, PARADISE, POISON *

* available from Severn House

HAVANA HIGHWIRE

John Keyse-Walker

SEVERN
HOUSE

First world edition published in Great Britain and the USA in 2022
by Severn House, an imprint of Canongate Books Ltd,
14 High Street, Edinburgh EH1 1TE.

Trade paperback edition first published in Great Britain and the USA in 2022
by Severn House, an imprint of Canongate Books Ltd.

severnhouse.com

British Library Cataloguing-in-Publication Data
A CIP catalogue record for this title is available from the British Library.

ISBN-13: 978-0-7278-5073-7 (cased)
ISBN-13: 978-1-4483-0691-6 (trade paper)
ISBN-13: 978-1-4483-0690-9 (e-book)

All Severn House titles are printed on acid-free paper.

Typeset by Palimpsest Book Production Ltd.,
Falkirk, Stirlingshire, Scotland.
Printed and bound in Great Britain by
TJ Books, Padstow, Cornwall.

To J.C. Wm. Tattersall
Special Agent, US Air Force Office
of Special Investigations (1951–1954)

ONE

I never saw the punch coming. Part of the reason was because the Cuban boys would never think of throwing a punch at an American. They are always polite, insistent but polite, in a way that bouncers in the States never are. See, they never know if the American they are trying to escort out the door of the club or casino or brothel is connected to the Syndicate. But they do know that if the drunken or belligerent American is a mob associate, even a low-level one, rough treatment of him will, at best, cost their job, and, at worst, find them stuffed in a fifty-five-gallon drum with a .38 slug behind their ear and no one to bring home the beans and rice to *mamacita* and the little kiddies. So, I never expected the punch.

That was my mistake. A private investigator, which is what I call myself and what the Cuban government license issued at a cost of five pesos over the table and a one-hundred-peso bribe says I am, should always expect trouble in the form of physical violence. Even on a simple case of catching a philandering husband in the act, a PI's bread and butter and the type of case I had expected to finance my permanent vacation in the land of sun, balmy breezes, rum, gambling, and compliant señoritas.

The problem was the photograph. The client, you see, always wants a photograph, never just a report. They have this masochistic need to see hubby *in flagrante* whatever with that floozy, tart, hussy, whore, tramp – pick your favorite description for the other woman, who is usually just trying to earn a living or have a little fun.

This client, my second referral from a prominent Midwest detective agency, had insisted on a photo to confirm her suspicion that her beloved was doing her wrong. 'He's cheatin' on me, I know it, but my lawyer told me I gotta have a picture of the weasel doin' it to come out right in the divorce,' her voice whined over the line from the far-off cornfields of Iowa.

'If you don't get me a picture, I don't get as much from the judge in the property settlement, and I don't pay, got it?'

'Yeah, I got it,' I said. 'I should be able to get you a picture, no problem.'

'OK. Charlie is flyin' to Havana on the tenth of the month. He says it's for business, to open the Cuban market for American brassieres his company makes.' I could hear her snap the gum she was chewing all the way from Dubuque. 'I asked if I could go with him and he said, no, it was just goin' to be a bunch of dull meetings, I'd be bored. Then I find the tickets. That's right, tickets, as in more than one, with the second one for his executive secretary, Miss Bouchard. The tramp. You gotta get that picture.'

'No sweat. It'll be in living color,' I'd promised, fool that I am.

Charlie from Dubuque had proven himself a capable and cautious adversary. I was in the airport arrivals terminal when he and Miss Bouchard – a red-haired stunner – deplaned. Charlie wasn't much to look at, overweight and myopic, but he was cagey. The two of them kept their distance from each other in baggage claim and took separate cabs from the airport. I followed hers in a cab of my own and ended up where most Americans end up, at the Hotel Nacional. She marched briskly inside and was gone in the elevator by the time I paid my fare and followed.

In my short time in Havana, I'd already made a valuable acquaintance at the Nacional – Alvaro, the front desk clerk. An American sawbuck slipped across the polished mahogany bought me a look at the hotel register. Charlie and his secretary were signed in as mister and missus under his name. I settled down in the lobby – the sawbuck bought me an undisturbed seat in addition to the peep at the register – and waited for the four hours that they presumably spent doing the horizontal hula until nightfall. At seven, Charlie stepped lively through the lobby to a cab and departed. The charming Miss Bouchard emerged five minutes later and was picked up by Charlie's cab, which had doubled back. Thus, no photo opportunity in the Nacional's lobby.

I hailed another cab and we cruised a few cars behind,

tailing them along the Malecón and over to the Capri, where Charlie and Miss Bouchard went inside. I followed at a discreet distance. The happy couple made a beeline to the roulette table, blending in with all the other couples consisting of older, portly, Anglo men and younger, beautiful, well-endowed women, Cuban and American.

After an expensive hour at the wheel, Charlie and Miss Bouchard moved to a table near the dance floor and ordered drinks. While the band of frill-shirted local cats played mambo after mambo, the happy couple imbibed Cuba libre after Cuba libre, with the end result being a lessening of their guard to the point where she climbed onto his lap and applied her tongue to his ear. My chance for the damning photo had arisen.

I tried to be circumspect. My Comet Five 12mm camera wasn't large but there was the matter of focus. I was at the bar, which was crowded but not overwhelmed. When the barman was down bar attending to a particularly demanding customer, I slipped the Comet out of my pocket and up to my eye to focus. Charlie chose that very moment to shift his attention from his ear-swabbing sweetheart and look straight at me. The band chose the same very moment to take a breather between tunes.

'Hey,' Charlie said, loudly enough for me, a few surrounding tables, and a local in a tuxedo lingering at the other end of the bar to hear. 'Hey, you! Wadda ya think you're doin'? No pictures of me and my girl.'

I shot a few fast frames, figuring it was the best I'd be able to do now that the cat was out of the bag. Charlie popped his flame-tressed date from his lap and headed across the dance floor toward me. The Cuban in the tux, one of the house men, did the same. They arrived at the identical time, bumping into each other in the process.

'Excuse me, sir,' the Cuban apologized to Charlie. He had slicked-back hair, a veneer of unctuous politesse, and the lightness and balance of a boxer. A welterweight, I guessed.

Charlie ignored the bouncer, addressing me. 'Gimme that film, asshole.'

'Oh, I'm sorry. I can't do that. I promised my mama some

pictures of my Cuban vacation when I get back to Dayton,' I said.

Charlie pushed toward me. Now that he was close, I saw that he was a head taller and fifty pounds heavier than me. And steaming mad.

The bouncer, like most of those in his profession, began with diplomacy. 'Please, gentlemen, relax. Is there a problem here?'

The house man's approach seemed to work to defuse the situation. Charlie took a step back and undoubled his fists. 'Damn right there's a problem. This asshole's took my picture and I don't want my picture took.'

By then I'd slipped the Comet back into my coat pocket. 'Sorry, mister. No harm intended.'

You could see the light bulb go on above Charlie's head, just like in the cartoons. 'Say, what are you, some kind of peeper? A private dick? Did Annabel hire you?'

Bingo, Charlie, I wanted to say, but the house man preempted any remark. 'Are you a private investigator, señor? If so, I will need to see your credentials.'

'I don't want to see his damn license,' Charlie fumed. 'I want that film, and now.'

I figured I'd do better with the polite bouncer and turned in his direction. The whole vignette had brought the band, and the dancers, and some of the action at the nearby gaming tables to a halt. Since I had whatever photos of Charlie and the voluptuous Miss Bouchard that I was going to get, I figured I'd better play along and get out the door with a minimum amount of disruption of the Capri's flow of sin and cash. I spoke to the bouncer. 'I'll be glad to provide my credentials.' I reached into my jacket pocket.

That was when the punch hit. It wasn't from the direction where Charlie stood, huffing and frustrated. It came from an unexpected quarter, my blind side, and it was a doozy. No Hollywood roundhouse aimed at a chin and easily parried, the blow hit my ear and the side of my face with the force of a Spanish fighting bull having a bad day. I dropped to my knees, dazed but congratulating myself on staying conscious, when the second punch came. No slouch, the guy delivering the belts put number two in exactly the same place as the first, for maximum effect in both pain and damage.

I can vouch for the pain because it seared through my ear, head, and jaw like hot lava. I can vouch for the damage because it put me out like a light.

TWO

There was an odor of cloves and cinnamon, with a distinct and recognizable earthiness in the background. The fuzzy edges of my brain stumbled for a moment on the scent and then declared 'bay rum' in recognition. Spurred on by the success of this identification, the brain pushed on to an association. My old chum from the Air Force, Ray Weltman, wore bay rum cologne. What was he doing here? And where was here?

I squinted both eyes open then; they had apparently been closed, though I had no recollection of closing them. The collision of light with my optic nerves brought pain, a sharp, tearing agony pinballing around inside my cranium. Despite the pain, my addled brain, with wavering sharpness and much effort, performed another feat of association. It remembered several recent events. The punch, or rather, punches. Charlie from Dubuque and Miss Bouchard, his lady friend. The polite Cuban bouncer. My brain willed my eyes to focus and there he was. He had a paper in his hands. My PI license.

The polite bouncer was standing sideways. Well, not really sideways but at ninety degrees to my field of vision. Now that pain and sight had kicked in, other senses followed suit. I heard a loud ringing in one ear. I tasted sand, the funk of stale beer, and cigarette ash, and realized that my tongue was lolling against an infrequently cleaned sisal rug.

'What's it say, Osvaldo?' The voice asking the question was behind me. I rolled my head toward the words and my vision narrowed almost to a pinpoint, then expanded wide when the adrenaline from a latent burst of pain kicked in.

'He is a private investigator, license issued by La Habana province.' Osvaldo, unruffled in his tuxedo, directed his words over and behind me to the man who was the source of both the voice and the bay rum scent.

'The hell you say! We pay off all the cops and now we

have private dicks snooping around the place. How does this shit happen?' Bay Rum asked. Rhetorically, I guess, because Osvaldo and another man in the room, represented in my line of sight by a set of brown and white wingtips below brown pinstriped trouser legs, offered no answer.

A wave of nausea swept over me. I was unable to suppress a groan. The groan brought me unwanted attention from Bay Rum.

'You puke on my carpet, asshole, and I'll let Larry have some more fun with you,' Bay Rum said from above like the Voice of Doom. Larry, I guessed, was associated with the wingtip-pinstripe combo that quickly moved to fill my field of vision.

'On yer feet, shamus.' Larry hauled me up by the lapels of my once-white linen suit to face Bay Rum behind a battered desk. I assumed the room that contained the desk, myself, and Bay Rum *et al.* was the casino office and was surprised by its small size. Then again, maybe it wasn't the office. Maybe it was just the room where they brought people to beat them up.

Bay Rum eyed me. 'What's your name?'

'Henry Gore.' They had my license, so Bay Rum already knew.

'You a private dick, like the paper says?'

'Yeah.'

'What are you doin' here in my casino?'

'I'm on a job.'

'Against the casino?' There was so much menace in the way Bay Rum put the question, I couldn't conceive of any sane man answering it in the affirmative.

'No.'

'Who then?'

'Just that sportsman, the one complaining about his picture being taken.'

Bay Rum raised an enquiring eyebrow to his minions. Osvaldo provided the explanation. 'He was taking a photograph of a couple of patrons and the man objected.'

Bay Rum shifted back to me. 'Why you in the Capri takin' pictures of people don't want their picture took?'

'The sportsman is traveling with a lady not his wife. His wife wanted me to document the fact.'

'That's what this is about? Jesus Christ, Gore, how long you been in this town?'

I knew if I was going to catch any kind of break here, an honest answer to that question was probably the only way. 'About a month.'

'A month.' Bay Rum was incredulous. 'You been walkin' around Havana with your eyes closed during that month, Mr Private Dick? Ain't you noticed during that month that this town is all about sportsmen or husbands or pussy chasers or whatever you call 'em comin' down here to get away from Peoria or Pittsburgh and their wives and girlfriends? To whore and drink and gamble until they can't stand up? Ain't you noticed that it's the business of this town, and the fine establishments in it like the Capri, to provide a place to do that, without pryin' eyes reporting it back home to the wives and girlfriends those sportsmen come down here to get away from? I'll put it to you simple, since it seems you can't see what's right under your nose. Guys like you sniffin' around here disturbing my customers is bad for business. I'm a reasonable man and a nice guy, so I'm gonna give you a break this time, but let me make it clear so you can get it through your dense noggin – me and my partners, who have business interests in almost all of this town's fine entertainment establishments, do not want our guests' enjoyment disturbed or distracted. We don't want them trailed, photographed, approached, or admonished for their behavior, moral or immoral. That applies not only to the Capri, but to all of my and my partners' business establishments. If you ever do what you did here tonight again, I won't be so reasonable. Your PI license might get revoked. Permanently, *capisci*?'

'Yeah, I understand.'

'Good, Henry Gore. Larry, escort Mr Gore out. The back way.'

Larry smiled, revealing, of all things, a set of braces on some of the worst-looking teeth I'd ever seen. 'Hard or soft, boss?'

'Have your fun, Larry, to help Henry Gore's memory.'

THREE

Larry's idea of fun was to pitch me headlong into the black darkness behind the Capri, plant his brown and white wingtips in my gut a couple of times while I was down, and finish with another blackout-inducing wallop to the side of my head. Up to then he'd seemed a decent sort, even returning my camera to me after stripping out the film and crumpling it in his big hairy paw.

I ended up in the same resting position as I had in Bay Rum's office, face down with tongue extended to savor the taste of the surface Larry had chosen as the cradle of my repose, the four-hundred-year-old cobblestones of the alley behind the Capri. My first sensation on awakening from my involuntary nap was the appealing taste of rotting vegetables, horse dung, and my own blood. My second sensation was of small hands at my shoulder, struggling to roll me over, finally succeeding, and then frisking through my jacket.

I still hadn't opened my eyes when I caught the hand removing my wallet by the wrist. The hand's owner grappled gamely but was no match for my strength and bulk, even in my debilitated state.

I willed my eyelids apart and saw, for the first few seconds, only the brilliant stars above me in the velvet tropical night. I shifted my gaze to the wiggling prey I had captured using my wallet for bait and was greeted by a wizened face, indistinct in the lightless alley. An old man, trying to roll me like a drunk, I thought, but the figure shifted from shadow to starlight as it struggled and I saw it was a boy of maybe fourteen or fifteen. He was small – no, stunted, really – and wrinkly-thin, his withered look the product of hunger bordering on starvation, a not uncommon appearance for many of the street kids in Havana.

The kid stopped struggling for a second and relaxed, causing me to do the same. I realized my mistake too late. He twisted and pulled free but not before I was able to snatch my wallet back.

'Beat it,' I slurred, as the kid broke away. But he didn't run, only retreated a few steps into a shadow against the Capri's back wall, lingering there like a vulture at the edge of the highway, waiting to see if I would scramble to my feet and move or expire into a convenient meal.

I sat up. The world spun, then stabilized. I did a quick inventory. Warm blood trickled from my ear. A molar was loose on the same side as my bleeding ear. My guts felt . . . well, they felt like they had been stomped on. I hadn't been beat up since grade school and never by a professional. I ached all over, confirming Larry's skill at his chosen vocation.

'You might as well get lost, kid,' I said. 'I ain't gonna croak, so you can't steal my wallet.' The kid just squatted there on his heels, thinking, analyzing, calculating. His eyes glittered in his old-man face. You could see the wheels turning.

'My sister, she a virgin. Very boo-de-ful. Only thirteen,' the kid finally piped up. 'She blow you for one peso, fuck you for two. You like, mister? Very boo-de-ful.'

'Kid, can't you see I just had the crap beat out of me? I'm in no mood or shape for that kind of thing. And your sister shouldn't be selling blowjobs and you certainly shouldn't be hawking her virtue.' The last I added as an almost-puritanical afterthought.

'Oh, you like boys, mister? I got this friend, Rodrigo, he a boo-de-ful boy, he . . .'

'No, I don't like boys.' I cut off the kid's sales pitch sharply. 'Can't you see I'm hurt. Go away.'

'You need help, mister? I help you get home, one peso only. I am the best helper in Havana, all Cuba, you see?'

The kid's persistence was kind of appealing, now that he'd gotten away from trying to entice me to commit abominable crimes against children. Still, it had only taken me a few days after I arrived in Cuba to learn not to trust Havana's street kids when a cute, curly-haired eight-year-old 'accidentally' ran into me while chasing a soccer ball on the Malecón. I didn't realize he'd picked my pocket until I got home. It was a cheap lesson, I guess. He only got a couple Cuban pesos and fifteen American dollars, and I got an abiding distrust of Cuba's youth. I ignored the old-man kid and tried to get up.

I did all right until I put weight on my right leg, which uncooperatively buckled at the knee and sent might-be-broken darts of agony into my already agonized brain. Apparently Wingtip Larry's toss of Mama Gore's son onto the cobblestones had landed me on that knee.

'You see, Joe, you need help,' the kid said. 'I a good helper, the best.'

'I don't need help,' I grunted. 'And the name ain't Joe.'

My street-urchin pal sensed that he had cracked my anti-social facade. 'My name is Benito Francisco Echayabal y Fernández-García.' I must have looked incredulous at the extended moniker. 'But my friends call me Benny. You can call me Benny, mister . . .?'

I tried ignoring the kid, and put weight on the bad leg until I forced out a grimacing, 'Ow.' Benny scampered to my side and planted himself in the right place to support me, kind of like a human cane.

'OK, kid. Benny. I'll bite.' I placed my hand on his shoulder. The relief to my knee was sufficient to allow me to concentrate on my other injuries. I dabbed at my bleeding ear with a handkerchief. The support was suddenly removed and I almost went down.

'One peso, mister.' Benny's eyes were steely now, insisting on the bargain.

'When I get home,' I said.

He stepped away and crossed his arms. I balanced on my good leg like a beaten-up Karl Wallenda.

'OK, OK, kid. Here's your peso,' I said, sliding the muddy-gray banknote out of my wallet. I held it out to Benny, judging the odds at eighty–twenty that the kid would snatch the bill from my hand and sprint into the night. After all, to that point, everyone I had encountered in the tropical paradise that is Fulgencio Batista's Cuba had the morals of a whorehouse madam and the scruples of a grifter. Why should I expect this poor kid to be any different?

Benny took the money and didn't disappear into the night. Instead, he rubbed it with his thumb and forefinger in the same

manner all Cuban merchants use to detect the greasy
counterfeits that circulate everywhere in Havana. Satisfied, he
planted himself next to me.

'Which way, boss?'

'Henry,' I said. 'Calle J y Calle 21.'

'OK, Mister Genry,' Benny said, and started us on the three
and a half block journey to the place I call home in Cuba, my
walk-up apartment over the Panaderia Casa Rojas.

FOUR

My apartment on Calle 21 is not like I expected it would be when I decided to move to Cuba. I had expected beauty, and luxury, and languid late afternoons lazing in the cool shade on a tiled veranda, a rum drink and a sultry Cuban sweetheart close at hand. True, there is beauty – the fiery cascade of bougainvillea clinging to the cast-iron rail of the narrow balcony outside the window of my bedroom-living-room-kitchen-office. There is luxury – the luxury of fresh *pastelitos de guayaba* and espresso for breakfast, the smoking-hot bitter-and-sacchariferous brew providing the perfect counterpoint to the flaking pastry enfolding the carnival-red gumminess of the guava-paste filling.

But there is ugliness and poverty, too. My mean little flat has no bath, not even a sink. I wash and take care of other needs in a toilet room with a sink shared with the bakery on the ground floor. My neighbors and my neighborhood are poor, with rundown housing and equally rundown mothers and fathers getting by on the pittance that they earn cleaning hotel rooms and trimming hedges for the American gangsters and corrupt Cuban politicos who suck all the wealth from the country. As an American, they think me rich, because I have two suits, a pair of shoes, and a livelihood where your money isn't earned with your back.

Or on your back. The last part of my Cuban fantasy, that exotic girl, she of dark skin and liquid eye, compliant but still clinging to large portions of her innocence, is nowhere to be found in Havana, I have learned. Purity, chastity, even simple discretion have been sold into whoredom in this town. You can get a 'trip around the world' for a dollar; a threesome with your choice of brunette, false blonde, or bottle redhead in any permutation; and all the whips, chains, spanking, and dominance you could ever desire or tolerate, but it is impossible to find what my mother would call 'a nice girl' anywhere in town.

'OK, Benny, this is it,' I said at the bottom of the stairway to my flat. It was three in the morning and the lights were on in the *panaderia*. Bakers start their days early.

'You need more help tomorrow?' Benny said expectantly.

'No, kid. I'll make it just fine from here on out.' I followed with an attempt to climb the stairs that would have been laughable if it hadn't been so agonizing. Benny obliged by getting me the rest of the way to my door.

'*MERCADO Y GORE. INVESTIGADORES PRIVADOS. INVESTIGACIONES CONYUGALES, NAVIAZGOS, LOCALIZ-ATIÓN DE PERSONES, EMPRESARIALES,*' Benny read aloud from the placard outside my door as I fumbled my key into the lock. 'Are you Mercado or Gore, Genry?'

'Gore.' I was impressed that the kid could read.

'You need some help with your *investigaciones*? I can help you with your investigations. I the best *investigadore* in Havana.' I was fast learning this kid was the best at – you guessed it – everything.

'Sorry, Benny, we're not hiring right now. Thanks for the help getting home.' I closed the door none too ceremoniously in Benny's expectant face. Five minutes and four aspirins later, I kicked off my shoes and fell into bed, hoping my aches and pains would be gone in the morning.

FIVE

A short four hours after retiring for the night, the tropic sun came blazing through the magenta riot of flowers outside my window and struck me in the eyes with all the subtlety that Wingtip Larry had used on the side of my head the evening before. The soreness from Larry's ministrations had not departed overnight; if anything, it had doubled and redoubled, to the point where I considered more aspirin and opted for something stronger.

Unlike so many *norteamericanos* in Cuba, I was not a morning drinker but I considered my current condition to provide an exception to that rule and shuffled to my sidebar, which with my bed, desk, and a single chair make up the entire furnishings of my apartment. It took a few seconds of searching to find a clean glass among the half dozen adorning the bar top, during which time I considered drinking from the bottle. Deciding against barbarity, I picked out a glass that passed for unsullied, poured four fingers of Matusalem rum from the half bottle that comprised my remaining bar inventory, and drank it off.

The haze of the rum took the edge off my pain and some of the brightness out of the incoming sun. I was teetering back to my bed when I heard a knock at my door. I opened it to find Señor Rojas, my downstairs neighbor and landlord, with a tray of cream-cheese *pastelitos* and black coffee.

'This *esqueleto rumbero* says you ordered breakfast,' Rojas growled. His mood was not improved by the fact that I was a week overdue with the rent.

'*Esqueleto rumbero*?'

'It means "dancing skeleton."' Rojas stepped aside to reveal a bright-eyed Benny.

'We – I mean you – need breakfast to help get your strength back, Genry.' Why hadn't a dog followed me home? It would have been simpler.

Rojas barged past me, pushed the dirty glasses aside, and thumped the tray onto the sidebar.

'I'm afraid, Señor Rojas, I'm a little short on cash,' I said.

Making martyr eyes, Rojas said, 'You can pay me when you pay the rent.' He was out the door and gone almost before he finished his sentence, undoubtedly hoping to avoid me asking for anything else on credit.

Benny lingered at the threshold. On the sidebar, inviting wisps of steam arose from the chipped coffee cup. The ubiquitous bakery scent, usually nothing more than olfactory background music, was multiplied by the pile of *pastelitos* there.

'Did you sleep on the landing last night, kid?'

Benny nodded. 'It was not cold. I thought you might need something, Genry.'

'You hungry, Benny?'

'*Sí.*'

I shared out the food between the two of us, and poured half the coffee into my breakfast rum glass, passing the other half over to Benny. He wolfed his share of the pastries before I had my second bite. In my defense, though, the loose molar slowed me considerably.

While I chewed – left side only – I pondered my fate. Now that I had been made by Charlie and the lovely Miss Bouchard, there wouldn't be any other chances to catch them in public. Nothing for the two of them but nookie and room service in their suite at the Nacional from here on out, I guessed. That would mean providing only a written report, *sans* photographs, to my client, Annabel. She would likely pay something for the report, even though not obligated, but certainly not enough to keep me afloat for long. Worse, my formula for a happy and easy existence of spying on philandering husbands was now all but impossible. And all I had wanted to do was get away from the cold.

I was born in the cold, on January 12, 1930, in Warsaw, Indiana. I passed the winters of my youth on the dreary, frozen plains of Indiana. I was a good kid, no trouble to my parents, a decent athlete in school, a capable student. No great shakes at anything, really, but very good at getting by at everything.

I passed the winters of my college years on the dreary, frozen shores of Lake Michigan, at the University of Chicago. When I graduated with a degree in English History, I faced the end of my draft deferment and the prospect of a stint doing Uncle Sam's bidding on the dreary, frozen battlefields of Korea.

This did not appeal to me. While there was no way to completely avoid my obligation to my country, I believed it might be possible to avoid the mud, brutal cold, and bloody ground combat taking place in the far east if I wasn't drafted into the Army. Following this logic, I enlisted in the fledgling US Air Force.

Long story short, my college degree landed me in something called the Office of Special Investigations, a kind of Air Force version of the FBI. I dodged Korea and was posted as the sole OSI agent at Presque Isle Air Force Base in Aroostook County, Maine.

For three years, I prevented the Soviets from conducting espionage in the Maine woods and did background checks on the sons and daughters of potato-farmers who wanted to work on the base.

Overall, I didn't have it bad. Certainly not as bad as the boys in Korea. I was bored, yes, and cold, but no one was shooting at me.

Then my parents were killed by a drunk driver. I was granted emergency leave for the funeral and sought a discharge to assume care of my little sister Janet. Uncle Sam had other ideas. As a trained counterespionage officer, I was apparently too valuable to be released from my duties, even though I was applying my training where the chances of espionage were the same as the chances of porcine flight. Janet was sent off to live with our Uncle Pete and Aunt Ruth in New Jersey.

When my stint in the Air Force ended, I traveled to New Jersey to see Janet, Uncle Pete, and Aunt Ruth. Janet had blossomed as a teen; the kid sister I'd last seen when we laid Mom and Dad to rest was starting to become a woman. She and Aunt Ruth had formed a bond and, in the matter of a few days, I knew that with her and Uncle Pete was where Jan should stay. I set off on my own, to Cuba, to get warm once and for all.

*   *   *

'Are you OK, Genry?' Benny's old-man eyes said he knew I was not.

'Yeah, kid, I'm fine.'

'Then why you stop eating?'

'Just thinking about how I'm going to eat from here on.'

'You are a rich American. You have no worries.'

I guess I was rich in Benny's eyes. I changed the subject. 'Hey, don't you have somewhere to go, something to do? What about that sister of yours? Don't you have to take care of her?'

'You mean the sister I try to sell to give you a blowjob?' A sly smile passed over Benny's face. 'She is not my sister.'

'Do you have a sister?' I asked.

Benny perked up, perhaps thinking that now I'd had some time to recover I would be in the mood for paid female companionship.

'I don't want a blowjob. Got it, kid?'

'OK, Genry.'

'So, do you have a sister who needs you?'

'No, Genry.'

'Then just who was going to supply the blowjob you were trying so hard to sell me?'

'I just get the closest . . . evening lady . . . if someone say they want my sister. If the lady sell a blowjob, she give me ten centavos. Twenty if she sell a fuck.' Benny described this as normally as if he were describing having a paper route. 'So, Genry, you need money. I know how to make money. I am the best in Havana at making money. We could be partners, Genry.'

'Thanks, kid,' I said. 'But I already got a partner.' Which reminded me that I did. 'Tell you what, Benny. You can run some errands for me.'

'You pay?'

'Sure, Benny, I'll pay.' And I sat down at my desk to scribble a note to the Mercado half of the firm of Mercado y Gore, Investigadores Privados.

SIX

I had to write a note to my partner, Ramón 'Moncho' Mercado, because he didn't have a telephone. Odd, you say? Why would a private investigator not have a telephone, an item so useful for the receiving of tips, the gathering of information, the acceptance of contacts from potential and current clients? In the case of Moncho, it was because the presence of a telephone might cause him to become involved in work, a circumstance he abhorred and tried studiously to avoid.

I did not know of Moncho Mercado's aversion to good old-fashioned labor at the time we became partners. I hooked up with him through Dean Conner, an old OSI chum who had gotten out of the Air Force a few months ahead of me and set up as a private dick in Miami. I had asked Dean for a job, Miami fitting my criteria of being snowless in winter.

'Sorry, old buddy,' Dean said. 'Private dicks are a dime a dozen here in the Magic City. I'm barely making ends meet, let alone having enough of a caseload that allows for hiring an employee.'

'Too bad. I was hoping for someplace warm,' I said over our echoing phone connection.

'Say, do you speak Spanish? I hear there's plenty of opportunity in Cuba for someone with an investigative background.'

'Not related to the Syndicate, I hope.'

'Naw, just run-of-the-mill stuff. You know, put enough American tourists in a place and the need follows. I'd go down myself but the wife don't want to leave the country and she sure ain't letting me go down there on my own, given the señorita situation.'

'Señorita situation?'

'You know, lots of unattached señoritas? Wives hate that kind of thing.'

'Not a problem for me. No wife keeping me in the country.'

'Well, I got a contact in Havana if you're interested, name of Mercado. Says he's connected. I sent a couple of small matters his way. He's slow but thorough.'

'Sure, why not.'

My casual 'sure, why not' got me a name and address, and, by letter and cable, I made a deal with Moncho. He would handle the local stuff, bread-and-butter investigations that he said would keep the lights on and the doors open. I would bring in and handle the less-frequent but higher-dollar gringo trade.

It was a symbiotic relationship. I figured the angle of making a bundle chasing cheating husbands and boyfriends on holiday from the States. Moncho figured the angle of how to get half of what I made without lifting a finger.

'Henry, a boy brought your message. What can I do for you this fine day?' Moncho's voice was high-pitched and staticky over the line from the pay telephone at the corner of his block. He used the phone there for calls on the infrequent occasions when he felt compelled to make one.

I thought about telling him that what he could do for me this fine day was to come to work at our business office, aka my apartment, in the manner that business partners often do when they are not shiftless slugs who try to live off their partners. Then I remembered I was calling him for help, and thought better of lighting the bridge between us on fire.

'This day isn't starting out so fine, Moncho.'

'Why, Henry? The sky is blue. The birds sing sweet songs. We are young, but not so young as to be naive. What is not fine about that, my friend?'

'You remember that case I had, the *hausfrau* from Dubuque who wanted me to get a picture of her one true love making the rounds of our fair city with his girlfriend?'

'The one who wouldn't pay unless you got a photograph of him with the other woman?'

'That's the one,' I said. 'I got the picture at the Capri.'

'That's great, Henry.' In the background I could hear a fruit vendor crying his wares, along with the adding machine in Moncho's head clicking away to tally his half of the take.

'There's a hitch. The subject saw me pop the photo. He made a stink and the house brought me in for a rather stern discussion of their no-photography policy. I have the bruises to prove it. And they took the film.'

Moncho's mental adding machine whirred to a stop. 'That's too bad, Henry.'

'That's not the worst. The meatballs who took the film also took me to see one of the higher-ups, who warned me not to trail sportsmen from Dubuque into any of his or his friends' emporiums.'

'Who was this higher-up, Henry?'

'I didn't catch his name while I was face down on his carpet. But he looked Cuban and he wore Bay Rum cologne. A lot of it.'

Moncho sucked air through his teeth on the other end of the line. 'Santo Trafficante. *Oye*, Henry, you are lucky that all that happened was a little bruising.'

I touched the loose molar inside my mouth with my tongue and thought about setting my partner straight about how much 'little bruising' I had suffered, then opted to get to more important matters. 'A Cuban wouldn't whack an American. The Syndicate wouldn't stand for it.'

'So true, Henry, so true. But Santo Trafficante is an American, from Tampa. First generation with a Cuban *papa*, but still an American. And the Syndicate? He *is* the Syndicate, or at least a big man in it, second only to Lansky.'

I hadn't been in Cuba long but I knew the name Lansky. Meyer Lansky, a friend of President Batista and the mastermind of the American crime organization in Havana, was feared by all and not to be crossed. Nor, I knew by logical extension, was his second in command. 'Jesus, we're screwed, Moncho. If Mr Bay Rum really is who you think he is, our business model for the matrimonial PI trade is no more. Unless we want to cross the Syndicate.'

'Please, Henry, do not use the word "we" when you speak of crossing the Syndicate. I wish to see many more fine mornings like this one.'

'Don't worry, Moncho. I'm not about to risk my neck, either. But the simple fact is that Mr Santo Trafficante's edict declaring

Syndicate properties off limits for my detecting activities pretty much kills the golden goose.'

'Kills the golden goose? What is this golden goose?' Moncho's voice brightened, doubtless from the mention of something with the word 'golden' in its description.

'There's no goose, Moncho. And no gold. It means it destroys an opportunity that would be profitable to me. To us,' I corrected.

'You think you will lose your American referrals?'

'If I can't produce results, word will get around fast among the referring agencies in the States. And I can't produce results if I can't operate in the casinos, hotels, and nightclubs owned by the Syndicate. The sportsmen who come to Havana don't come here to go to the art museum.'

'Henry, *acore*, my friend, I think the world of you, you know this.' I pictured Moncho, if our conversation were being held in person, eyes brimming with crocodile tears. 'But this has grave implications for our partnership.'

'Are you saying you're cutting me loose, Moncho?'

'Henry, you must understand, the private investigation business in Havana runs on a very tight margin. I cannot afford a partner who brings in no business.'

'Oh, that, Moncho, that is rich. You and I both know that is exactly what you were intending to do to me. Hell, you haven't even paid your half of the rent on the office.' I conveniently omitted the fact that I had only paid the first month's rent on our office – which doubled as my apartment – myself.

'Henry, Henry, let us not allow our parting to become ugly. I will have my half of the rent to you soon, very soon. And to show my generosity to you, I will not even ask you to vacate our office.' The line clicked dead before I could think of a snappy reply.

Benny, hearing half the conversation from his seat in the doorway of the office, said, 'What happen, Genry?'

'You spent last night and half of this morning trying to get me screwed, Benny, but I think my partner just beat you to the punch.'

SEVEN

'Genry, do we have any detecting work to do today?' Every morning for the two weeks since Benny had taken up sleeping on my stair landing, he had greeted me with the same question. Every morning I'd had to provide the same answer. 'None today, Benny.'

It became more and more disheartening to open the door and receive Benny's expectant question and then his response of 'maybe something come tomorrow' to my dejected negative. I arose later and later, avoiding the pregnant query, dreading the need to respond to the ever-optimistic Benny. As I shared my dwindling supply of food with him, he still considered me rich and worth hanging around, a stray dog at the fringe of a rusting junkyard.

The day finally came when I vowed not to get up at all. I had used the previous evening to drain the dregs of the most recent bottle of Matusalem and a minor hangover – there had not been that much of the dark rum left – seemed to be my punishment for not facing my unofficial mascot. I lay, watching the late morning breeze stir the window curtains, contemplating how to lay off my uncompensated employee, when I heard him speaking to another on the landing.

'You cannot go in,' Benny whispered. 'Mr Genry is sleeping.'

The baker Rojas made no attempt to speak quietly in his response. 'That must be why he cannot pay the rent, sleeping until noon.'

Deciding it wasn't fair to allow Benny to act as a shield for my financial dereliction, I jumped up and flung open the door, causing an uneasy lurch in my alcohol-bruised stomach.

A sullen Rojas greeted me. 'Señor Gore.'

I checked my watch. Eleven forty-five. 'Good morning, Señor Rojas.'

'Señor Gore, I must require your rent to be paid by this Friday. If it is not, I must ask you to leave.'

'I understand, Señor Rojas. You have been most accommodating. You shall have your rent.'

'By Friday,' Rojas growled.

'By Friday, Señor Rojas.'

The baker turned and clumped heavily down the stairs to his *pan* and *croquetas*.

Benny turned to me. 'How will we get the rent, Genry?'

I noted the 'we' in his question. The kid sleeping on my stair landing was more concerned about my well-being than my now-former business partner had ever been. Which reminded me, Moncho owed me money.

Not that I thought I'd ever see it. But it surely wouldn't hurt to remind old Moncho. 'Come in, Benny, while I write a note for you to take to Señor Mercado.' I figured if I showed up at Moncho's place he'd just lock the door and draw the curtains. Maybe he wouldn't remember Benny, would open the door to him, and actually accept and read my note. Maybe, too, President Eisenhower would call me up, invite me back into the Air Force, and make me a general. I put the odds of either event at about the same – nil. I wasn't optimistic when Benny set off for Moncho's with my scribble.

The funk of my rum-induced indisposition had just begun to recede that afternoon when the phone rang. It had not done that – rung – for days. I lifted the receiver, wondering if my Ike-makes-me-a-general fantasy was about to come true. But no, it was an occurrence even more fantastic. Moncho had called in response to my note.

'Henry, how are you?' Moncho's voice was full of bluff good humor.

'I've seen better days, Moncho.'

'I received your note, Henry. You did not think I was forgetting you, did you?'

'More like avoiding me.'

Moncho's broad laugh reverberated over the line, an aural good-natured backslap. 'You are such a comedian. Why would I avoid my good friend Henry Gore?'

'Because you owe me money?'

'Ah, yes, the subject of the note your urchin messenger

insisted I read in his presence. Persistent little devil. But, Henry, you know I am – how is it said? – strapped for cash.'

'So you called to give me the brush-off.' I realized too late that I had said exactly what I was thinking.

'No. No, Henry, not the brush-off. I call you with something better than money, something which, when you hear all the details of it, will undoubtedly cause you to forgive the paltry debt I owe to you. Something rare, valuable, far more valuable than the thirty-five pesos which stand between us. I call you with an opportunity.'

'I'm a little dubious when people call me with opportunities. The last time that happened, Uncle Sam was calling me with the opportunity to serve my country. Next thing I knew, I was in Maine, up to my ass in snow and thanking my lucky stars that I wasn't on a hill in Korea providing some Chi-com with an opportunity for target practice.'

'This opportunity will allow you to put your skills to use. It begins with an introduction to a very important man. Are you agreeable to it?'

'I'd rather have the thirty-five pesos.'

'Alas . . .'

'OK, Moncho, I'll bite. Where and when?'

'Meet me at three this afternoon, on the steps in front of El Capitolio.'

'And who am I being introduced to, Moncho?'

'A very important man, Henry. A man who can make your future.'

EIGHT

El Capitolio is a massive pile of a building in the heart of old Havana, right on the Paseo de Martí. Designed by an American as the seat of the Cuban Congress, it is a dead ringer for the Capitol Building in Washington, DC, except that the Cubans insisted that it be taller than its *norteamericano* counterpart by a few feet. I spent one of my last four pesos to take a taxi to get there, figuring I didn't want to appear before whatever grand personage Moncho had me meeting in a suit stained with sweat from a two-mile walk from my apartment in the afternoon heat.

Moncho Mercado was late. Or, rather, not late but on 'Cuban time'. That was the first thing I learned about Cuba when I arrived – things happen when they happen and few people, other than *norteamericanos*, seem to mind. Don't get me wrong. Everything gets done. All events occur somewhere close in time to when they were scheduled but never *on* time.

The steps of El Capitolio lacked shade, a breeze or any other form of relief from the afternoon sun. By three-ten, I had sweated through my beige linen suit and the hatband of my Panama. By three-fifteen, I was cursing Moncho for his arrogance, and myself for my foolishness, when he strolled up the granite steps, cool in seersucker and a white fedora.

'You're late, Moncho,' I grumbled.

Moncho obviously missed to whom my remark was directed. 'No, Henry, we are right on time. Our appointment inside is for three-thirty.'

I fumed but bit my tongue. It seemed that the steps were not just a convenient meet-up point; Moncho had a connection *inside* the capitol. In a country where connections are everything, this was too valuable for me to grouse about my former partner's tardiness.

Moncho took my elbow and began to steer me up the steps. Twenty feet away, another group ascended, a man in a tropical-weight military uniform bedazzled with medals, flanked by three others in dark suits, obviously security men. The uniformed man climbed rapidly, the three bodyguards almost breaking into a jog to keep pace.

Suddenly, to the left and slightly lower on the steps, a man shouted. The noise caused me to turn back to look, in time to see the shouter drop a newspaper he was carrying to reveal a rusty sawed-off twelve-gauge.

The military man had halted at the sound of the shout, turning instinctively in the direction of the noise. His body-guards pivoted as well, reaching for shoulder holsters inside their jackets when the shotgun made its appearance.

'Down!' Moncho yelled, and shoved me to the ground as he ducked. The first shotgun blast ripped through the sodden heat of the Havana afternoon, catching the security man nearest me full in the face. A gory shower of the man's flesh and bone sprayed over Moncho and me. The shotgunner was quick, but had a poor aim, felling a second security man with a load of shot in the lower legs.

Another man, wearing a vest but no coat, with a green armband on his shirtsleeve, charged from the top of the steps with a wicked butcher knife in his hands. He ignored the third security man, a mistake as the guard felled him with two snap shots from his 1911 .45 semi-auto. The knife-wielder, despite his wounds, continued to crawl down the steps as the third bodyguard turned his attention to the shotgunner.

The sawed-off was a double-barrel, and when its operator tried to reload after emptying the spent shells from the weapon, he fumbled as he drew fresh ammunition from his pocket. The new loads dropped to the ground and the shotgunner bent to pick them up. The third bodyguard shot him in the top of his head. The shotgunner's body dropped heavy and lifeless as a sack of cement.

Until then, only shooting could be heard and only the scent of gunpowder was in the air. With the death of the shotgunner, the wounded security man began to shriek and writhe, twisting and rolling to the bottom of the steps, a wash of bright blood marking his progress. A woman's screams from down on the Paseo de Martí matched those of the injured bodyguard.

The coppery odor of blood rose in the heat as the smoke from the firing cleared.

The man with the knife continued his deliberate crawl toward the military man, shouting, '*Viva Cuba libre!*' His target easily sidestepped the assailant. The uninjured guard interposed himself between the two men, leaned over, and shot the assassin in the forehead.

A squad of soldiers, helmeted and armed with rifles, appeared and deployed along the top of the steps. People ran down the steps away from the soldiers and the carnage, out to the Paseo de Martí and down that long avenue.

'Get up. Let's get out of here, Henry,' Moncho said, standing and casually brushing dirt from the knees of his pants. As I stood, I glanced at the dead shotgunner. He, too, wore a green armband.

'Walk, Henry. Don't run,' Moncho said quietly. We walked down the Capitolio steps and away from the scene just as two jeeps, with more troops, and a half-dozen blue-and-white police cars, sirens wailing, careened into view.

Moncho picked up our pace when we reached street level. I didn't look back until we hit the corner, and turned in time to see the military man, the object of the assassination attempt, on the landing of the Capitolio, his bodyguard still at his side, weapon in hand.

'I guess our meeting is cancelled,' Moncho said. Moncho Mercado, master of the obvious. 'I will call you when it is rescheduled.'

NINE

Walking away down the streets now teeming with police, Moncho had been tight-lipped about the assassination attempt we had witnessed. No matter, I thought. I'll learn all I need to know from the morning papers. But, after forking over five centavos, I got *basebol* scores and news of events in New York and Madrid but nothing about an attempt on the life of an obviously important military officer on the very threshold of the nation's capitol.

I'd sent Benny, who had now fully assumed the position as my unpaid factotum, for the newspaper. I thought maybe he had purchased the wrong one. I'd asked for an English-language paper and he'd brought one. Maybe that was the mistake – maybe the local Spanish-language rags had covered the shooting.

'Benny, did you see if any of the papers had headlines about a shooting at El Capitolio yesterday?' I asked as I shuffled pages and sipped my breakfast of sugary coffee.

'No, Genry. The papers do not cover news such as the attempt on Duranona.'

'Who?'

'Colonel Duranona, the Chief of Naval Aviation. The Directorio Revolucionario, the Green Armbands, are the ones who tried to kill him, if that is what you are trying to find out.'

'Why isn't it in the papers?'

'The papers carry no news of the bombings and assassinations. To learn of these things you must hear it on the street or see it with your own eyes and live to tell it, as you did.'

'You seem to know a lot about what happened.'

'Yes, Genry. I hear of things. You want the news, I tell you. I am . . .'

'I know. You are the best in all of Havana at finding out the news.'

Benny grinned, teeth still pink-red from his morning *pastelitos de guayaba*. I didn't want to know what he was telling Rojas the baker that convinced him to keep giving us food on credit.

Just as I was about to pick Benny's brain for more information on Duranona, my long-silent telephone rang.

'Gore Investigations,' I answered, formulating the moniker of my new, Moncho-less, agency on the fly.

'Ah, Henry, so quickly I am forgotten.' Moncho's voice was exceptionally jolly considering our brush with death less than twenty-four hours before.

'Ah, Moncho, how can I forget you? You nearly got us killed yesterday,' I said with false jollity. 'And you still owe me thirty-five pesos.'

'Henry, why dwell on such trivial matters between friends? And, before you make some unnecessarily testy comment, you should know that I'm calling to square my debt with you by rescheduling the meeting that yesterday's unfortunate circumstances prevented.'

'Should I bring my bulletproof vest?'

'You are such a kidder, Henry. But, no, no bulletproof vest is needed. Your best suit will do nicely instead.'

'I would wear it but I seem to have torn a sleeve and ripped a hole in the knee of the pants diving to the ground at the last iteration of this meeting. Will this next shootout . . . er, meeting, be held at the same place?'

'No, Henry. Instead, we meet in a venue that is more secure. The Hotel Nacional, for the grand opening of its Club Parisién.'

'That's a pretty hot ticket, Moncho. I'll have to pass. It's one I can't afford just now.'

'Not to worry, *acore*, it is my treat. See you there at seven, Henry.' Moncho was still laughing when he hung up.

'We have business tonight, Genry?' Benny asked.

'Yeah, Benny. Let's just hope it's not monkey business.'

TEN

When I arrived that evening, there was a line of burnished Lincolns and Caddys winding around the driveway entrance of the Nacional, waiting for sprinting white-jacketed valets to take possession and steer them like ocean liners into their berths in an isolated corner of the hotel grounds. A second stream, consisting of what seemed like most of Havana's fleet of taxis, merged with the valet line to turn the entire scene into one of happy chaos, honking horns and shouted curses. Sportsmen with their wives, or mistresses, or some hot number they had picked out and paid for earlier in the day, sweated in the cars in the tropic heat, the ladies too dignified to disembark before being deposited within inches of the actual entrance.

I had no such difficulties. I had no wife or mistress and lacked sufficient funds to decorate the arm of my second-best, and now only, suit jacket with a compensated hot number. My shortage of money also meant I was not required to participate in the vehicular fray. I had walked from my humble apartment to the Nacional, the pinnacle of Havana's guest accommodations, traveling from poverty to luxury in the course of six blocks.

Inside, I navigated the crowds to the entrance of the Club Parisién and presented myself to the maître d', realizing only then that I didn't know whose party I would be joining. Unflustered by my flustered state, the maître d' asked my name, and my response garnered me an immediate trip to a table for four located the optimal distance from the club's intimate stage. I was just beginning to wonder who my host was when Moncho appeared, dapper in a tan linen suit and butter-yellow tie and matching pocket square.

'Good evening, Henry.' Moncho sat down beside me. 'A great table, is it not? And the headliner tonight is Miss Eartha Kitt.'

'Yeah, it's great, Moncho. Is it on your dime?' I said, remembering the thirty-five-peso deficit in our relationship.

'No, Henry. This and the entire evening are on our host's "dime", as you say.' A waiter sidled up with four champagne coupes, a bucket of ice, and a bottle of Dom Pérignon '49. Pretty high-toned booze, compared to what I'd been reduced to drinking.

'And who is our . . .'

'Ah, here he is now.' Moncho rose and extended a hand to a dignified Cuban with most un-Cuban green eyes. 'Senator Bauza, may I present Mr Henry Gore. Henry, Senator Guillermo Bauza.'

I shook Bauza's hand, which was cool and dry as a lizard. 'Good to meet you, Senator.' My grasp of Cuban politics was still rudimentary but even I knew that Bauza was a political powerhouse – senator for Las Villas province, a job for which he had been handpicked by his predecessor, President Batista; Chairman of the Senate Armed Forces Committee; and the reputed friend of and fixer for Meyer Lansky. If it had been an official position, he would have been the Cuban government's liaison to the Syndicate.

'The pleasure is mine, Mr Gore,' Bauza said. 'Moncho has told me of your exploits for the US Air Force's OSI. It speaks well for Cuba to have a man of your stature coming to establish his home in our country.'

Just then the senator's attention was diverted to the stage, allowing me to give an eye-roll in Moncho's direction and to receive a mouthed '*de nada*' in return. I wondered exactly what lies Moncho had told to Bauza and where the evening was headed as a result.

What had grabbed Senator Bauza's attention was the start of the show. A handsome Desi Arnaz-type, in a white dinner jacket and black patent shoes so buffed out that they reflected the stage lighting like mirrors, stepped to a stand microphone as the band played a flourish.

'Ladies and gentlemen,' began the master of ceremonies in heavily accented English. 'Señores y señoras. It is my pleasure to welcome you to the grand opening of the hottest cabaret in Havana, the Club Parisién. It's going to be a

memorable night, as we have two of America's best song-
stresses gracing our stage, including our main act, the sultry,
the seductive, Miss Eartha Kitt.' A roar of applause greeted
the mention of the name. 'But first, direct from a string of
sold-out performances in Des Moines, Lincoln, Indianapolis,
and Chicago, join me in welcoming the luscious, the lovely,
Miss Lola Loring.'

The applause didn't roar for Miss Lola Loring but Senator
Bauza was so enthusiastic that he got to his feet and stood
clapping until all others had ceased.

Seating himself, Bauza nudged me confidentially and
said, 'Such a beautiful woman, and with a voice as smooth
and smokey as honey from the flower of the black mangrove
tree. She is exquisite, you will see.'

The lights went down and a single spot focused on the
microphone stand. Lola Loring stepped from the darkness into
the dazzle of the spotlight. She wore a full-length deep green
satin gown, cut low to reveal a respectable, but not buxom,
bosom and high to reveal long, long, shapely legs. Her hair
was real blond, not from a bottle, her skin fair to the point of
translucence. She had pale blue eyes that looked like someone
had just surprised her with a not-unpleasant surprise. Her nose
was a little pugged; it reminded me of my kid sister Jan's
nose before she grew into a more womanly face. A slash of
the brightest of red lipsticks accented a plain mouth that seemed
to contain too many teeth.

As a blond, she was as exotic in Cuba as the dark tropical
beauties I had dreamed of were in Maine. I pegged her for an
upper-Midwest farm girl originally, maybe from Minnesota or
North Dakota. I suspected that the alliterative Lola Loring
moniker replaced something like Ella, Anna, Gretel, or Ingrid
on the front end, and Olson, Anderson, Larson, or Ericson on
the back. I'd have put money, if I had any, on the fact that ten
years ago she was milking cows in a dairy barn somewhere
on the Great Plains.

She caressed the mic stand, nodded to the band, and did a
passable rendition of 'The Man I Love' – not powerful, but
polished, sweet, and steady, of opening-act quality in
Indianapolis, Chicago, or Havana.

Senator Bauza paid rapt attention to the singer, ignoring me, Moncho, and the waiters who kept refilling his rapidly drained champagne coupe. After three more torchy and service-able numbers, Lola Loring took her bows. Bauza gave her a standing ovation which others around him, including Moncho and me, felt obliged to join.

'Is she not wonderful?' Bauza effused. Not waiting for an answer, he went on. 'She will be a star, the greatest star in Cuba, far better than that mulatto.' He waved toward the stage where Eartha Kitt was slinking and purring through a tune, playing the crowd, male and female, like the proverbial violin.

'Yeah, I'm sure she will be a star, Senator.' I was currying favor for a reason I couldn't fathom. I suppose it had to do with Moncho's cheerleading for this meeting. I hoped it wasn't a snow job.

The senator looked my way as if taking the measure of something in me and, satisfied, said, 'Señor Mercado tells me that you have just concluded an important case for a private client.'

Boy, Moncho had laid it on pretty thick. At least it wasn't a total lie; there had been a client. Probably my last. 'It's correct that I have just concluded a case,' I said, remembering that just that morning I had stared in the mirror and decided that the bruising inflicted by Wingtip Larry was no longer visible. 'But I would hardly call it an important case.'

'Your modesty only confirms what Moncho has told us of your character.' Us? Who was us? Or maybe Bauza spoke in the papal collective. He drew on his American cigarette, a luxury most Cubans forgo in favor of less expensive, locally grown cigars. 'But regardless of how we describe your most recent case, are we to understand that you are now available to undertake a new matter?'

Damn, I'd underestimated Moncho. Actual work for a client who clearly had money to pay! I could have kissed my conniving ex-partner. 'That is correct, Senator. I'm available. I assume it is you who are in need of my services?'

Ignoring my question, Bauza said, 'Moncho tells me you witnessed the unfortunate incident involving Colonel Duranona yesterday afternoon.'

I nodded, remembering how close I had become to being an active, and dead, participant instead of a mere witness.

Bauza continued. 'There is an element, a small . . . no, a minuscule element, of the population who seeks to disrupt and overthrow the legitimate government of President Batista. They are nothing more than bandits, really, common criminals, and their efforts have had little effect in Cuba.'

Other than attempted assassinations taking place on the very steps of the capitol, I thought to myself, as well as rumors of bombings in Havana, Cienfuegos, and other major cities throughout the country.

'Nonetheless,' the senator savored the fancy English word. 'They have proven themselves to be a . . . nuisance in the last few months, to the point where President Batista has decreed that they must be halted.'

'I can understand the president's concern,' I said, and I could. From what I'd heard, Batista and his cronies in the government had their hands in the till of every casino, night-club, and hotel in Cuba. Who would want a few revolutionaries to derail a gravy train like that? Not that I cared in the least about any of them. Batista took graft from the mob who stole from the suckers who came in from the States for gambling and sex. The only undeserving victims might be the Cuban people, but maybe not. Maybe that was just the way the world worked here, and, after all, Cuba wasn't my country anyway. I'd already saved my country, battling the Red Menace in the snowy potato fields of Maine. I'd done my honorable time and now, I'd stick my neck out for no man. Well, not for free.

'But what, Senator Bauza, does the president's concern about the . . . bandits have to do with me?' I asked.

Bauza leaned in to me, the yeasty odor of the Dom on his breath mingling with the smoke from his Camel. 'The police, in Havana and elsewhere, are lazy and corrupt.' He made a distasteful face. Corruption, which makes the world go round in the high places of Cuba's government, was apparently unsavory and embarrassing when practiced by mere policemen. 'Our military intelligence service, the SIM, has been diligent but not very effective in cracking down on the bandits. Proper intelligence on these criminals, to uncover their operational cells, weapons caches, and the like, through well-conducted espionage activities would be invaluable.'

'How invaluable?' As the words left my lips, I realized I was asking a question that had been asked a hundred, a thousand, maybe ten thousand times before in Havana. Asked in connection with building permits, casino licenses, proposed legislation, drugs, and women, with all the details of life, large and small, in this sunny font of sin beside the glittering Caribbean. I was, at last, being integrated into the community.

Bauza smiled. 'We are prepared to pay ten thousand pesos for your assistance.'

ELEVEN

Ten thousand pesos is a respectable amount of money, one of the many things I'd learned since my flight in from Miami. Ten thousand pesos will buy a modest but comfortable house on the beach in Vedado, or five automobiles imported from the US to start a taxi company, or several hundred nights of debauchery in the fleshpots of the City of Columns, or enough rum to float a boat and ruin your liver. Ten thousand pesos would set me up nicely, with enough for rent and living expenses until I got on my feet, and plenty left over to start a first-class private-investigator operation.

Moncho Mercado had done a helluva sales job. I knew he would expect his cut, and the amount expected would dwarf the debt he owed to me. But it would be worth it, and I would pay him gladly for getting me this job doing . . . what?

'Ten thousand is an interesting amount, Senator. You certainly know how to get a guy's attention. But, what, exactly, is expected in return?' That was the sixty-four-thousand-dollar, or, rather, the ten-thousand-peso, question.

'We would have you work with the head of our military intelligence, Colonel Ernesto Blanco Rico, to formulate espionage and counterespionage strategies to combat the bandits who plague our country.' The senator had managed to give me a name but not much more. I guessed I would have to meet with this Colonel Blanco Rico to get the full scoop. 'I certainly hope you are interested, Señor Gore.'

'It is an interesting proposition, Senator.' The mental image of Señor Rojas, in his flour-dusted apron, standing with a hand outstretched for the rent money on my doorstep on the upcoming Friday sealed the deal. 'What is the next step?'

'You will be contacted by Colonel Blanco Rico in the next twenty-four hours. He will – how do you say? – fill you in on the details.'

I reached for my wallet. 'Here, let me give you a card with my address and phone number.'

'That will not be necessary, Señor Gore. I can assure you that the colonel already has the information. He will be in contact with you.' Bauza half-turned and brightened. 'Ah, Lola, my dear, a wonderful performance.'

The senator rose and planted a chaste kiss on Lola Loring's cheek. Up close, she was less the seductive chanteuse and more the girl next door, a kid not much older than twenty-one or twenty-two. Away from the white glare of the stage lights, her skin was less pale, with a smattering of freckles across the bridge of her upturned nose.

'Mr Henry Gore, Señor Ramón Mercado, this is my . . . good friend, Miss Lola Loring.' Senator Bauza, thirty years Lola Loring's senior, beamed with unmistakable pride. When middle-aged Cuban men had female 'good friends' less than half their age, the unspoken but clear message was that the young woman was a mistress. Senator Bauza's excess pride stemmed from the fact that Lola Loring was an Anglo and blond, something only the most wealthy and influential Cuban men could hope to obtain.

'Pleased to meet you, Mr Gore,' Miss Loring said, pressing her hand to mine and giving it a pump like a water well. You can take the girl off the farm but you can't take the cow-milking, hay-bale-slinging farm out of the girl. 'Where you from, Mr Gore?'

'A small town in Indiana that nobody's heard of – Warsaw,' I said.

'Like Poland?' Lola said. It was kind of a dim question but the arch smile that accompanied it said mischief to me.

'What about you, Miss Loring?' I asked. 'You don't look like you grew up in Havana.'

'Nope. I'm from a small town in North Dakota – Warsaw.'

'Like Poland?'

She laughed, a merry, musical sound that conjured up those little chimes the drummers use in some of the mambo bands. 'Like Poland, only in the Red River Valley. You know:

Just remember the Red River Valley
And the cowboy that's loved you so true.'

'You're a long way from the Red River Valley, Miss Loring,' I said.

'Yes. And you're a long way from Warsaw, Indiana, Mr Gore. Did you come here for the waters, like that Casablanca guy?'

'Something like that,' I said.

'And, like him, were you misinformed?'

'Let's just say my eyes have been opened.'

'Well, you Americans are all such fast friends when you meet,' Bauza interrupted, with maybe a touch of irritation. 'Perhaps we should sit.'

A second bottle of Dom Pérignon was ordered. The fourth champagne coupe that had sat unused at our table was filled. Lola took a seat between Senator Bauza and me, and the next hour passed with the senator holding forth about the United States and its investments in Havana, Cuba's new status as a tourist destination, and the benefits from that status for the Cuban economy and its people. Also passing in the next hour was the third bottle of Dom. The room started to get fuzzy around the edges and I could swear at one point that Lola Loring looked deeply into my eyes. I could also swear, not just good old regular swearing but on-my-dear-departed-mother's-grave-serious swearing, that shortly after Miss Loring returned from a trip to the ladies' room, her hand slipped into my outside jacket pocket and left something – a note? – there.

'Thank you for your hospitality, Senator Bauza,' Moncho said, shortly after the note was passed. 'But Henry and I should be giving you and Señorita Loring your privacy.'

I and my champagne-loosened tongue were about to object that we really didn't need to leave just yet, but Moncho had me up by the elbow as Senator Bauza and Miss Loring said hasty good-byes.

On the street outside the Nacional, while the doorman hailed a cab, Moncho said, 'All the *chocho* in Havana and you have to pick Bauza's mistress! What is wrong with you, Henry?'

'Hey, just a little harmless conversation between expats. It meant nothing.'

'For your – no, for our sakes, I hope she says the same

thing. I think I got us out of there just in time. The senator was starting to get – how do you say? – miffed.'

'Oh, very nice vocabulary, Moncho. We'll turn you into a Yankee yet.'

Now it was Moncho's turn to look miffed. 'I think maybe you should get your own cab, Henry.'

'Maybe I'll walk,' I said, starting into the night.

I'd covered a block when Benny came out of an alley and fell in beside me. 'We have business, Genry?'

'We'll see, Benny. I'm not sure.'

'OK, just as long as it's not monkey business.' Benny grinned.

Right then I remembered the sensation of Lola Loring placing her hand in my coat pocket. I reached in and felt a slip of paper. Stopping in the light from a corner *bodega* we were passing, I read the schoolgirl scrawl:

> *I want to see you again,*
> Lola
> *4–8751*

I recognized the digits as a telephone number.

'Is business, Genry?' Benny asked.

'Yeah,' I said. 'Monkey business.'

TWELVE

Nights in Havana are electric with the excitement of sin, the main streets lit with dazzling invitations to peccancy, the alleys dark with its wicked fruition. In contrast, days in Havana are languid affairs of lazy mornings and indolent afternoons, the sleepy Caribbean side of an island that tourist brochures and travel agency posters would have you think never stopped hopping.

Two of those drowsy days passed without any word from Senator Bauza or Colonel Blanco Rico. I began to think that Moncho was right, that my harmless almost-flirting with Lola Loring had gotten on Bauza's bad side. Maybe I had killed my chances. With this in mind, I decided that I had two courses of action. I could forget that the meeting had taken place, sit in the morning sun on my balcony, and contemplate where I might acquire my next meal. Or I could dial the number given to me by Lola Loring, and spend the afternoon with her, in a bar or a bedroom, and *then* contemplate where I might acquire my next meal.

I was wavering between the balcony and the telephone, between lethargy and iniquity, when a third possibility presented itself in the form of a knock on my door. Thinking it was Benny with a street-kid scheme to save both of us from starvation, or Señor Rojas with a final threat of eviction, I said, 'It's open.'

The door swung inward, framing two mutts wearing suits that must have come straight from the Sears-Roebuck catalogue. Not hoods, I could tell, because no self-respecting hood, not even muscle, would be caught dead in such cheap clothes. I didn't ask them to come in. I didn't need to. They stepped inside without hesitation, obviously used to entering rooms where they had not been invited.

'Señor Henry Gore?' The lead mutt was the smaller of the two, with bright eyes and a brisk manner.

'Who wants to know?' I said, sounding more gutsy than I felt. The second, bigger mutt took a step forward. You could tell he wasn't used to even minimal push-back against his authority. The lead mutt put a hand on his arm, stopping his advance.

'We are here with an invitation for you, Señor Gore, from Colonel Ernesto Blanco Rico of the Servicio de Inteligencia Militar to visit him at his headquarters.' Mutt One's English was flawless and unaccented. He'd had some schooling in the States, I thought. Maybe he even grew up there.

'When's the invitation for?'

'Right now, Señor Gore.' His voice said acceptance of the invitation was nothing less than mandatory.

I tossed on a jacket and hat and left with my escorts, Mutt One in the lead down the stairs and Mutt Two a step behind me. When we hit the bottom of the steps, Two grasped my elbow like I was in custody. I shook it off and drew a silent glare, but he didn't touch me again.

An olive-drab Pontiac was at the curb, the acronym SIM stenciled in white lettering on the front doors. The mutts marched me straight to its rear passenger door. I hesitated as Mutt One opened the door, glancing around the street. Benny was nowhere to be seen. Neither was anybody else. The usually bustling neighborhood street was silent and empty. A hand pulled back a curtain for a furtive look from a second-floor window across cobbled Calle J. Señor Rojas could barely be seen in the deep shadows of his *panaderia*, peering over the counter.

'Please get in and slide over,' Mutt One said. Mutt Two pushed down on my shoulder – slightly – as I did just that, then went around to take the wheel. One joined me in the back seat for a wordless ride to a fortress-like building in the Old Havana part of town.

'Where are we?' I figured the question was innocent enough to keep Mutt Two from giving me the beating it appeared he was itching to deliver.

'The Comandancia General,' Mutt One said as we crossed a drawbridge over a dry moat and entered a courtyard behind the building's stone walls. 'The main police station for Havana.'

I experienced a moment of panic. 'I thought I was going to see Colonel Blanco Rico of Military Intelligence.'

'We have a facility here,' Mutt One said as the Pontiac stopped in front of a heavy wooden door in the interior wall. The Mutts got me out and walked me to the door, which was guarded inside by two helmeted soldiers with slung Thompson sub-machine guns.

As my eyes adjusted to the dim lighting in the hall we had entered, I heard a brief but unmistakable scream from the far end. I was concerned but then remembered the cacophony from the Air Force stockade back at my posting in Presque Isle. Jails are noisy everywhere, I decided; why should this one be different?

'This way to Colonel Blanco Rico's office,' Mutt One said, directing me to the end of the hallway furthest from where the scream had emerged. Mutt Two dropped out of sight. Apparently there was enough horsepower loitering behind the hallway's closed doors to provide any assistance if I became belligerent.

A knock on the door at the end of the hall, an almost-salute touch of his hat brim tip, and Mutt One handed me off to an army sergeant pecking at a typewriter inside. The sergeant wore a sidearm, despite being behind two sets of foot-thick stone walls, a dry moat, a pair of guards we passed on the drawbridge, and the sentries with the Thompsons inside the door of the SIM 'facility'. These guys were loaded for bear.

While I was deciding if I should feel very safe or completely unsafe, the sergeant knocked on a wood-paneled inner door behind his desk, entered, and after a second emerged. 'Colonel Blanco Rico will see you now,' he said, swinging the door wide to admit me.

'Mr Gore, a pleasure.' Colonel Blanco Rico stepped from behind his desk and extended a warm, firm hand. In physical appearance, he reminded me of my old commanding officer from the Air Force – medium height, slightly taller than me; dark, close-cropped hair; a uniform without a button, ribbon, or emblem out of place or unpolished; keen eyes; and a decidedly friendly air, the type of demeanor that puts folks at ease.

'Thanks for the . . .' I struggled for the appropriately ironic word. 'Invitation.'

'Ah, the little charade by Lieutenant Trujillo and Sergeant Alvarez. I hope you do not mind. They are good men. They treated you acceptably?'

'If I was being taken into custody they did.'

'Good. Good. That was the point, to make it appear as though you had been arrested. You see, if you simply came here on an invitation from me and were seen by certain criminal elements, you would be suspect as being a spy or informant for our government.'

'Do you believe the Comandancia General is being watched that closely by these criminal elements?' I asked. 'My experience is that criminals are not so sophisticated that they monitor police stations.'

'That may be one of the ways you need to reform your thinking, now that you are a resident in our fair country, and if, as I am told, you are prepared to be of service to your new home.'

'For a price I am.' Why beat around the bush? Besides, my belly was grumbling. Señor Rojas had cut off my credit for breakfasts.

Blanco Rico smiled. 'You are direct. I like that in an officer. And I understand you were one, in the American Air Force, in its Office of Special Investigations.'

'I assume Senator Bauza told you that. I also assume you know the price offered to me was ten thousand pesos. For some consultation on counterespionage, from what the senator said, to keep the criminals from watching the Comandancia General without you knowing it.'

'Ah, that is amusing, Mr Gore . . .'

'Call me Henry, please.'

'Henry, then. And Senator Bauza correctly informed you that we need your expertise in espionage and counterespionage. But something a bit more direct than consulting.'

'What would that be, Colonel?'

Blanco Rico lifted the lid on a humidor on his desk. 'Have a cigar, Henry. They are excellent. A gift to me from President Batista.'

'Thanks, I'll pass for now. What do you mean by "a bit more direct than consulting"?'

Colonel Blanco Rico rolled a cigar between his fingers and lifted it to inhale its scent. 'Field work.'

'Field work? Don't you have spies and informants of your own? What do they call them? "Thirty-threes", because you pay them thirty-three pesos and thirty-three centavos per month, isn't it? Seems to me you could get a lot of field work done at that rate for the ten thousand pesos you want to pay me for it.'

'This is a special circumstance and you meet our requirements exactly.' The colonel smiled amiably.

'How so?'

'We need a *norteamericano* to play a role.'

'What kind of a role?'

'As a gunrunner.'

I thought about that. It meant I would probably be in contact with some revolutionaries, like the Green Armbands I'd seen in the failed assassination attempt at the Capitolio. They might have been poorly armed, and inept, but they were still plenty dangerous, ready to kill and ready to die trying. And I had to assume Colonel Blanco Rico didn't have too much concern about losing a *gringo* during one of SIM's operations if it came to that. Still, there was my stomach that had had no breakfast and now no lunch, the unpaid rent, and the lack of a ticket back to the States.

'I'll need some cash now, for operating expenses.' I heard the words and couldn't believe they were coming from my lips.

'Of course, Henry. I assume a thousand pesos will be enough,' Blanco Rico said. He reached into his desk drawer for an envelope and counted out five gray hundred-peso notes and a red-backed five hundred from it. 'Until the operation concludes, it is best that you make no further visits to this office. This is for your safety and the security of the operation. You will have a contact, a woman. Meet her tomorrow night at the Tropicana. She will be wearing a white feather in her hair. Ask her to join you for a drink. She will respond by telling you she will only drink with you if you order champagne. Order it. She will give you information on the particulars of your mission and help you to make contact with the criminal elements.'

'I suppose the champagne's on my dime?'

'From your expense money, Henry. You choose the vintage.'

'No surprise there.'

At this point, in the Air Force, my commander would stress to me the importance of my mission for the country and the free world. Following that patriotic pep-talk, I'd be sent on my way. In Cuba I got, 'Will there be anything else, Henry?'

'Yeah, Colonel. I'll take that cigar now.'

THIRTEEN

Benny was nowhere to be seen when I returned to my place but he showed an hour after I'd strolled in with a bottle of Havana Club and a bag of groceries from the *tienda* around the corner on Calle K. I'd decided that I would pay the rent tomorrow, the less to link the visit from the SIM mutts in the morning to the money in the mind of Señor Rojas.

'The SIM come for you, Genry. I think you dead,' Benny said, talking around the sandwich I had just made for him.

'No, Benny. They asked me a few questions about what I'd seen on the steps of the Capitolio and let me go.' Might as well practice my cover story with a receptive audience.

'Then, Genry, the work you were talking about, she come through?'

'It, Benny. Not she. It came through. Yes. We're back to eating. Tomorrow I'll pay the rent arrears and we're sure of a roof over our heads.' Of course, Benny's roof was over my open stair landing but there was no way I was going to move him in with me. There were already too many American visitors to Havana who were real *pájaros*; I didn't want to be lumped in with them as a flit.

'The work is over, you have been paid?' he asked. Visions of sugarplums, Benny?

'No, kid. I just got an advance against expenses. There's still plenty of work for me to do.'

'Good. I help you, Genry. You see, I am the best investigator in Habana. What we investigate?'

'That, Benny, I find out tomorrow night.'

The Tropicana is, simply, the most fantastic place I have ever been. Situated far on the outskirts of Havana, it ought to be a place where no one other than a dedicated chiropterologist ventures after dark. Nestled at the edge of a lush jungle, you'd think the only suitable after-dark activity would be the study of the nocturnal habits of the Cuban fruit bat. And that was pretty much the case until just before World War II, when an ambitious Habanero opened a small cabaret there. It limped through the war and its aftermath, catering to Cubans with a taste for sin but not much money. When the Syndicate finally got Havana rolling in the century's second half, the Tropicana was first a place for those in the know, then a venue for *norteamericanos* to go slumming. By the time I got to town, it was to 1957 Havana what Rick's was to the fictional Casablanca of 1942 – the place to which everybody comes. Every American who visited Havana, every mobster who invested there, every Cuban politico, military man, or public official, and every Cuban woman who had beauty, ambition, a desire to dig gold, or all three, congregated there, dancing, drinking, carousing, and watching the famous show, night after night. It was New Year's Eve, Christmas, and St Paddy's Day, all rolled into one, every night of the year.

Moncho Mercado introduced me to the Tropicana just four days into our then-new partnership and my sojourn on Cuban soil. I didn't even mind when he stuck me with the tab for the evening, so dazzled was I by the overarching modernist pavilion mingling with the verdant plants and trees, the jungle night sounds, and the celestial show overhead in the clement tropic darkness. The sensual percussion of the mambo filled my ears. The delicate fragrance of gardenias, real gardenias, weaved its way through the harsher odors of cigars and rum to fill my nostrils, and my brain, with seductive enchantment.

And the women, my god, the women. Petit, statuesque, voluptuous, slender, dark, fair, girlish, or ripe to the point of perfection, the Tropicana has them all, and any and everything else the male imagination can conjure in its most erotic dreams. Stunning women nestled in the arms of elderly fogies; took in hats and mink stoles at the coat-check counter; and lingered at the long mahogany bar with inviting eyes and high price tags. Even the young lady who circulated through the cavernous dining area with a tray of cigars, cigarettes, chewing gum and mints would have stopped male traffic on the streets of St

Louis, Portland, and New York City, if only someone had the presence of mind to transport her to one of those places.

Yet all those lovelies paled in comparison to the Tropicana's showgirls. Like the Coldstream Guards, they were selected for their height, with silken legs that seemed to go on and on. Their comeliness was legendary, not only in Cuba but across the globe. Hence, every beautiful woman in the melting pot of beautiful women that made up Cuba's female population aspired to be a Tropicana showgirl, to wear the scant sequined costume and the massive gaudy headdress of feathers. Being a Tropicana showgirl meant the chance to parade before the richest men in the country, the hemisphere, the world. And it meant a chance to be selected from that perfect chorus line to become a wealthy man's mistress, concubine, or even his wife.

At eight in the evening, I took a taxi to the Tropicana. My off-the-rack suit and somewhat worn Florsheims labeled me as unworthy prey for the higher priced ladies who frequented the place, and I passed the first hour undisturbed by anyone other than my waiter, from whom I ordered a Cuba libre, and the heavenly cigarette girl, from whom I bought a pack of Lucky Strikes just so I could get a lingering close-up view of her perfect olive skin.

Pérez Prado, the Mambo King, was the headliner that night. By ten, he and his orchestra had both the locals and the high-rollers from the States swiveling their hips and tossing their shoulders in a frenzy of Latin lust. Then, just when the amateurs were about to expire, the dance floor was cleared and the pros took over, cascading into the room in a torrent of skin, sequins, and feathers. They were led by a black-as-night six-footer, with a face that managed to convey innocence and lust in the same instant, and a body that assured you that the message from her face was all true.

I'd spent the evening with an eye out for the woman with a white feather in her hair, to no avail. Then I realized it was of the plural – feathers – that Colonel Blanco Rico had spoken. And there was only one woman in the room with an elaborate headdress of white feathers in her hair – the chorus line's lead dancer. All the other chorus girls had red plumes sprouting from their headpieces. I watched the lead dancer – who in the room didn't? – and wondered how I could make contact with her in front of all these people. I was still pondering the problem when the chorus number ended and all the feathers, and the legs, hips, and breasts attached to them, exited the dance floor.

Pérez Prado reappeared and took his boys through some more subdued dance music, no doubt to avoid exhausting the revelers too early in the evening, before they had parted with all of their cash. I ordered another Cuba libre, to my waiter's disappointment. He probably would have preferred a free-spending couple at my tiny table instead of a slow-drinking piker who nursed his rum-and-Cokes. I was contemplating how to tell Blanco Rico that his ace spy of spies couldn't even succeed in making contact with his handler when she showed, approaching the table from the dark shadows on the jungle side of the room.

'Good evening, señor. This seat is not taken?' She had changed from her costume to something more, shall I say, modest. High at the neck and drifting well below the knee, it reminded me of the uniforms worn by the Catholic schoolgirls around town, only more chaste, if that was possible. She had removed her stage makeup, too, adorning only her lips with a touch of color.

'Not at all. Will you join me for a drink?' I said, thinking it best to conclude the sign/countersign part of the evening before we got down to names.

'I will drink with you only if you buy champagne.'

The waiters at the Trop have a nose for the collision of local females with unattached males. My guy materialized as soon as my companion spoke the magic word – champagne.

'A bottle of Dom Pérignon, waiter.' I was learning that Havana was a Dom Pérignon kind of town. After the waiter vanished, I said, 'My name's Henry Gore.'

'You may call me Marta. Marta Serrano,' she said, leaving it quite ambiguous as to whether it was her real name.

'Well, Marta Serrano, how do you come to be in this kind of life?'

'What kind of life is that, Señor Gore?'

'Henry, please, if we are to be co-workers.' I thought the term had a sterile air that would please Marta, who to that point hadn't been free with so much as a smile.

'Henry, then. Of what kind of life are you speaking?'

'A life as someone who convinces others that she is someone who she is not.'

'Let us get something straight at the outset, Henry Gore. You are, I know, doing this strictly for money. My motivation is the same. That should take care of any philosophical discussions you feel the need to have. Now let's get down to business. Kiss me.'

'What?'

'Kiss me, now, damn you.'

I obliged, kissing her in a way I thought someone in a pseudo-Catholic schoolgirl outfit ought to be kissed.

Out of the corner of my eye, I saw the waiter approaching with the Dom. So, apparently, had Marta. And, apparently, Marta did not consider the kiss I was applying to be vigorous enough. The next thing I knew, Marta's tongue was in a throat that wasn't hers. Then she broke the clench slightly to whisper a command in my ear. 'Slide your hand up my skirt.'

Not wanting to shirk my duty, I complied, moving my hand along her silken thigh until I encountered silken panties.

The waiter arrived at that moment. 'Your champagne, señor,' he said, arching an eyebrow. Marta sat back and readjusted her skirt as I drew my hand away. Two coupes were filled and the waiter departed. Marta raised hers in what I thought was to be a toast. But when she spoke, it was no toast.

'I will explain your mission as we drink. Every once in a while, kiss me, like we are lovers, and be free with your hands.' She stroked my hair. 'But if you are ever *that* free with your hands again, I'll twist your balls off.'

'Just trying to follow orders,' I said. The hand caressing my hair expertly sliced the top of my ear with a sharp fingernail. 'OK, OK, message received.'

'Good,' Marta said. 'As of tonight your detecting business becomes a cover for your real profession as a gunrunner. I will be your mistress. Don't get excited – you just got as close to getting inside my panties as you are ever going to get.

Tomorrow you will use some of your expense money to rent a nice little house for me on a quiet street in Miramar. We will meet there most days from now on, although you will occasionally come here to watch me perform.

'I have infiltrated a cell of the Directorio Revolucionario, the Green Armbands, at the University of Havana. They wish to acquire guns. They are fools, a half-dozen wet-behind-the-ears children who think they are going to overthrow Batista and make Cuba a model for democracy in Latin America – free speech and fair elections, the elimination of bribery and corruption, quality education and health care for all. It is a fantasy, of course.'

'Of course,' I agreed. I covered her mouth with a kiss, lusty in appearance but restrained in actuality.

'Very good,' Marta said when we came up for air. She took a sip of champagne, rubbing her free hand across my cheek. 'I will present you to this cell as an American who has guns to sell. You will offer to deal in only large quantities of arms, which will be, I suspect, beyond the financial capability of the cell. The idea will be to get them to involve those higher up the chain of command in the transaction, to expose the very top leadership of the Directorio Revolucionario.'

'A straightforward plan,' I said. 'Just one problem. I have no guns to sell. No merchandise to show your little friends.'

Marta reached in a large purse she carried, pulled out a folded newspaper, and placed it on the table between us. 'Guns are impossible to obtain in Cuba. Even having one gun will mark you as capable of supplying more. Take this and be discreet.'

I lifted a fold of the newspaper and saw the butt of a pistol in a holster inside. 'I'm going to the gents' room, doll. Be back in a minute.' I tucked the paper under my arm.

The men's room at the Tropicana was as luxe as the rest of the facility. An attendant standing by a stack of towels and a tray of colognes on the sink counter bowed as I entered. I went into one of the marble-walled stalls, unfolded the paper, and looked at the gun. A Colt Woodsman. My father had given me one for my seventeenth birthday back in Indiana. Firing a .22 caliber long-rifle shell, it was more of a plinking gun than a man-killer. I'd used mine to shoot at tin cans and bottles in the town dump. Hardly the weapon I'd pick to start a revolution. But, as Marta said, guns were hard to come by in Cuba. Maybe SIM had given her this gun for me in case I screwed up and it fell into the hands of the schoolboys at the university. As a popgun, it couldn't cause much harm, if it did. I would have preferred something with more punch.

The Woodsman was in a shoulder holster. I took my coat off, wriggled into the holster, and threw the coat back on. The gun was long-barreled and awkward, but light, and its narrow profile fit well beneath my left arm. I checked the clip; it was full. I flushed the commode, washed my hands, tossed the attendant a five-centavo coin, and returned to Marta.

'OK, I've got a gun. What's next?'

'You take me to your place for the night,' she said.

FOURTEEN

Being the chivalrous sort, I spent the night on the hard wooden floor of my apartment, while Marta occupied the bed. Our amorous play act had ended as soon as the door to my place had closed and recommenced in the morning only when Marta stood in the open doorway, locked onto my lips one last time, and took her leave.

Benny was witness to her departure, as were a few of the nearby residents sweeping the sidewalk and shaking out their rugs. I hoped my overnight visitor would enhance my reputation among my neighbors or, at least, quell any rumors of homosexuality that Benny's lingering presence had set in motion.

'Genry, that was the job you get? To make us money?' Benny asked, as Marta Serrano made purposefully slow, enticing progress along the street.

'None of your business, Benny.'

'But you not even fuck her.'

'Benny, you gotta stop using that word. And how do you know what I did?'

'I have ears, Genry. And you and that *chica* no make the fucking noise.'

'I told you, stop using that word. And no more listening at the door when I have guests. Or otherwise.'

'OK, Genry.'

'Now, go see if you can scare up some coffee and breakfast.'

'Señor Rojas say no more credit.'

I handed Benny a ten-peso note. 'Here. That should pay up the food and coffee account.'

Benny disappeared down the stairs and reappeared shortly with coffee and *quesitos*, trailed by Señor Rojas.

'*La renta*, Señor Gore,' Rojas grumbled.

'Here you go, Señor Rojas. Fifty pesos to clear the arrears

and thirty-five in advance for next month.' The smile that had
seemed less of a possibility every day the rent had remained
unpaid reappeared on Rojas's face. Benny, too, was smiling,
his belly full of *quesitos* after a couple of lean days.

I was the only one without a smile. Now, I'm not one for
introspection. I take life as it comes, try to enjoy the day – that
carpe diem thing – and figure that the past is past and the
future will take care of itself. Considered on that basis, I was
in pretty good shape. True, my original business plan had gone
to hell in a hand basket, but I'd come out of my encounter
with the Syndicate in decent shape. No permanent injuries,
anyway. And this new gig, while it had its risks, had some
great upside. Big-time connections with real movers and
shakers in the government. Possible additional work when it
was over. And let's not forget the substantial cash involved.
Champagne. Visits to the Tropicana. A beautiful woman on
my arm. That, I realized, was the problem.

No, not the fact that Marta was beautiful, per se. But the
fact that there was something missing in my life. Love 'em
and leave 'em had always been my philosophy. And I had
practiced it religiously. Not that it had been difficult with
the wholesome, thick-ankled farm girls of Indiana or their
equally wholesome but more slender-ankled counterparts from
my Air Force days in northern Maine. Both types were not
adverse to a little fun but the honey-trap of marriage was
always their ultimate objective and I hadn't been about to fall
for that. In Havana, the girls had proven more commercial and
much more short-term in their orientation. I'd engaged in a
few transactions in my first weeks in town, like any self-
respecting unattached *gringo* would when confronted with that
much unrelenting advertisement. But that grew hollow after
the first dozen times, and no 'nice' Cuban girl would be caught
in the presence of a *norteamericano* because that automatically
branded her a whore.

In short, I wasn't smiling because I was lonesome. For a
friend. For, of all things, a girlfriend, something I had never
had, a true steady woman in my life. Maybe it was because I
was a stranger in Havana. Maybe I had taken leave of my
senses. But here I was, twenty-seven years old, and I wanted

to sit down with someone nice, someone with whom I was not engaged in a commercial transaction, someone who didn't see me as a meal ticket for the night or for the rest of her life. Someone from home.

My assignment for the day from Marta was to acquire a love-nest for the two of us in Miramar. Easy enough to accomplish, I figured. Now that I had money, I would just throw money at the task. I estimated it would take a couple of hours, tops, to find a place, hand over some of my thousand-peso advance, and get a key. I could do it later in the afternoon.

I fished in my coat pocket for the note from Lola Loring. I didn't think about it. I just dialed the number.

'Yeah,' a voice, thick with drowse, answered.

'Hello. It's Henry Gore.'

'Who?'

'Henry Gore. We met at the Club Parisién two nights ago. You slipped a note into my pocket.'

'Yeah . . . Oh, yeah. Hi, Henry. Sorry. I'm a little fuzzy. I just woke up.'

I glanced at my Orvin. It was eleven forty-five.

'But, but . . .' Lola realized my hesitation. 'It's great to hear from you. I was wondering if you'd call.'

'Listen,' I said. 'Would you like to get some lunch?'

'Breakfast.' The drowse was gone from her voice. 'We entertainers sleep late. There's a hole-in-the-wall place near my house called El Siboney. On 5th Avenue. They make great ham and eggs. I'm in the mood for ham and eggs.'

'I could use some myself. Twelve-thirty OK? I'll pick you up.'

'I'll walk, Henry. Meet you there at twelve-thirty.' The phone clicked off.

FIFTEEN

One thing you can say without hesitation about Cuba is that the weather is relentlessly nice. This point was proven by my cab ride to El Siboney to meet Lola Loring. The cabbie, a porcine fellow in a dirty captain's hat, had exhausted the usual offers of women, virgin girls, boys, and sex shows by the time we reached the Malecón and fallen silent. I leaned my head back against the seat and watched the aquamarine of the Florida Strait, punctuated by whitecaps, slide by. The whitecaps were the product of a collision between the eastbound Florida Current – the beginning of the Gulf Stream – and the gentle trade winds that caress the island for six months of the year. The southeast winds take the edge off any heat produced by the agreeable sun, rendering the temperature a Goldilocks-perfect not-too-warm, not-too-cool, just right.

Lola had not given me her address, nor the address of El Siboney, but the cabbie knew the latter and I figured the former could wait until such time as she saw fit to divulge it. The hack dropped me at the Teatro Miramar on 5th Avenue, and pointed across the street to a nondescript commercial storefront. A window sign, so small it almost seemed geared to prevent detection, labeled the place as El Siboney. I crossed and entered the dark interior, where an elderly maître d' greeted me. 'Is just the señor for lunch today?'

'No. I'm meeting someone,' I said.

'You come to meet Señorita Loring?'

'Yes.'

'She say you come. She is a favorite, a regular.' He smiled a grandfatherly smile. 'You come this way.'

The old man led me through the small dining room and out to a courtyard with four tables on its coral stone floor and a cascade of bougainvillea along its walls. All the tables were empty except the one where Lola Loring sat. She wore a green floral-print sundress. When she rose to greet me, she seemed all straight lines and angles, long legs and sharp shoulders. She had on almost no makeup, with the effect of appearing too pale to risk time in the tropical sun.

'Hello, Henry,' she said. She was exactly the same height as me but managed to tilt her head down so that her blue eyes looked up to me through blond lashes. Without the glamour of the Club Parisién surrounding her, she was just a kid, I saw, a kid alone and fetchingly vulnerable in a country far from her home.

'Hello, Lola.' I was suddenly at a loss for words, until I stammered out, 'Ready for some ham and eggs?'

'You betcha,' she said, her almost-Norwegian northern Midwest accent fully unleashed with the idiom. 'They make the best here. The eggs are fresh, like at home. I have 'em two, three times a week. You gotta try 'em.'

'OK,' I managed, as the elderly gent who'd shown me to the table reappeared. Evidently, he was the waiter as well as maître d'. Probably the busboy, too.

Lola gave him a warm look. 'The usual, Gustavo.'

'Times two,' I said.

'The gentleman wishes the milk, too?' Gustavo asked.

'I have mine with milk to drink,' Lola explained.

'Yeah, sure.' I hadn't had a glass of milk since the day I entered the Air Force. Gustavo nodded and scurried away.

'Guillermo scolds me when I want to drink milk. He says it's for children,' Lola said. She was lovely, and delicate, and a little sad. 'What do you think?'

'I think you should drink whatever you want.'

Lola's eyes reminded me of the summer sky at the edge of the horizon. She looked directly into mine. 'Why did you call me?'

'Not to be sarcastic, but why did you smuggle me a note with your number on it?'

'Because I thought you were kind. Why did you call me?'

'Because I thought you were nice. Sweet. And I'm not kind, by the way.'

She smiled a luminous smile, showing too many teeth. The paint-spatter of freckles across her nose beckoned. I leaned in and kissed it.

She colored and said, 'You shouldn't do that.'

'Isn't that what you wanted?'

'I don't know.'

'If it's not what you wanted, what do you want?'

'A friend. Someone I can talk to, really talk to. Someone who will be honest with me. Someone I can be honest with.'

'All right, I'm game. Talk to me. Tell me something you want to be honest with me about.'

Gustavo chose that moment to appear with two platters of ham and eggs, the ham smokey, with a crispy edge of fat, the eggs sunny side with yellow-orange yolks that jiggled in the center. And two tall glasses of cold milk, condensation beading their outsides. Lola dug in and we ate in silence for a minute.

'My real name is Fannie.' She looked up from her eggs. 'Fannie Knutsen. And I know I can't sing. Not good enough anyway. I'm OK but I'll never be a star. But it was the only way I had of getting off the farm. God, I thought I was going to be milking cows for the rest of my life, first on Daddy's farm and then on one of the boys from school when I finally made a mistake and got knocked up an' had to get married. I was the best singer in the county and I ran away thinking I'd come back someday as a big star. Now all I am is an old man's kept woman.'

I thought she might cry but she didn't, just stopped talking and looked at me with moist eyes and a forkful of eggs. I didn't know what to say, so I said, 'I think you sing just fine.'

'Fannie.'

'What?'

'I think you sing just fine, Fannie.'

I said it.

'You're the only one who knows my story here,' she said. 'You're the only one who even pretends to care.'

'Bauza seemed like he cares.'

'Guillermo thinks he cares, maybe, but he really doesn't. All the men here treat women like crap and no matter how much he seems like he cares, he doesn't. He's like all of them, wants to be a big man, *el hombre grande*. If you're gonna be *el hombre grande*, you have a very high-class Cuban wife.

And then you cheat on her. Oh, so very discreetly, with some hot number from the local trade, or, even better, with a blond *norteamericano*. A performer is the best, because then you can bring your friends, your fellow big men, and show her off in a way that you couldn't if she was just a whore. Guillermo makes sure he can do that, makes sure I can work, helps my career, even twisted arms to get me the gig to open for Miss Kitt at the Parisién. Yeah, he's helped me, helped me a lot. Given me a place to live. Helped me get work. I don't blame him. Everybody's got something going on the side in this town.'

'Everybody?' I said.

'Everybody,' she said. 'Now, Henry Gore, tell me something you want to be honest about with me.'

This all seemed like too much too soon, and then it didn't. 'I'm homesick.'

'For Warsaw, Indiana?'

'I guess so. I don't know. Warsaw, Indiana isn't really there anymore for me. My parents are dead, got killed by a drunk driver while I was in the Air Force. My sister, Janet, was just a kid at the time. Now she lives with my Aunt Ruth and Uncle Pete, in New Jersey. I tried to get out of the service to take care of her but I was in the AFOSI and they said it was a matter of national security that I finish my enlistment.'

'AFOSI? What's that?' she asked. 'From what Guillermo mentioned, it sounded like you were some kind of a spy.'

'I wasn't a spy,' I said. 'More of an investigator. I had a college degree – English History – which got me a position as a clerk-typist in Washington, DC, in something called the Office of Special Investigations, a kind of Air Force version of the FBI. My boss, a chicken colonel whose specialty was counterintelligence, saw something in me that nobody else, including me, did, and the next thing I knew I had a direct commission as a second lieutenant and a trip to OSI Training Command. I made it through the course by the skin of my teeth and was slotted for the worst duty assignment as a result, to Presque Isle Air Force Base in Aroostook County, Maine.

'I was the only OSI agent on the base, which allowed me to wear civilian clothes, carry a Colt .38 Aircrewman revolver, and come and go as I pleased, answering only to the base commander. I spent three years there.'

'Was it tough, what you did?' she asked.

'Overall, I didn't have it bad. I was bored, but no one was shooting at me. At the end of my enlistment, I went to see Janet, Uncle Pete, and Aunt Ruth and saw that they were a family, a family that I wasn't really a part of. I decided to get out of the cold, come to Cuba, and make a new life. Only now, it seems like something's missing.'

'A girl, Henry? Is that what's missing?' she said. 'Or maybe there was a girl back there, back in Indiana, or Maine, or somewhere else in the States.'

'There's no girl back there. Unless you count my kid sister. But, no, no girl the way you're thinking,' I said. 'Maybe I'm not really homesick; maybe I'm lonesome.'

She suddenly stood. 'I've got to go, Henry.' Her hands shook. She seemed like brittle broken glass.

'Can I call you again, Lola?'

'Fannie.'

'Yes. Fannie.'

'Guillermo can't find out. But, yes, you can call me.' She brushed her long fingers against the top of my hand and looked away. 'Like I said, everybody's got something going on the side in this town.'

I watched as she moved with a farm girl's grace through the courtyard and out to the street. I thought about following her to see where she lived. But I didn't. I had a task to perform yet, the acquisition of a love nest for my mistress. After all, everybody's got something going on the side in this town.

SIXTEEN

F inding a place in Miramar to keep one's mistress was a surprisingly easy errand. I asked the taxi driver who picked me up at El Siboney's front door if he knew of places to rent in the area. He was exceptionally knowledgable, driving me by a half-dozen houses with *se alquila* signs in their windows. I settled on a small cottage, very precious and out of the way, and I hoped not very expensive. My cabbie knocked on the adjoining property door, which proved to be the house of the landlord, and, after some desultory haggling in Spanish, most of which seemed to be over the cabbie's commission for producing a *gringo* with cash, a monthly rent of fifty pesos was settled on. I had a key by the cocktail hour.

As I dressed for an evening at the Tropicana, the irony of my situation was prominent in my mind. I had just rented a home for my Cuban mistress, the kind of exotic woman I had fantasized about meeting when I made my plans to come to Havana. Despite the public necking, I really wasn't attracted to her. I was, however, falling for a North Dakota farm girl, the kind of woman I had spent most of my bachelor days avoiding. And who, by the way, was someone else's mistress.

One thing I was certain of was that I could do nothing to resolve my romantic issues that night. I had to focus on my work, which meant appearing to romance the woman who didn't interest me.

The maître d' at the Tropicana's eyes sparked with recognition when he saw me. Apparently Marta had put in the word. I received a table close to the dance floor but off to the side, in the dark recesses of the club. I watched the show with detached interest, amused that the statuesque beauty who was the center of the performance would soon join me and be unable to keep her hands off me, and more amused that every second of it would be an act on both our parts.

As happened every night, the floor show concluded with

a shaking of tail feathers and the delectable flesh beneath them, and the dance floor was returned to the amateurs. Marta eased into the seat beside me twenty minutes later, planting a lusty buss on my lips and moving from there to my neck just below my ear. I guess she wasn't in the mood to waste time.

I had been drinking a Greenall's martini in an effort to wean myself from the steady diet of Dom Pérignon, which left me with a dull headache each morning. The waiter appeared when Marta finished her neck-nuzzling act.

'Havana Club and lime,' she ordered. When the waiter departed, she nodded to the almost-empty martini glass in front of me. 'How many have you had?'

'I didn't know we were already married.'

A flicker of anger crossed Marta's brow. Then she smiled sweetly. 'I need you to keep your wits about you, *hombre*. I've arranged a meeting with members of the Directorio cell from the university for tonight.'

'OK. I've had one for starters and the partial you see in front of me. I think I can handle a meeting with some college brats without blowing our cover or slurring my words.'

I felt her bare foot slide against the side of my ankle and wondered how much of this under-the-table action might be seen by anyone watching us. I decided to go with it; it set the mood.

'We'll have our drinks and leave,' Marta said. 'Do you have the gun?'

'Yeah.' I'd strapped on the Woodsman in its shoulder holster when I dressed, thinking it was silly to wear a gun, and thinking what a silly gun it was to be wearing, too long to be easily concealed and too light in caliber to do any serious damage. 'You think I'm going to need it? I really didn't sign on to be a gunslinger.'

'You will need to show it.' The waiter brought an old-fashioned glass with a couple of fingers of amber rum and a slice of lime in it. Marta sipped and, on her smiled approval, the waiter drifted away. 'Did you get us a place in Miramar?'

'Yeah. A real love nest on a quiet street.'

'Good. Take me there.'

'What about our meeting with the kids from the university?'

'The Directorio will have someone follow us from here to Miramar. They will let us know at your "love nest" where the meeting will be.'

'So they didn't give you a time or a place?'

'No, Henry.' Marta gave me a deep kiss, a take-me-home kiss.

'Maybe these college boys aren't as dumb as I thought.'

'If they were, Henry, they would already be dead.'

It was almost one in the morning when the cab dropped us at the love nest. The ride from the Tropicana had been one long necking session in the back seat of the hack, in case the driver was with the Directorio. Marta was so vigorous I felt like I needed a cigarette by the time we reached our destination and I paid the fare.

The cottage seemed particularly quaint when we entered, quaint being another word for cramped and tiny. Marta sniffed and made a little sound of displeasure in the back of her throat, but said nothing. I flipped on the lights.

'Take me to the bedroom,' she said. She was wearing a frock almost identical to the Catholic schoolgirl number she had worn on our first 'date', and flats. She kicked off the shoes when we entered the room, moved to the bed, and stretched out on it. 'Turn out the lights and lay down beside me.'

I did and we spent the next hour in the pitch black, beside each other, not touching. Whispering, Marta filled me in on the meeting with the Directorio. 'Sometime before dawn, an escort will knock on the door. Once we exchange passwords, he or she will take us to an after-hours place somewhere on 5th Avenue. Don't ask, Henry; I don't know which one. There we will meet Máximo Quintana, a law student and the leader of the cell. There may be others with him but probably none from the highest leadership of the Directorio, a group of five known as the Council of Leaders. It will be up to you to convince Quintana that you can supply large numbers of guns to the Directorio, and to wrangle a meeting with the Council of Leaders.'

After a discussion of some details to the overall plan, Marta fell silent. In a few minutes, her regular breathing told me she was asleep. Despite being in bed with a beautiful woman, and being about to falsely portray myself as a gunrunner to a bunch of revolutionaries, I, too, drifted off to sleep.

At about three in the morning, we were awakened by a sharp rap on the bedroom window.

SEVENTEEN

'Don't turn on the light,' Marta said, moving toward the living room and the entrance door. I followed, the way illuminated by a three-quarters moon that streamed yellow light in the front windows.

When Marta opened the door, a dark figure there said, '*Viva Cuba libre.*' The voice, though muffled, sounded familiar. Marta responded, '*Libre y soberana.*'

'Hello, Genry,' the figure said.

'Hello, Benny,' I said. 'How did you get all the way to Miramar? And how did you find this place?'

'I ride in the trunk of your taxi. The driver, he is Directorio.'

'Wait, wait,' Marta interjected. 'You two know each other?'

All this was taking place on the cottage's doorstep, and, while we all spoke in whispers, there was no telling who might be watching and listening. I pulled Benny and Marta inside and shut the door.

'Genry and I know each other long time,' Benny said brightly. 'We investigate together.'

Marta turned to me. 'You did not tell me this.'

'I don't know exactly what "this" you are talking about, but if you mean knowing Benny, the answer is, I know him. For the last few weeks. I didn't know he was going to appear at the door here at three in the morning. And he doesn't work with me on investigations.' I omitted the fact that I'd had no investigations on which to work since Benny had helped me home from the dingy alley behind the Capri. It seemed like a long time ago, now that the bruises had healed. 'He kind of acts as a . . . messenger or office boy for me.'

'You and El Máximo are working together to make the *revolución*? That is your new business, Genry?' Benny asked.

'Quiet, you,' Marta hissed. 'You don't need to know and you surely should not be saying it, to anyone. Do you want to get Henry killed?'

'No, señorita.' Benny's figure, already small beside Marta's six-foot frame, seemed to shrink at the thought he might endanger me.

'Now, take us to Máximo.' Marta pushed open the door and we three stepped into the warm Cuban night. Unlike downtown, Miramar had no streetlights, but we still moved easily in the bright moonlight. Benny's preferred path was the utility alley behind the houses rather than the public street in front. I suppose it lessened our chances of being seen by an insomniac or someone staggering home after a late-night assignation but I worried we might be mistaken for prowlers. Both Benny and Marta moved silently, though, sticking to the shadows and disturbing none of the trash cans and tomcats we encountered.

After covering a dozen blocks through alleys, Benny brought us out on a residential street, walked us another quick block, and steered us onto a stretch of 5th Avenue that was populated with storefronts. Even the grandeur of one of Havana's most glamorous thoroughfares was subdued at this late hour, with no automobiles or pedestrians in sight. There was watery light coming from a clerestory window above the door of one of the storefronts. Benny pointed silently at the door, and when we looked back from the building, he was gone.

We crossed the street to the door, which had a hand-lettered sign hanging on it that said, *Bar La Finca – cerrado*. Marta knocked and a man wearing a spotlessly white *guayabera* pulled the door open a crack, looked us over, and let us in. The place was full, lively with talk and laughter, the air a blue fog of cigarette and cigar smoke. Seeing who was inside the establishment, it was difficult to determine who the doorman might actually exclude. There were two men in tuxedos at the bar. A working man still dressed from his labors drank at a table by himself. A couple, very middle-class and ordinary, argued at another table. One corner table was populated by four ladies of pleasure drinking highballs and looking spent. Others around the room appeared to be tradesmen or businessmen, and their wives or girlfriends. The only thing I didn't see were any *norteamericano* faces.

Parked behind a bottle of rum at a corner table were two

men and a woman. Both of the men were slight in stature. One was darker, with heavy eyebrows and a neat mustache. For some reason, I imagined him to be a barber. The other man was really just a kid dressed up like a man. He had a baby face, without even a wisp of peach fuzz on his jaw. He wore a decent suit and tie, which seemed out of place. One should either be in a tux or casual clothing at this hour of the night, I thought.

Marta steered me toward the group. So these three were our contacts with the Directorio Revolucionario cell. With that knowledge, I paid some attention to the woman. She was stocky, thick through the middle, with wiry hair swept up and back from her forehead. She had bags under her eyes – no, circles, really, because they extended all the way around her upper lids, like both eyes had been blacked. Her eyes made her appear older, until one of the men said something, and she smiled, and then you could tell she was young. She wore a khaki shirt and men's pants, something I'd never seen a Cuban woman do.

As we approached the table, the three took note. That told me all I needed to know about their experience as operatives, or revolutionaries, or freedom fighters, or whatever they fancied themselves to be. If they'd had any training or field experience, they would have had their eyes on Marta and me from the moment we entered the bar. These were just unseasoned kids, playing at a dangerous game, no match for the pros at SIM. It made me wonder why Senator Bauza and Colonel Blanco Rico thought they needed me.

Marta walked right up to the trio and spoke to the baby-faced one in English, I assume for my benefit. 'Hello, Máximo.'

'Good evening, Marta.' The young man's voice was as immature as his face, high-pitched like he was still waiting for puberty to arrive. 'Let me introduce Miguel Gomes' – he gestured toward the other man at the table – 'and, of course, you know Celia Nunez. And who is your friend, Marta?'

'This is El Tío,' Marta said, much to my surprise. We had not discussed me using a cover name.

'And whose uncle is he, Marta? Yours?' El Máximo sneered

the question. Maybe he didn't appreciate anyone other than him going by a *nom de guerre*.

'I prefer not to disclose my real name, given the nature of my business,' I said. 'I find I live longer that way.'

'It also makes it more difficult to check references,' El Máximo said. I could tell his back was up, that he had a short fuse and it was already lit.

'I didn't think this was an interview for the job of shipping clerk,' I said to Marta. 'In my line of work, there's not much call for references. I provide the goods, you provide the cash, no references required. On either side of the deal. But maybe I should ask for some in this instance.'

The woman named Celia spoke. 'There is no need for acrimony, Uncle.' She locked intelligent brown eyes on mine, her expression and body language sending a placating message. 'Máximo merely meant that we need to exercise care in who we deal with. I am sure you feel the need to do the same.'

'You're right about that, miss,' I said. 'I exercise care in who I deal with. Marta, in whom I place explicit faith, has said that you folks are to be trusted.'

Celia smiled, the smile lighting her plain face with a warmth that bordered on beauty. 'And, as Marta has vouched for you as well, we should all be comfortable. Please, sit. Join us.'

We sat. The barman appeared with two empty glasses, some sliced limes, and a bowl of chipped ice, the latter no doubt in deference to my *gringo* sensibilities. No self-respecting Cuban would ever take ice in their rum. Celia poured from the unlabeled bottle on the table and moved to add ice to my glass.

'Just lime, thanks, Miss Nunez.'

'Celia, please. You are welcome, Uncle.'

El Máximo seemed irritated by these niceties. 'We understand you have product to sell.' He bit off the word 'product' like it had a bad taste.

'I do. For the right price.'

The heretofore silent Gomes spoke for the first time. 'Marta said that you would make us a good price. That you support our cause. That you are a friend of the *revolución*.'

'I'm sympathetic to your cause, Mr Gomes, but it will

require cash, pure and simple, for me to be a true friend to your revolution.'

El Máximo quivered with suppressed anger at my remark, like a baby about to throw a tantrum. He turned to Marta. 'So, this is who you bring to us, Marta? Well at least we know what kind of *hombre* we are dealing with.'

'I thought you wanted me to sell you product, Máximo,' I said. 'Not pass some kind of character test.' El Máximo was such a hothead, I decided about the only thing he was suited for was fomenting revolution. I wondered who would govern if this angry infant succeeded in toppling Batista. Not that I considered such a result even a remote possibility.

'I've seen nothing to indicate you have any product to sell,' Máximo said.

I held open my jacket just enough for the three to see the shoulder holster and the butt of the Woodsman inside. In the States, that would mark me as nothing more than a guy who had gone to the hardware store and plunked down fifty dollars. In Cuba, though, with gun ownership highly restricted, possession of just one pistol made me a credible arms dealer.

'I will buy it,' Máximo said. 'What is your price?'

'Buy what?'

'The "product" you just showed us. I will give you money for it, right now.'

'Hold on, Máximo,' I said. 'That's my personal weapon, and not for sale. Did you think I came here to sell you just one pissant pistol?'

'We need many, that is true,' Celia said. 'But in Cuba, most guns can only be acquired one at a time. We thought one was all you had.'

I chuckled, which seemed to irritate Máximo even more. 'Well, you're right. I only have one gun with me. But I deal in volume. I have access to weapons by the crate. I don't sell small quantities. The risk isn't worth the reward.'

Máximo, Celia, and Gomes all leaned in at the mention of guns by the crate. 'What types of weapons do you have available?'

'Military rifles. M-1 Garands, never used, in crates with the Cosmoline from the factory still on them. Two hundred units.

And Thompson sub-machine guns. Korean War surplus, not new, but in good condition. I can get you fifty of them.'

There was a glimmer usually associated with greed in El Máximo's eyes. 'You have ammunition as well?'

'I can supply you with a hundred rounds for each Garand and two thirty-round stick magazines for each Tommy gun.'

'What is the price?'

'Three hundred fifty US dollars for each Garand, in lots of ten or more. Six hundred dollars for each Thompson, also in lots of ten. Delivered to Havana.'

Máximo colored, his angry-baby face a deep red. 'Those prices are outrageous!'

I pushed my chair back and stood. 'I thought I might be dealing with amateurs. Come on, Marta, let's go. Thanks for the drink, Máximo.'

'Wait.' Again it was Celia who spoke. 'I am sure what Máximo meant is that those prices are somewhat more than we have paid in the past.' The smile from her again. A winning smile.

'Bought a lot of arms, have you?'

'In truth, no.' Máximo winced when Celia made the admission. 'To this point, our group has acquired only two revolvers' – two! – 'but the high leadership of the Directorio is usually involved in the purchase of any significant quantity.'

I took a gamble, grinned at Máximo, and said, 'Here I am thinking that I was dealing with the organ-grinder when I'm really just talking to the monkey. C'mon, Marta.'

'We can arrange for you to meet with the *jefe* and the other leaders of the Directorio.' Celia's voice was calm but tinged with urgency. 'They will have the money to buy in quantity from you.'

I stopped and swung back into my seat. 'Now that's more like it. When and where?'

That was the moment when the police came in the door.

EIGHTEEN

Cops in Cuba enter an establishment in one of two ways. If there is the slightest hint that there may be danger on the other side of the door, they come in by the dozens, with guns drawn and a hair-trigger attitude. If, on the other hand, danger is not part of the picture, they arrive in ones and twos, and stroll in as if they own the place, which they may as well, because they are usually there to wring a protection payment, or a free meal or drink, or both, from the owner.

The two cops who entered the Bar La Finca on the night when the revolutionary future of Cuba was being plotted at our table fell into the latter category. They made straight for the bar. The barman poured two glasses of Bacardi, and slid them across the smooth-worn wood of the bar to the lawmen. The larger of the two, with corporal's stripes and a two-day beard, picked up his glass, drained it, and then proceeded to do the same with his companion's. The companion, a fresh-faced kid I suspected was a trainee, didn't flinch at the loss of his drink. The one thing he'd already learned was to expect his mentor to filch his already once-filched rum.

The corporal, fortified by the drinks, leaned with his back against the bar and scanned the room. The efficient bartender slapped a fat envelope filled with protection money across the bar and the trainee took it, the corporal undoubtedly wanting to avoid the burden of carrying the cash during the rest of his shift.

The head cop's eyes fell on our cozy group. Conversation had ceased at our table, with all of us staring into our glasses, except Máximo, who glared toward the two policemen as though they had personally insulted his *mamacita*. Máximo's eye contact was taken by the corporal as a challenge to his authority. He slowly lifted himself off the rail of the bar and weaved among the tables until he came to a halt directly behind me, facing

Máximo across my left shoulder. The trainee trailed along after his boss, and positioned himself behind Gomes.

'I'll have your identification papers,' the older cop said. The thought crossed my mind that this was nothing to get excited about, just a little show of authority by the corporal, or maybe a minor shakedown. The man's tone of voice said that he had no idea that he was dealing with a dangerous group of rebels plotting an arms deal.

'Of course,' Máximo said. He reached in his suit jacket for what I and the corporal thought were his papers. What he came out with was a .25 caliber Galesi. I recognized the gun because I had taken one away from a drunken airman once back in Maine. The airman had called it a mouse gun, and it looked like that's all it would be good for – killing mice.

El Máximo didn't hesitate to use the miniature pistol. He shot the corporal in the left shoulder. I guess he had aimed for the cop's heart, but inexperience and the short barrel of the cheap gun led only to a wound that enraged the policeman and, worse, did nothing to incapacitate him. The corporal was carrying an old Smith and Wesson Military and Police .38 and he had no trouble drawing it with his uninjured right arm. The cop had the aim that El Máximo did not, hitting the hero of the revolution in the heart. Unfortunately for the corporal, the slug struck just as Máximo got off his second shot. The jolt caused Máximo's hand to pitch upward as he fired. The little .25 caliber slug doesn't do much damage but it didn't need to, as it caught the corporal directly in the right eye, exploding the orb in its socket and continuing on to the brain. The policeman dropped like a stockyard steer clubbed with a sledgehammer, twitched once, and was dead. El Máximo never saw his kill, dead where he sat.

The trainee cop had frozen when the shooting started but now he came around, drawing his own .38 in what seemed like slow motion. His eyes were on Gomes. Gomes, if he'd had any sense, should have raised his hands and called it a day. Instead, he reached in his pants pocket and, making the cardinal mistake of bringing a knife to a gunfight, flicked open a switchblade and lunged for the kid cop. The kid's eyes were white with panic but he must have gotten high marks on his training at the range; he put two, center mass, into Gomes. The switchblade clattered to the floor as Gomes slumped across the table.

All the gunfire had produced a reaction in me that could only be described as natural, given my AFOSI training. By the time the trainee had fired his second shot at Gomes, I had the Woodsman out of its shoulder holster, safety off, and was swinging it toward the young cop. I didn't want to shoot him. Hell, I didn't want to shoot anybody.

I yelled, '*Hacer alto!*', the only thing I could think of, but the kid didn't stop. I had the drop on him. But it didn't make any difference to him, given what he had already seen happen to his boss. I can't say I would have done any differently if I had been in his shoes. He swung his Smith and Wesson toward me. I put five shots into his chest as fast as I could pull the trigger. The kid never finished the traverse of his gun from Gomes to me. He fired one harmless shot into the wall above Celia Nunez's head as he fell over backward.

The explosive sound of gunfire in the tight space of the bar was replaced with the screams of women and the shouts of men. There was a mass exodus out the single door, led by the barman, who prudently took his cashbox with him. In less than a minute the place was empty except for Marta, Celia, me, and four corpses.

Marta was frozen in terror, her mouth open like Munch's *The Scream*, with the same amount of sound coming out as in the famous painting. Celia sprang to Máximo's side, checked for a pulse, and, finding none, did the same to Gomes, with the same result.

'Come on,' I said. 'Let's get out of here.' I'd thought for a second about staying and explaining when the guaranteed flood of additional cops arrived but then I remembered what the bodyguard had done to the wounded and disabled assassin on the steps of the Capitolio. Best not to take the chance that the corporal's and the kid-cop's comrades would be in a charitable mood when they saw the carnage inside the bar.

Marta was slow to move. Celia and I dragged her to her feet and pulled her along with us out onto 5th Avenue. The air seemed clear and clean after the olfactory confusion of burned gunpowder, spilled rum, and the copper-penny scent of blood in the bar. It was quiet, too, the screaming and the shouting done, the silence broken only by the soft tread of fleeing footsteps.

'This way,' I said to Celia, and steered Marta across 5th Avenue back to the shadowed street we had approached along earlier in the evening. When we reached a darker area, we stopped to catch our breath. A shape emerged from the shadows beneath an espinillo tree. I swung the Woodsman, which I had been holding against my leg as we walked, toward the figure.

'Genry, is everything OK? I hear the shooting.' Benny.

'Jesus, Benny, you scared the living daylights out of me.'

'What is this "living daylights", Genry?'

'Never mind about that. We've got to get out of here. You should, too. Don't come with us. The police are after us.'

Celia, Marta, and I moved off at a walk so as not to cause suspicion. Only now, five minutes after the shooting had started and two minutes after we had exited La Finca, did we hear the sound of police sirens in the distance. At most, we had another minute or so before the squad cars arrived at the bar, and another three or four minutes after that before they fanned out into the neighborhood looking for suspects. Looking for us.

Marta still had not uttered a sound. She was moving better now, keeping pace with Celia and me, no longer needing to be dragged along. We tried to skirt any lighted areas but once or twice light from a porch or window illuminated Celia's face. She appeared strong, resolute, fearless. Once, in one of those dimly lighted places, I spotted a small figure trailing us by a dozen yards. Benny again. There was no time to go back and chase him away. He was on his own. At least he didn't look like a cop-killer if the police caught him. And he knew the streets, and the hiding places along them, better than the three of us. He would be fine, I told myself.

The first sirens wound down to a stop. They must have reached La Finca. We had covered about six blocks by then, almost halfway back to the love nest. I allowed myself to become mildly optimistic about our chances of reaching the cottage when a new flood of siren wails rent the night.

The first police on the scene must have reported the quartet of corpses they'd found in the bar.

Now the sirens came from all directions. I glimpsed blue and white patrol cars speeding along 5th Avenue and then in the adjacent streets, their spotlights playing against houses and foliage. That was one thing I could never quite figure out about cops – when something really big hit the fan, their reaction was to come in with sirens blaring and lights blazing. They advertised their presence, and any sensible perpetrator went to ground and hid. Maybe they did what they did expressly for that purpose, to make sure the gunmen who had killed their fellow officers avoided them, thereby saving themselves from the same fate.

I knew it was only a matter of time, though, before they adopted a more stealthy approach and widened their search to the snicket where Marta, Celia, and I hid.

We moved to the end of the alley, where it intersected with a cross street. Just then a police car turned in at the opposite end. We dove into a large hibiscus bush. The blue and white Dodge crept along, its Detroit engine a low rumble, its spotlight scouring the garbage cans, board fences, and shrubbery edging the narrow lane as it inched closer to our hiding place.

'We must run across the street,' Celia whispered. She was right. A mad dash across the open street left us exposed and at risk of capture but staying where we were concealed guaranteed it. We had squatted down to be less visible. Now I stood and pulled Marta to her feet.

'OK, let's go,' I hissed.

At the same moment there was a commotion from the cop car at the far end of the alley. '*Alto, alto!*' the cops yelled. Looking back, I saw the hunched figure of Benny framed in the beam of the spotlight as he ran through it and sprinted directly past the passenger door of the squad car. The policeman in the passenger seat, a tub of lard who'd chowed down on way too many *bistecs de palomilla* and *moros y cristianos* in his day, rolled out and gave chase, gun in hand. His partner slammed the Dodge into reverse as Benny zigzagged down the sandy lane and off into an adjoining yard. The fat cop snapped off a shot just as Benny cut out of the alley. The cop was no more of a marksman than he was a sprinter; the bullet clipped off a banana leaf high above Benny's receding figure.

With the police focused on Benny, the three of us took our chance crossing the street. We made it easily, and continued along the side street at a dead sprint all the way to the door of the love nest. More police cars could be heard, converging on the block where Benny had made his move.

I hoped that Benny had made it. But I didn't see how he could.

NINETEEN

One of the benefits of having a hideout in Miramar is the number of important people who live there. Ambassadors, wealthy merchants, middle-ranking politicos – those who don't need extensive security to keep from being assassinated – foreign businessmen, and a healthy dose of Syndicate figures in the neighborhood meant the police couldn't just do a house-to-house roust like they would in some of Havana's less tony environs.

Once or twice during the night, the lights of the searchers played across the windows of the love nest but the expected knock on the door never came. Marta, Celia, and I hunkered in the darkness until daylight, and then waited out the morning, hungry and exhausted, behind closed curtains.

Celia rummaged through the kitchen for food. Finding none, she turned her attention to the bath, which contained only a lone bottle of hydrogen peroxide. 'It's time for me to become a blond,' she said. 'Marta, I'll need your help.'

Marta, still shaken by the bloodshed and danger of the night, was slow to assist. Eventually, though, the two women became engrossed in the project, giggling like schoolgirls at Celia's platinum-blond results. Marta had some makeup in her handbag, and, after liberal application, the mannish Celia was transformed. The problem of her masculine shirt and pants was solved when a very worn, very dirty, shift was located on the floor of the bedroom closet. When she donned the dress, she made a passably feminine prostitute. 'You make an excellent whore,' Marta remarked, admiring her handiwork.

The real test came a few minutes later. A police car had been parked at the corner of the block since early morning, the two cops inside taking turns dozing after their long night trying to locate the killers from the Bar La Finca shooting. Celia displayed steely nerve and a realistic hooker's gait as she marched out the front door and right past the cops. The only attention she drew was an *'Aiiee, chica!'* and a wolf whistle from the cop who wasn't sleeping. Her plan was to make her way to 5th Avenue and catch a bus back to the university from there.

'What about us, Marta?' I asked after we saw Celia pass safely on her way.

'You tell me how a six-foot-tall black woman and a *gringo* in dirty clothes can sneak by those cops at the end of the block,' she replied.

She had a point. I looked like I'd been on a two-week bender and gotten rolled at the end of it. The sleeve of my jacket was torn and the knees of my pants were dirty. As for Marta, she looked just fine but if anyone in the bar was able to describe any one of us to the police, it had to be her. The dumbest cop in Havana could pick her out of a crowd of a thousand based on a description from a nearsighted grandmother.

I thought for a minute and a solution, a very unsatisfactory solution, came to mind. 'I need a phone,' I told Marta.

'You'll never make it to 5th Avenue to call from a payphone. Maybe we should just stay here.'

'It's only a matter of time before the boys in the blue-and-whites start knocking on doors in the area, and kicking them in if there's no answer. We've got to get out of here. I think I can get us out if I can make a call.'

'What about the landlord? Does he have a phone?'

The space between the love nest and the landlord's adjoining house was mostly blocked by a variegated forest of overgrown crotons. Using them for cover, the only time I would be visible from the street would be when I knocked on the front door.

It had all happened so quickly at La Finca that I hadn't even broken a sweat until we began to run from the police. Now, though, there was plenty of time to contemplate how I would die if the police caught me in the open. Casual was the way to play it, I decided, but I was sopping wet with perspiration by the time I reached the landlord's door and waited the interminable minute it took him to answer my knock.

He eyed me with the contempt all landlords have for their tenants when the rent has been paid and the tenant's appearance can only mean a request or demand for which they will receive no additional compensation. '*Que?*' His voice dripped with suspicion.

'*Yo quiero teléfono,*' I said, in my limited Spanish.

Surprised that my visit did not involve a stopped toilet or leaking roof, the man waved me into the foyer of his house, where an ancient Bakelite telephone rested on a small table. He motioned to a chair beside the phone.

'No long distance,' he said, wagging a finger at me and leaving the room.

I dialed Fannie Knutsen's number.

TWENTY

Fannie Knutsen's drowsy morning mumble came on the line. 'Hullo?'

'It's Henry.'

'Henry.' The voice was more pleasant now.

'I'm in trouble. Police trouble. I need your help and I need you to not ask too many questions.'

A second's hesitation and then, 'Sure, Henry. I'll help. Whatever you need.'

'You have a car?'

'Yeah.'

I gave her the address of the love nest. 'I'm there now. Back the car down the driveway to the garage door. And bring me some clothes, if you have them.'

'Guillermo keeps some stuff at my place. What do you need?'

'Casual pants and a shirt. And a hat.'

Twenty minutes later Fannie showed up in a white '54 Cadillac convertible, a gift, I suspected, from Senator Bauza. The car had government license plates on it, a real break for me. And an indication of just how corrupt Cuba was, when the mistress of a senator could drive around in a car with government tags in public and no one even flinched.

Fannie backed the Caddy close to the garage, as instructed, and got out and marched to the front door. She appeared to have dressed to match the automobile – a gauzy white sundress, short white gloves, white sandals, and a white straw hat with a shallow crown and a broad brim that resembled an inverted dinner plate.

When she reached the door, I opened it and pulled her inside. 'Whose place is this?' she asked, scanning the living room.

'Mine,' Marta said, emerging from the kitchen.

The two women eyed each other. I was reminded of the

time when my sister Janet brought home a stray cat and introduced it into the room where our long-time pet kitty, Tiger, had reigned for the last decade. 'And who are you?' Fannie asked.

'I'm Marta Serrano.'

For a moment, I expected the two to hiss at each other. During that moment, I was flattered that, if they did, it would be over me. Instead, Fannie put out a gloved hand. 'I'm Lola Loring. Pleased to meet any friend of Henry's.'

'The same here, Señorita Loring,' Marta said. 'Thank you for coming to our assistance.'

Fannie turned to me. 'Does this have something to do with all the cops snooping around the neighborhood? They even have a checkpoint set up on 5th Avenue. It's the only way into the area. Or out, I suspect.'

'Yes,' I said. 'They're after me, and Marta. There was a shooting last night, involving the police.'

Lola's baby blues widened. 'You shot a cop?'

'Look, Lola, if you don't want to get involved, I understand . . .' I began.

She shook her head like she was awakening from a deep sleep. 'No. No, I mean, I'll help you. Do you need to get to the American embassy?'

'We just need to get out of here.'

'Both of you?' Fannie placed a lot of emphasis on the 'both'.

'They haven't started searching houses yet but it's only a matter of time,' Marta said.

'What do you want me to do?' Fannie asked.

I noticed she carried a large handbag. White, of course. 'Did you bring the clothes?'

Fannie dug into the bag and produced a pair of black pants and a white *guayabera*. 'Guillermo's,' she said. 'They should fit you. I've got one of his Panama hats in the car.'

The pants were baggy but the loose-fitting Cuban shirt covered the bunched waistband. After I'd changed, we cut through the house to the interior garage entrance. There, Marta said, 'I'll climb into the trunk.'

'What?' Fannie said. 'Why?'

'If the police have our descriptions, they are looking for an

Anglo man and two Cuban women. One of the women very tall and black,' Marta said. 'I would, as you *norteamericanos* say, stick out like a sore thumb. You two in the car should pass through OK. Whatever you do, don't let the police look in the trunk.' Or we're all dead, she could have added.

While Marta stood out of sight in the garage, Fannie and I opened the door and popped the Caddy's trunk. It didn't appear that anyone was watching, so I walked Marta to the trunk, shielding her from view as best I could. She rolled herself inside and I closed the lid. I got in the passenger side, sliding the Woodsman under the seat and putting on the Panama I found inside.

'You paint a handsome picture in that hat, Henry.' Fannie tried to sound casual and confident but her voice was edgy when she spoke.

'Everybody wore a Panama in Maine when I was stationed there, to keep cool under the blazing tropical sun.' My poor attempt at a joke should have fallen flat but we were passing a squad car parked at the corner of 5th Avenue then, and Fannie made a great show of laughing at my line. She was proving herself a better actress than singer.

We had traveled only six blocks toward downtown when the street was barred by a checkpoint. Blue-and-whites were parked to funnel traffic to a barricade where three cops checked papers and looked in back seats and trunks. Other officers loitered nearby, casual in the manner of all Cuban cops, but a few of them had riot guns in the crooks of their arms. I shuddered to think what the buckshot from them would do to Bauza's white Caddy. And Fannie. And me.

'I'll handle this,' Fannie said under her breath, while smiling sweetly at the cops lining our path.

A cop with sergeant's stripes approached the driver's side window. 'Is there something wrong, officer?' Fannie asked in English.

The sergeant mumbled something in Spanish and held out his hand. Fannie said, in her best Spanglish, '*No comprendez Spanish.* I don't speak. English only, *por favor.*' The sergeant did what most cops do when confronted with linguistic non-compliance – repeated himself in a louder voice, still in

Spanish. Fannie gave him a quizzical look and sat, unmoving, with both hands on the wheel.

This caught the attention of a middle-aged lieutenant who was speaking to three patrol officers behind the barricade. He strolled over. 'Is there some difficulty, señorita?'

'Yes, officer,' Fannie said. 'I cannot understand what this officer' – inclining her head toward the sergeant – 'wants because he won't speak English to me.' Fannie had obviously decided to go with the clueless American act.

'The sergeant asks for your and the gentleman's identification papers, señorita.'

'Why, officer? We have done nothing wrong. And you and your men have already made me late for an appointment with my friend, Senator Bauza.'

The lieutenant had eyed the government license plate on the Caddy when he'd approached. That, combined with the mention of Bauza, sent him into full obsequious mode. 'I am sorry, señorita. I had no idea. Please move on through the barricades. And please excuse any delay that we may have caused you and the señor.'

'Certainly. Thank you, officer . . .?' Lola said.

'Flores, señorita. Lieutenant Armando Flores. I am pleased to provide any assistance.'

'There is a special favor you could do for me, Lieutenant, for which I would be most grateful.' Fannie gave the cop her best shy farm-girl smile. 'It would be best if Guillermo – Senator Bauza – did not learn of the señor's presence with me in the car today. Do we understand each other, Lieutenant Flores?'

'Of course, señorita.' Flores managed a both knowing and gallant expression in a way that only Latin men can do. 'I can assure you that my daily report will make no mention of your . . . companion, señorita . . .?'

'Loring, Lieutenant. Lola Loring. I'm most grateful and will be sure to mention your courtesy to Senator Bauza.'

Flores made a slight bow. His men removed the barricade and stepped aside. In five minutes we were cruising along the Malecón, sea breeze in our hair.

Before we reached downtown, Fannie steered the Caddy

into a deserted alley and we unlocked the trunk. Marta emerged from the cramped space, hot but none the worse for wear. There was a bus stop a couple of blocks away. There she could catch a bus to the Tropicana in time to appear for her evening show. Once she took the stage, no one would suspect that the Trop's lead dancer had been involved in the shooting of two policemen at Bar La Finca that morning.

After a silent drive, Fannie dropped me on a corner six blocks from my apartment on Calle J. When I closed the car door, I leaned in the window to explain about Marta but she drove off before I could. I hoped I would get the opportunity to explain later but at that moment it didn't seem likely.

The sun is a particularly lustrous gold on the day after the night when one is almost killed. The breeze is sweet and gentle in the afternoon of the day when one escapes a police dragnet. True, I was still a hunted man. True, I was a man haunted by being forced to kill the poor kid-cop who was little more than a teenager. But my situation was looking up compared to what it had been only hours before. I didn't feel good, especially about the kid, but I almost felt human. I wasn't optimistic but at least I wasn't hopeless.

Strolling along the street shaded by palms and ceiba trees, I told myself the worst was over, that I would find a way out of the fix I was in, that, somehow, I would get out of Cuba and never look back.

It was about then that I glanced to my right and saw the olive-drab SIM car keeping pace with me as I walked.

TWENTY-ONE

T here was a fleeting moment when I considered bolting for the nearest side yard, hoping that the mutts in the SIM Pontiac weren't fast enough to catch me on foot or good enough with a gun to plug me in the back as I tried to scale a fence. There was a fleeting moment when I considered shooting it out, 'Two Gun' Crowley-style, but me alone, with the few shells remaining in the small-caliber Woodsman, against two or more of them – they always traveled in force – using their standard-issue .45 semi-autos didn't seem like good odds. So, like many people in trouble, I chose to ignore the problem. I walked steadily, facing forward.

'*Mi madre*, God rest her sainted soul, taught me that you can never outrun your difficulties.' The voice which dispensed this bit of wisdom was accompanied by a hand which firmly seized my right elbow. 'I can assure you that you cannot out-walk them either, Señor Gore.'

'Lieutenant Trujillo, what brings you out from the rock you live under on this fine day?'

'I've come to save your scrawny ass from the blue-and-whites, and if you know what's good for you, you'll thank me and come along quietly.' A nudge in the ribs from Trujillo's automatic convinced me that I should do just that.

'Why, thank you, Lieutenant Trujillo,' I said. As the SIM car pulled to the curb, I saw it was driven by Trujillo's humorless sidekick, Sergeant Alvarez. 'And thank you, Sergeant Alvarez, for the scenic drive I'm sure we are about to take.' Alvarez scowled, got out, and stuffed me in the rear driver's side door. Trujillo got in beside me.

'Down on the floor,' he ordered. 'Unless you want the police to see you.'

I didn't want that, so I spent the next fifteen minutes inspecting the floorboards as we weaved left and right through the light midday traffic.

'Where are we going?' I finally asked.

'To see Colonel Blanco Rico.'

'Not at your "facility" at the Comandancia General, I hope.' Havana's main police station and jail didn't seem like a prudent destination for a day when I'd killed a cop.

Trujillo chuckled. 'No, Señor Gore, even SIM could not guarantee your welfare there today. Colonel Blanco Rico will be meeting you at another, safer location.'

The safer location turned out to be a fairly new, fairly nondescript middle-class home in a block of similar homes, save for a commercial building on the nearest corner. I got a glimpse of the street sign painted on the wall of that building – Calle 17 and Calle 26. Plunk in the middle of the Nuevo Vedado district – a nice, family-oriented neighborhood. It didn't seem like a place where SIM would have one of its 'facilities' but I suppose that made it the logical place for it. Maybe Colonel Blanco Rico was going to put me up in a safe house for a few days until the heat was off with the cops. I didn't think he was going to have me killed. He could have had Trujillo and Alvarez do that right on the street where they picked me up, and then disappeared my body. Or he could have made some points with the police by turning me over to them at the Comandancia General, where the cops would have enjoyed a few days of torturing me before they finished me off.

'Come this way.' Lieutenant Trujillo walked me up the front steps and rang the doorbell. A woman of middle age answered the door. With her incurious eyes and plain blue housedress, she reminded me of my mother.

'Enjoy,' Trujillo inexplicably said as he waved me inside.

'This way,' the lady of the house said in English. She led me to a room that, from its size and where it was situated, had once been the living room of the residence. It had been reconfigured to accommodate a small crescent-shaped stage at one end of the room and a well-stocked bar, complete with a bartender in a white shirt and dapper bow tie, at the other. In between the bar and the stage were a sofa and a number of overstuffed chairs, all facing the stage. At one end of the sofa sat Colonel Blanco Rico, sipping from a glass of rum, a corona smoking in a pedestal ashtray beside him.

'Henry, so good of you to join me,' Blanco Rico said, not rising. He pointed to a nearby chair. 'Come, sit.'

I thought about making a wise-guy response about the voluntariness of my presence. Instead, I opted for, 'Thanks, Colonel,' and sat as directed.

The barman hustled over and asked if I wanted a drink. 'Momo makes an excellent daiquiri,' Blanco Rico said. A double martini, up, would have suited my mood and taken more of the edge off than the local fruit drink, but I said, 'Sounds good.'

'Cigar?' the colonel offered. All of this sociable offering of drinks and cigars had me wondering if the next offer was for a last meal, followed by a SIM bullet behind the ear.

'No, thanks.'

Blanco Rico got straight to the point. 'When we gave you a gun, we had no idea you would put it to use so quickly. And against the police, no less.'

'Believe me, Colonel, it was not by choice. That was one dance I would have just as soon sat out.'

'That is what I told the Chief of Police, that if you used the gun it was because his officers had forced you into it.'

'You talked to the Chief of Police about me? Jesus, Colonel, every cop in Havana will be after my scalp now they have my name to go with any descriptions given by witnesses.'

Blanco Rico took a long draw on his cigar. 'Please, Henry, do not become agitated. Chief Delgado assured me he will not disclose your name to others. He even made certain that his Lieutenant Flores allowed you and Marta to slip through the police perimeter earlier today. And, tonight, a flying squad of police officers will capture, if possible, but, more likely, will be forced to kill, two known bandits – a white man and a black woman – who will be declared responsible for the deaths of the brave officers who were ambushed last night in the Bar La Finca. That, and the funerals of the police officers, should bring this ugly matter to a close and allow you to continue your mission.' The curtain on the stage rose. 'Ah, good, the entertainment.' Blanco Rico sat forward in his seat in anticipation.

Was I going to get off scot-free for the killing of those

policemen, I asked myself as the lights dimmed, theater-like, and a set of spots illuminated the stage? Was life that cheap and so easily tossed away in this town? And what was expected of me in return now? The appearance of a muscular man and three women on the stage barely distracted me from these thoughts until Blanco Rico spoke.

'Pick one,' he said.

'What?'

The colonel waved his cigar toward the three women on stage. 'Pick one, Henry.'

The women and the man were all wearing silken bathrobes. The women were all markedly different from one another – a well-endowed blond, a tall mixed-race woman with dyed-red hair, and a child-like brunette.

'Pick one for what?' I asked.

'For the entertainment. The *sata* you select will provide the entertainment along with El Toro, the big man.'

Still distracted by my narrow escape, I said, 'OK. I pick the blond.'

Blanco Rico waved toward the blond. The other two women, indifferent to the fact that they had not been selected, wandered off the stage to the bar. Momo the bartender set them each up with a glass of rum, which they drank with their backs turned to the upcoming performance of their colleagues.

The man called El Toro shrugged out of his robe, revealing a well-defined torso and arms, and the largest male member I've ever seen in my life. It hung between his legs like a thick and distinctly unappetizing sausage. Once naked, El Toro looked for a moment toward the two of us, his audience, and then turned his attention to the woman, drawing off her robe. Like El Toro, she was totally nude beneath the robe. Like El Toro, she was an impressive example of her sex, with large, firm breasts and a cloud of blond hair at the convergence of her thighs.

The woman dropped to her knees without hesitation, taking El Toro into her mouth, jaws and tongue working until a ring of her red lipstick encircled his erection. She stood and presented her backside to El Toro. He entered her with a brutal thrust.

I cut my eyes toward Colonel Blanco Rico. He watched the woman and El Toro with cool appreciation, a sign that he had been to this place and witnessed this vulgar performance before, often enough to watch without being shocked and yet not so many times that he was indifferent to it.

I tried to keep my eyes from the couple, embarrassed for the woman's degradation, but unable to do so completely. There was no enjoyment for me in watching their gyrations, more a sickening fascination of the kind that one experiences when passing a bloody car accident on the road. You know you should look away. You know what you see will be upsetting. But you can't help but look, and after you do, you feel a mixture of shame and sick exhilaration, though you would never admit it to a living soul. And you try hard not to admit it to yourself.

The ugly spectacle continued for a quarter of an hour, brought to a conclusion by a grunt from El Toro and the withdrawal of his relaxed member from his victim. The woman slid to the floor of the stage for a minute, exhausted, before recovering enough to stand and walk off, defiled beyond debasement, a once-child, a daughter, a human being now nothing more than a piece of meat cast before hungry canines. Canines like Blanco Rico. Canines like me.

'The most impressive thing about El Toro, after the size of his *pinga*, is that he can repeat his performance immediately,' the colonel said. 'And again after that. That is why there are three girls, you see, so he can fully display his prowess, like a champion athlete. Who do you choose to be next?'

I wanted to call him a sick bastard, to call everyone in this quiet suburban house on this quiet suburban street sick and perverse and disgusting. But all I said was, 'This really isn't my kind of show, Colonel.'

'Ah, Henry, I had no idea.' Blanco Rico was smug. 'Boys? I would not have suspected, you conceal it so well. Not my preference, but in deference to the difficult last twenty-four hours you have experienced, I can have Lula send in three boys for El Toro. It will take but a moment.' He raised his hand to the motherly woman, who I realized had been watching from an alcove near the bar.

'No. No, Colonel, what I mean is that this type of . . . entertainment, this . . . sex show is not something I particularly enjoy.'

Blanco Rico smiled a close-lipped smile. 'My friend, the American businessman Meyer Lansky, who owns this establishment, would say, "All work and no play makes Henry a dull boy." Still, if you wish to get to work.' He turned to the stage. 'Most impressive, El Toro, but my friend and I must talk.'

El Toro picked up his robe from the stage and walked from the room. The redhead and the brunette left the bar, drinks in hand. The barman busied himself polishing glasses.

'Now, Henry, to business,' Blanco Rico said. 'It is well that one member of the Directorio cell survived the shooting at La Finca and even better that you aided in her escape. This can only serve to establish your credibility with the bandits, something for which two lowly policemen are a minor price to pay. Before the shooting, was it going well? Were you and Marta able to convince the bandits that you are an arms dealer?'

I couldn't believe it. Clearly, the colonel viewed the deaths of Máximo Quintana, Miguel Gomes, and the two policemen as incidental, a mere hiccup in the operation.

'Yes, I guess so,' I said. 'Máximo Quintana was being difficult but I got no sense that he was not convinced.'

'He is a problem which no longer exists. What of Celia Nunez?'

'She seemed to believe and she seemed ready to deal. And ready to involve those higher up in the organization,' I said. 'I'm just not so sure I am, Colonel. I didn't sign up for a shooting war.'

'Henry, Henry, I am surprised. You know that matters of this nature often involve some personal risk. Or are you asking for more money?'

Blanco Rico was right. I knew there was risk involved when I signed on. And no one was more concerned about the welfare of Mrs Gore's only son than me. I was just too broke to assess it objectively. 'I knew there was risk,' I admitted. 'And I'm not asking for more money, Colonel.'

'Good, Henry. A – how do you say it? – shakedown would have been so unseemly and beneath your dignity.'

'But I want out,' I said. 'I'm not a killer. Especially cops. Especially cops who look like they haven't graduated from high school. This operation just isn't for me.'

'Of course, Henry. I understand. Simply return the thousand pesos we advanced to you and we will call things even. It will be difficult but I'm sure we can locate another American "arms dealer" to work with Marta.'

'There's a problem with the thousand pesos, Colonel. There's only about five hundred left. I'll need some time to repay the rest to you.'

'That *is* a problem, Henry.' Blanco Rico took a long draw on his cigar, pursing his lips to exhale the smoke and watching it curl away toward the ceiling. 'The payment would need to be immediate. As you must be aware, Cuba is a cash economy. Credit is contrary to the Cuban spirit.'

The colonel studied the end of his cigar, allowing the silence to hang as heavy as heartbreak in the room. I glanced over to the bar, I guess hoping for help to somehow appear. Momo the barman rubbed a cloth along its surface and avoided eye contact.

No choice. 'OK. I guess I'm in, Colonel.'

'Good, Henry. I knew you would see the light. Be assured we will keep a closer eye on you from this point forward. To be ready to assist, of course, so that no unfortunate incidents like that of last night occur again. For now, stay out of the public eye, and away from your home. I wouldn't want any zealots from the Havana police to find you before tonight's capture of those responsible for the two police officers' untimely demise. Lieutenant Trujillo and Sergeant Alvarez will give you a ride to wherever you wish to go.'

TWENTY-TWO

B lanco Rico's two curs were waiting in the SIM Pontiac, engine idling, when I stepped out the door. They put me in the back seat, alone this time. I guess they thought I could be trusted not to bail out and run, now that the colonel had worked his magic on me.

I had them drop me outside a tourist bar called El Toucan, just off the Malecón in Vedado. I picked it because I thought it unlikely that the cops would visit a tourist bar looking for killers, because there was a payphone on the street nearby and because it seemed like the best place to put the two pesos and twenty centavos rattling around in my pocket to work. Just before they dropped me off, Trujillo leaned over the seat and slapped two loaded clips for the Woodsman into my hand. 'Try not to use them too quickly,' he said. 'And make sure, if you do, that you're shooting the bad guys this time.'

Inside El Toucan, I used one peso for a glass of Bacardi at the bar, and gave the bartender a ten-centavo tip. Then I went outside to the payphone and called Fannie Knutsen.

'I need help, Fannie,' I said, dispensing with the formalities, when she came on the line. It had been four hours since she had dropped me off. It might as well have been a thousand years.

She didn't seem kindly disposed when she responded. 'Again? You're like a baby, Henry, you need help every few hours. If I'd wanted to live my life that way, I'd be on a farm on the banks of the Red River right now, with one squallin' on my hip and a second in the oven.'

'C'mon, Fannie. I'm in a jam. I need a place to stay for a day till the heat's off. Just for a day.' Saying the time frame made me think of the two unsuspecting 'bandits' who were going about their regular business right then, eating meals, working, maybe making love, real love, not knowing they were going to be bumped off tonight for something they had no hand in. Just to save my skin.

'There ain't gonna be another dame along with you, like the last time, is there, Henry?' Her voice was as cold as the winter wind off the North Dakota plains.

'No. Just me.'

'Where are you?'

'At a bar. The El Toucan, a block off the Malecón.'

'All right. I know the place. I might show up in a half-hour, if I don't have an attack of common sense between now and then.' The line clicked dead.

I went back inside El Toucan. The bartender hustled down the bar to me in a flash after the ten-centavo tip, and I used my remaining peso on another Bacardi, wondering how I'd get along on my remaining five centavos if Fannie had that attack of common sense she'd spoken about.

I didn't get to find out. After ten minutes, Fannie stepped in the door, a vision momentarily backlit in the afternoon sun, wearing a white halter top, black cigarette pants, and red ballet flats. She looked like a farmer's daughter trying to look like Audrey Hepburn. She could have carried it off if she wasn't so tall, so blond, and so blue-eyed. She scanned the place, picked me out at the bar, and marched over.

'Would you like a drink?' When I asked, I realized I didn't have the money if she said yes. Maybe I'd have to ask her to pay for it. El Toucan, you see, was a pay-in-advance kind of place.

'No,' Fannie said. 'I didn't say anything before but I'm saying something now. What I would like is to know who that Amazon was you were with earlier? What I would like is to know why you need so much rescuing and why I'm the one you call when you need it? What I would like is to know if I'm being played for a sucker?' Her eyes sparked like angry azure diamonds as she spoke.

'Those are all legit questions,' I said. 'The Amazon means nothing to me. She's a co-worker and nothing more. You gotta believe me on that. I'm not trying to play you for a sucker. And as for why you get the call when I'm in trouble, it's simple – you're the only one I trust in this whole damn town.'

The fire left Fannie's eyes. They softened into concern, or maybe something deeper than that. 'Guillermo is off in the countryside for a couple of days. Doing the politician thing and probably cheating on his wife. And me. I can hide you at my place until tomorrow.'

'Thanks. That'd be great.'

She smiled. 'Let's get out of this dive, then. How did you pick this place, anyway?'

'It looked like a place that the cops didn't visit very often.' I tossed my last five centavos on the bar and took Fannie's arm. Her white Caddy was parked right out front.

'I put the top up, figuring you didn't want to be seen in broad daylight,' Fannie said. She drove us back toward Miramar, taking streets that hugged the southerly edges of the neighborhood, avoiding the main drag of 5th Avenue and its hordes of police. She finally stopped on a side street which had no signage, and was shaded on both sides by massive ceiba trees.

'Get down on the floor, Henry.'

'This is getting to be my preferred mode of transportation,' I mumbled from the nylon-carpeted floor of the Cadillac. In another three minutes, we pulled into a garage.

Fannie drew the garage door shut and took me out a side door which opened onto a narrow colonnade leading to a rather grand house. The outside was all stucco and tile roofs in the classic Spanish style. The inside foyer was in the same vein – dark wood, heavy furniture, and wrought-iron banisters on the stairs leading up to the second floor. The walls were dotted with portraits of cavaliers and ladies in mantillas. The whole place looked as if it had been plucked from a duchy near Seville or Madrid and dropped intact into the Caribbean.

'What do you think, Henry?' Fannie wasn't fishing for a compliment about the massive pile she lived in. She seemed to really want to know what I thought.

'I feel like I neglected to wear my sword and buckler,' I said.

'I know what you mean. I feel like Rapunzel, stuck in the castle, only I don't have enough hair to let down, and no prince to climb it if I did.'

'I take it you didn't choose the decor.'

'No. Guillermo picked out everything. He says he's

descended from Spanish nobility. There's even a Bauza family crest over the bed in the bedroom.' Fannie blushed when she said 'bed in the bedroom'. That was nice to see, in a town where visits to the bedroom are just another commodity. Recovering her composure, she said, 'You can stay in the guest room, third on the right on the second floor. I've got to change and leave. I have to work tonight. There's food in the pantry. No one will bother you. No one ever comes here but Guillermo.'

'Thanks,' I said, and brushed my palm against her cheek.

Fannie's eyes stayed on mine for a long, long time, so that it was by no means certain that she was going to change clothes or leave to go to work. Then she said, 'You meant it, didn't you? About me being the only one in Havana you trust?'

'Yes, Lola.'

She turned quickly and went up the curved stairway to the second floor. I took a seat in the foyer, in a chair made from an old wine barrel. She came down twenty minutes later, in full makeup and wearing a sapphire-blue evening gown. She purposefully avoided eye contact with me. Her hand was on the door latch when she stopped and said, 'Remember, Henry, call me Fannie. That's my name. Fannie Knutsen. From Warsaw, North Dakota.' And then she was gone.

I sat in the barrel chair, like a Spanish grandee, and stared at the door for a long time after Fannie left. I was bone-tired and hungry and confused about Lola or Fannie or whoever she was. I ached for her. I'd never ached for anyone before. I didn't know what to do about it, so I went to the pantry, found bread and ham for a sandwich, and ate. Then I climbed the curved stairs to the guest room, put the Woodsman on the nightstand, and fell into bed. Thoughts of the farm girl from the bare Dakota plains occupied my mind as I lay and watched the pewter light of a half-moon work its way across the room.

Fatigue must have supplanted the thoughts of Fannie, as I awakened from a deep sleep after several hours. The moon had continued on its path, high enough then that only a wedge of silver light, at the side of the bed, remained. I heard the latch work on the door downstairs and reached

for the Woodsman. There was a click-click of high heels on
the tiles; I recognized the timing of the steps. Fannie had
returned from work. I thought about getting up but reasoned
that she had to be tired and just wanted to get to sleep. And
reasoned that now was not the time to further complicate
her life or mine. I'd just complimented myself on how
virtuous I was when the door pushed wide.

Fannie was a shadow in the indirect light of the moon. She
still wore her evening gown but she had removed her high
heels. She padded across the floor to the side of the bed, stopping in the silver light. When she stopped she didn't look at
me. She faced upward, toward the light streaming in. Her
hands went to her shoulders and slipped away the straps that
rested on them. Her gown dropped to become a pool of fabric
at her feet. She wore nothing underneath, her body slim and
pale and virginal. She turned from the moon and eased into
bed next to me. We curled into each other. She breathed
into the crook of my neck, her fine hair fanned lightly against
my chest.

'Lola,' I said.

'No. Fannie.'

'Fannie then.'

'Make love to me, Henry.'

It was slow and sweet and had an air of sadness to it.
Afterward, Fannie wept quietly until we fell asleep in each
other's arms.

TWENTY-THREE

Marta Serrano sighed and blew a ring of smoke from her Cabañas Elouisas Listos. She had been smoking the diminutive cigars for the last four hours as we lay on the bed in the love nest in Miramar.

'It's settled then. Tomorrow I will make contact with Celia Nunez and try to get discussion of the gun-buy back on track,' she said.

It had been three days since my night with Lola Loring. Or Fannie Knutsen. I really didn't care which name she wanted me to use. I just knew that, for the first time in my life, I was absolutely, irrevocably, uncontrollably in love with someone who loved me as much as I did her. I knew this because, at breakfast after our night together, she had smiled at me, and then cried again, and cursed my name before she told me she loved me.

It had also been three days since it was safe for me to walk Havana's streets again, the confirmation of which had been an article in one of the newspapers loyal to Batista. POLICE MURDERERS KILLED IN SHOOTOUT the headline had blared. The story that followed described the attempted apprehension, resistance, and demise of the two perpetrators who had been at large since the Bar La Finca shooting of hero policemen Roberto Ortiz and Nico Perez. Below the story were the death photos of the bandits, a white man bearing some resemblance to me, and an attractive black woman, together with a short description of their criminal past. Police Chief Delgado, the article said, had pronounced the case closed and the officers' killing avenged.

To keep our cover story intact for any prying eyes, Marta and I remained in bed until dawn. Then we rose, and breakfasted, discussing what would be required after renewing contact with Celia.

'We will need to show them something more than just your

pistol, Henry.' Marta had resumed her hard, professional persona with me. By tacit agreement we made no reference to her fear and near-panic on the night of the La Finca shootings. 'Celia can't go to the Directorio leadership and ask them to meet you without being able to say that she has seen a sample of the goods herself.'

'How big does the sample need to be?' My question might as well have been rhetorical; I couldn't fathom where I might obtain even a single Garand or Thompson. It certainly didn't seem that Colonel Blanco Rico and SIM would part with anything more than the Woodsman.

Marta frowned into her coffee. 'I'm only guessing but I'd say a case of ten Garands. And a single Thompson should do. And some ammunition for both.'

'Well, then, nothing to it. I'll just stop by the corner *bodega* on the way home and pick those up.'

'Don't be sarcastic, Henry. It does not become you.'

'I didn't know you cared.' Might as well heap on the sarcasm. I wasn't in a very convivial mood after a night of choking on cigar smoke in the stuffy love nest.

'What makes you think I do?' Touché. And so much for gratitude for shooting that young cop to keep him from killing her. And me.

'Enough nonsense.' Marta drained her cup. 'I will get word to SIM that we need a Thompson and some Garands. Let's hope there are some available and that Colonel Blanco Rico is willing to risk them with us. You'd better head out. It's not *macho* for men in Cuba to linger with their mistresses over breakfast.'

I walked the few blocks to 5th Avenue and caught a cab home from there. I'd stayed home the previous night – Marta had a late show and Senator Bauza was back in town, so there was no chance to see Fannie – and for the first time in weeks Benny had not been on my doorstep in the morning. No surprise to that. Either the cops had captured him or, like any smart revolutionary, he had given me the ten-foot-pole treatment until the coast was clear. Or maybe forever.

I washed my face in the pitcher and basin I kept in the room and was about to lay down for a nap when there was a knock at the door. The rent was paid and Colonel Blanco Rico wouldn't send his mutts Trujillo and Alvarez to my door as long as I was undercover, so I didn't know who it could be. I cracked the door and there stood the elfin Benny.

'Hello, Genry,' he said, stepping in without invitation.

'Benny! I thought the cops got you back in the alley in Miramar.'

'The cops cannot shoot straight or run fast, Genry. You see I led them away from you?'

'I saw that, Benny. You saved all three of us. I'm very grateful.'

'No need to be grateful, Genry. I do it for the good of the *revolución*. Like you. Your business is to help the *revolución*, too, isn't it?'

'Yes, Benny. I'm here to help the revolution,' I lied. Lied to someone who had done nothing except try to help me, in his own way, since I'd met him. Someone who had been unfailingly loyal to me with absolutely no reason to be so, other than he liked me, I guess. And I liked him. He was the kind of bright, sunny, genuine kid I could see myself having as a son someday, a son who looked up to me. And I was on a mission to repay his loyalty and admiration by selling out his revolution, bringing down its leaders, and ending its chances of toppling the cruel and corrupt regime of Batista and the Syndicate, a regime of men who exploited the Bennys of Havana, and their parents and sisters and brothers, for nothing more than personal gain. I was doing it for the same reason all those men did what they did, for nothing more than a peso or a dollar. I was no better than them.

'When the *revolución* comes, all will have food, Genry. All will have a roof over their head and a soft bed to sleep in at night. Our babies will no longer die of illness. Our daughters and sisters will no longer need to sell their virtue in the street.' Benny's voice carried his excited anticipation of the day the revolution would arrive the way kids in America talked about their birthday or Christmas. 'Is that not so, Genry?'

'Yes, Benny. That's so.'

'You are a big man in the *revolución*, I know. I am proud to help you.'

Oh, Jesus Christ, I wanted to say. Can't you see me for what I am, Benny? I'm not making sure the Cuban people have food or a place to sleep. I'm not saving babies from the dysentery and infection that take so many before they reach the age that you have reached. And I'm one of the ones victimizing the sisters and daughters of Cuba. Open your eyes, I wanted to say.

'The revolution will save the Cuban people from those who exploit them,' is what I did say.

'I help you, Genry. Together, we make the *revolución*. You see. I am the best *revolucionario* in Havana.'

'Sure you are, Benny.'

'OK, Genry. Now what we do to make the *revolución*?'

'For now we lay low until the heat is off. I'll let you know when you're needed, or someone will. Maybe the person who gives the instructions from the Directorio . . .'

'The person whose name I must tell no one?'

'Yes, Benny. That person.' I thought about trying to trick the name from him but I couldn't bring myself to do it. There was no doubt in my mind that if Benny gave me information exposing the Directorio leadership, he would be in danger. I couldn't repay his loyalty with that. I decided then and there to do everything I could to protect him. While at the same time destroying the revolution that gave him so much hope.

'OK, Genry. You want me to do anything, I be close.' He was out the door and gone. I felt like shit listening to him, felt guilty and deceptive. Well, Henry, you can sit here and listen to Señor Rojas make bread while you stew in your own juices, or you can get out. The cops aren't after you anymore. You're a free man in a vacation town in the sunny Caribbean. Get out and enjoy it. Maybe you'll feel better about yourself.

TWENTY-FOUR

The cab I caught at the corner of Calle 21 and Calle J was a brand-new Ford Fairlane, one of the five-model total remake of the Ford line for 1957. Of course, nothing can hold a candle to this year's Chevy Bel Air, maybe the best-looking car ever made. Still, the Ford reminded me of home, enough so that I delayed my plan for lunch at the Hotel Nacional to pick up my mail at the post office in hope of a letter from the States.

There aren't many people to write to me at home, with Ma and Dad gone and no girl back there. About the only ones are Uncle Pete and Aunt Ruth, who are pretty spare with the paper and stamps, and my little sister, Janet. Jan's a swell kid and she comes through with a letter for her big brother pretty often. I've come to look forward to them since I've arrived in Cuba.

The post office had placed one letter in the dusty corner of the big box I'd optimistically rented to hold all the referral requests expected from the States. The letter was not a referral but a note from Janet, something better than any referral could ever be. I didn't open it there, deciding to savor it over lunch.

I asked the Fairlane's driver, an old man with a maximum speed of thirty-five, to take the Malecón to the Nacional, a deviation of a few blocks from the more expedient route. He took the request in stride; I suspect I was not the first *norte-americano* to ask for a leisurely drive along Havana's most famous avenue on that day or maybe even that hour.

The day was sunny and temperate, with a north breeze riffling the cobalt waters that lapped and slopped against the seawall beside the road. It was close to noon. The lunch-time crowd of nice girls, who worked in offices and as store clerks, had supplanted the usual bevy of hookers who patrolled the seawall at most hours. With the nice girls arrived the nice boys, good Catholic husbands and boyfriends, who met their girls for a sandwich and soda beside the blue waters. The whole thing was reminiscent of the Spanish *paseo* I had heard of, a stroll by chaste girls and good boys to display themselves to each other under the watchful eyes of parents and grand-parents. I saw a slender, dark-eyed beauty steal a kiss from the handsome man she was with, and then take a furtive glance around to see if anyone had seen her brazen-for-a-good-girl display.

The young woman on the Malecón reminded me of Fannie Knutsen, the farm girl I was falling in love with, the alter ego of the provocative Lola Loring. I knew in my bones that Fannie Knutsen was a good girl, even if Lola Loring was the kept woman of a member of Cuba's powerful cadre of political grifters.

We approached the USS *Maine* monument. 'Drop me here, driver,' I said. I lingered for a minute before heading up the gentle slope to the Nacional, wondering what the sailors whose deaths had provided the cause for the Spanish-American War and America's long pseudo-colonization of Cuba would think if they saw Havana now. How would they feel about giving their lives to provide a foothold to corrupt politicians and a haven for the Syndicate to launder ill-gotten money and turn it into even more profit on the backs of the Cuban people? Would they, the honored dead, care? Or, like America today, would they turn a blind eye to what was happening and call Batista a friend? I guessed that those heroes of the last century probably didn't care. They probably had more important things on their plates, being dead, like playing harps and enjoying the hereafter, if there was a hereafter to enjoy. I decided I was in the same position as them, less the harps and the hereafter, as far as Cuba was concerned. I had my own business to mind and my own skin to save.

I walked the few hundred feet up the slope to the Nacional, through its busy lobby with a nod to Alvaro, the desk clerk, and out the rear doors.

The Nacional is a good hotel, maybe the best hotel in the city, with top-quality appointments and service. But what separates it from other places to lay your head down in Havana is what greets you when you step out those rear doors. First is a tiled terrace, with wicker chairs and sofas scattered about in casual elegance. Next, a broad expanse of manicured lawn, spring green and inviting, slants away to the deep ultramarine of the Florida Straits. Here and there, a chaise lounge is placed on the lawn, sheltered in the black shade of enormous palms and towering ceibas. A fountain provides the soothing burble of water as background music.

As if this wasn't enough, sited discreetly to one side of the lawn is the most attractive open-air restaurant in all of Havana, really nothing more than a collection of tables beneath a roof of fronds and wooden supports, its minuscule kitchen concealed on the side closest to the hotel. It was here that Gary Cooper and Errol Flynn took their morning coffee in the '30s, Rita Hayworth and Fred Astaire lunched in the '40s, and Sinatra, Brando, and Ava Gardner enjoy a simple supper these days before heading out on the town.

The head waiter, Jesus, who is said to know all the Hotel Nacional's rich and famous customers on a first-name basis, greeted me by name, though I am neither rich nor famous, and though I had only eaten lunch there one time before, with Moncho Mercado. 'Will anyone be joining you for lunch today, Señor Gore?'

'No. Flying solo today, Jesus. If you can, get me a spot in the corner.'

'Of course, Señor Gore.' Like I was somebody instead of nobody. 'This way.' Jesus led me to a tiny table in the farthest seaside corner, out of the way and with a commanding view of both the foaming sea and the restaurant.

A waiter followed sharp on the heels of Jesus, took my drink order – a Greenall's gin martini – and reappeared with the icy elixir in under a minute. I ordered the Cuban lunch spread of rice, black beans, plantain, and pork that had been spit-roasted for hours. The Cubans don't go in much for spice, and the result is plain and hearty, the kind of food a Midwestern boy like me appreciates.

I daydreamed about bringing Fannie Knutsen there, for a look at the sea and a taste of the homey cooking, but that would be impossible. As secret lovers – like almost everyone in Havana was to someone else – we could not be seen in public together.

I put aside my fantasy of a simple meal in a public place with Fannie and slit the envelope containing Jan's letter. It was written on lined paper in schoolgirl scrawl, looping and immature. Seeing it made me so homesick for America I almost cried. She wrote of ice-skating parties and going to basketball games, of Sunday dinners after church and a pet beagle named Spike that Uncle Pete had bought for her. She thought she liked a boy, who she shyly did not name. Janet was at that stage where she was still partly the kid sister I had known back in Indiana and partly on the way to becoming a woman, a woman who I knew would not just be my sister but also my friend for life. She closed the letter, as she always did, with 'Come home, Henry. I miss you.'

I folded the letter into my pocket and stared out to sea, north, to America, ninety miles and a world away. I ought to get out, I thought, ought to take Fannie and bring her to meet Janet, and make a home for the three of us. Ought to find a real job with real hours, one that didn't involve bloodshed, deception, and betrayal of trust. That kind of fantasy required a nest egg to get started. I was on my way to earning it, even if I felt dirty in my work. But, then again, lots of jobs are dirty jobs.

The restaurant had been crowded when I entered and Jesus had hustled me to my table so quickly that I hadn't paid attention to the other diners. A table of two couples on the opposite side of the place caught my attention as they now rose, together with four men at an adjoining table.

The first one I recognized was my old friend Larry, he of wing-tipped foot and ham-heavy fist, who was at the all-male table. Two of his table mates appeared to be men of equal intellect and physical capabilities, goons hulking in body and short on smarts. The fourth was of smaller stature, with a malevolent bearing, hard eyes, and a nervous quickness in the way he carried his hands. A gunsel, I guessed.

Shifting my attention to the two couples, I saw the reason for the table of foot soldiers. Meyer Lansky, mob emperor of the island, was easily identified by his high brow and prominent Roman nose. I'd seen his picture in the papers, though he seldom went out on the town like other members of the

Syndicate. With him was Santo Trafficante, who I recognized despite the dark Ray-Bans he wore. Trafficante was a handsome man, though he didn't appear as tall now as the last time I had seen him, when I was looking up at him from his office carpet.

With the two kingpins were two gorgeous women draped in diamonds and, incongruous in the tropics, fur stoles. The one at Lansky's side, I knew from the papers, was his wife, Teddy. I assumed the other woman to be Trafficante's Cuban mistress, Rita, a former showgirl young enough to be his daughter. Rita was famous among the members of her past profession as one of their number who had made good, rising to the pinnacle of showgirl success by snagging the gangster away from his wife.

Two of the soldiers led the way, followed by Lansky and Teddy, who, like the mob royalty they were, glanced neither right nor left at the peons ogling them. Santo Trafficante seemed less sure of himself, casting his eyes around the room like a ward politician at a fundraiser. His gaze settled on me. He spoke a word to his mistress and made his way across the room, Larry trailing loyally behind like a menacing golden retriever.

'Mr Henry Gore, isn't it?' Trafficante, arriving at my table, said. Larry sneered over his boss's shoulder, no doubt remembering the 'fun' we'd had together. I know I remembered it; the side of my jaw still ached sometimes to remind me.

'That's right, Mr Trafficante.'

'I hear good things about you, Mr Gore. I hear you are now on the right team. On our team.'

Not knowing what to say, I nodded.

Trafficante continued. 'I respect when a man meets some adversity and learns a lesson from it. It's good to know that you are doing what you are for the legal authorities and the business community of Havana.' I thought that was pretty generous, considering that the only things I'd really done to date were to kill a baby cop and plot to supply arms for a revolution.

Trafficante talked over his shoulder. 'You see, Larry, what I'm always telling you about learning from your reversals?'

'Reversals. Yes, boss,' Larry intoned.

Trafficante turned his attention back to me. 'Well, no hard feelings then, Henry Gore.' Like he was the injured party. 'Good to have you on the team. See you around.' The mobster turned and left. Larry, still puzzling over the multi-syllable word 'reversals', gave me a confused smile, and followed.

So word was out that I was on the team with the Syndicate. Not exactly the reason I had come to Cuba. Not exactly something I was in a position to deny.

Even to myself.

TWENTY-FIVE

L ieutenant Trujillo of the Servicio de Inteligencia Militar popped the trunk on the Willys Aero Ace. The Aero was not the kind of snazzy car you'd expect a successful gunrunner to have, even with its two-tone, white-over-mint color scheme. The car lacked the fins, and hence the flash, that you see in today's Chevys and Caddys and Lincolns, but it would have to do. Beggars can't be choosers.

It was really a bit of a surprise how easily Colonel Blanco Rico had acceded to my request, relayed through Marta, for guns and a nice car to help me play the role of arms dealer. I hoped that the guns were of better quality than the middling automobile. First-rate product made for a credible gunrunner, as with any merchant.

'Here you are,' Trujillo said, unfolding a blanket in the car's trunk. The light was poor in the stuffy warehouse near the harbor where we met. Marta and I leaned in to see the goods.

The first fold of the blanket revealed a Thompson sub-machine gun. The stock was worn and marred, the bolt handle smooth from use. Not that it mattered. I doubted the baby rebels of the Directorio Revolucionario would understand that the gun had seen better days. Even if they did, they were so eager for weapons it would not matter.

'It's not in the best condition I've ever seen, Lieutenant, but it'll do,' I said. 'What else have you got for us?'

Trujillo flipped back the blanket to display two stick magazines filled with .45 ACP cartridges and a long wooden box so dilapidated it could have come from King Tut's tomb. He lifted the lid of the box to reveal six rusted rifles with the words 'Légion étrangère' stamped on their receivers. While they were stamped for the French Foreign Legion, they were old Ross rifles, Canadian World War I design guns that were so poor in quality that our friends to the north had sent them at the outbreak of World War II to someone who would be unlikely to fire them – the French. When I was in the Air Force, I had once encountered a Canadian Mounted Police officer who had been issued one. He called it the most unreliable piece of dung he had ever fired, and carried his private Marlin 336 deer rifle in his patrol car in case he ever actually needed a long gun.

'I thought we were going to get Garands. What the hell are these?' I asked Trujillo.

'There are no Garands to spare,' Trujillo said blandly. 'And if there were, Colonel Blanco Rico would not risk them falling into the hands of the Directorio Revolucionario.'

'How the hell am I supposed to get to the top leaders of the Directorio with garbage merchandise like this to peddle to them?' I asked. Trujillo shrugged and said nothing. I was about to continue to argue when it dawned on me that Lieutenant Trujillo could do nothing, which was precisely why he had been sent to deliver the crappy guns. It also said a lot about the men in charge in Havana. They had thousands of pesos to pump into this enterprise without flinching. When it came to weapons, though, they were tight-fisted. They were so wedded to keeping control of the guns in the country that they wouldn't risk even ten workable rifles to eliminate their biggest problem. No wonder the revolutionaries were reduced to using shotguns, lady's pistols, and knives. Maybe the Ross rifles would do the trick after all. 'OK, Lieutenant Trujillo, we'll take it from here.'

Marta lay against me, her exquisite neck against my shoulder, her head nuzzled next to mine. We were cruising along the Malecón, headed for the love nest in Miramar. Because we were in public, the illusion that we were lovers had to be maintained for any prying eyes.

Despite the act, Marta was in a foul mood, sullen and silent for some reason. The silence allowed me to daydream while I drove. My mind conjured another, blond head next to mine, another woman, sweet and simple, curled against me. I thought about the ten thousand pesos and what they would buy, tickets for Fannie and me back to the States and a fresh start in a little town for the two of us and Jan. Someplace new and nice. Maybe somewhere out west.

After a minute or two, I shook it off. Now was not the time to dream. Better to focus and get the job done, or you can say goodbye to the dream, I told myself.

'What's the next step, Marta?' I asked.

She spoke into the curve of my neck. 'I will let Celia know we have the product samples – the guns – available to show to the Council of Leaders of the Directorio and we will wait for word from them about a meeting. She is in direct communication with the head of the Council, the one called El Fuerte.'

'El Fuerte?'

'"The strong one", Henry.'

'He must be a tough customer to have a moniker like that.'

'It is rumored so. Few actually know, as El Fuerte conceals his identity, like all the members of the Council of Leaders. According to Celia, only the three other members of the Council and the five heads of the Directorio Revolucionario cells around the country know who he actually is. She only met the man after Máximo Quintana was killed and she was elevated to head the cell at the university. And, though I pretended worshipful curiosity, she said she was sworn to reveal to no one his actual name, his location, or even his general appearance.'

'It sounds like he's got more in the smarts department than that fool El Máximo. Of course, so does Celia Nunez. We'll need to be careful with her.'

'I have been, Henry. And no matter how smart she is, she will end up dead like they all do. No one can overthrow Batista. He has too many eyes, too many ears, too many soldiers and police and guns.'

'You sound like you think you are backing a winner.'

'I always back winners. Life is about backing winners, riding along with them, their power and their money. Only fools bet on long shots.'

TWENTY-SIX

Waiting has never been an easy task for me. I was one of those antsy kids, squirming at my school desk, first out the door from the confinement of Sunday services at the First Presbyterian Church. Now the waiting was taking place in the warm tropical winter of the West Indies, in its old Spanish capital, but the waiting still wore on me.

I visited Panaderia Casa Rojas twice in the morning for coffee to kill time. The molasses-thick *cafecito* that Señor Rojas poured from his dented moka pot served only to further my restlessness. The hour of ten found me pacing the narrow balcony of my apartment. Benny, once again present on the landing when I awakened, had retreated elsewhere.

Back home and safe for a week, I'd avoided any contact with Fannie Knutsen. Congress was in session, trying again to find an excuse to delay elections and keep Batista in power. That meant Senator Bauza was in Havana, returned from the hinterlands and whatever female companionship he maintained there, back in the arms of his Lola Loring. That meant she was off limits to me.

By late morning I couldn't stand it anymore. If I called now, I reasoned, Fannie would be up but not gone to rehearsal yet and Bauza would be off legislating in some stogie-clouded back room at the Capitolio. The telephone rang twice before she picked up.

'*Oigo*,' she said, barely audible.

'You didn't learn that Cuban dialect in North Dakota.'

'Henry!' There was palpable excitement in Fannie's voice. Then, more quietly, 'You shouldn't call here.'

'Is Bauza there?'

'No. I'm alone. But this is Havana. Guillermo says the walls have ears. The phone might, too.'

'I want to see you, Fannie. I have to see you.'

'No, Henry.'

'I'll come there. I'll be careful.'

'No. It's too risky to come here.'

'Where, then?'

There was a long silence at the end of the line. Then a resigned sigh. 'The same place. The place where we met before.'

'Where we met for lunch?'

'Yes. Come around back. Gustavo will let you in there.'

'When?'

'In half an hour.'

The Willys Aero wasn't much to look at but it was a comfortable car to drive. I parked it in the sandy alley behind El Siboney and locked it, hoping that some ambitious kid with a screwdriver and hammer wouldn't jimmy the lock on the trunk and find its cargo of weapons.

An unpainted door next to some rotting cans of garbage swung open and Gustavo, the maître d', waiter, chief cook, and bottle-washer of El Siboney, beckoned, then led me to the courtyard where I'd lunched with Fannie Knutsen in what seemed like an age ago.

She was there alone. She rose from her seat when I entered. She wore a baby-blue sundress, white gloves, and her broad-brimmed straw hat. Her eyes were hidden behind Wayfarer sunglasses; I knew they smiled at me in accompaniment to her happy grin when she saw me.

'Oh, Henry, I thought I would die without you,' she said, and chastely presented a cheek when I took her hands and moved to kiss her. OK, I thought, the order of the day is no public display of affection beyond that which occurs between friends. I could live with that, especially when I kissed her smooth cheek and caught the scent of flowers, whole fields of spring flowers.

'It was pretty rough without you, too, Fannie.' The name still stuck on my tongue a bit and, at the same time, was the most delightful music to my ears. 'I'm glad you agreed to see me today.'

Gustavo reappeared to ask for drink orders. 'Double Havana

Club with lime, no ice,' Fannie said. Not her usual glass of cold milk.

'Hatuey, *por favor*, Gustavo,' I said. Beer was strong enough for me at eleven-thirty in the morning.

When Gustavo left to get our drinks, I asked, 'So, my lovely, what are we celebrating with drinks this early in the day?'

Her face turned grave, her lips pinched. I noticed then that she was wearing more makeup than usual. She'd gone heavy on the face powder. And she kept on her sunglasses, even in the shady courtyard. I almost asked her to take them off, so I could lose myself in her enchanting blue eyes.

'I wasn't sure I should see you, Henry.' No cause to celebrate there.

'What? Why?' Kidding, I said, 'You're not throwing me over, are you?'

Fannie didn't say anything, just removed her Wayfarers. Both of her eyes were blacked. Ugly, gray-green welts encircled her left eye. The right was worse, nearly swollen shut.

'What happened?' I took her hand in mine. She had removed her gloves and the bones in her hand felt like bird bones, light and frail.

She slipped her dark glasses back on, so Gustavo wouldn't see her condition when he returned with the drinks. She had no more than completed the act when he appeared, placed the two glasses on the table, and asked if we were ready to order.

'Give us a few minutes, Gustavo,' she said, her cool Lola Loring persona doing the talking.

'Of course, Miss Loring.' Gustavo backed away.

By then I had moved from shock to anger. 'Who did this to you?'

'Henry, it's best that you don't become involved . . .'

'Who?' I wanted to enfold her in my arms and cradle her like an injured child. I wanted to feel my fingers around the windpipe of the one who had beaten her like this, wanted to smash my hand into his face the way he had smashed hers.

'Guillermo.'

'The bastard. I'll kill him.'

'No, Henry. No. You'll do nothing of the sort. This is my business. I'll handle it.'

I had my own ideas about how, and who, should handle
Senator Bauza but the last thing Fannie needed was me
disagreeing with her. 'What made him do this?' I asked.

'He . . . suspected I was seeing you. Well, not you but
that I was seeing someone. When he returned from his trip
and we were alone he said I was cool toward him, withdrawn.
Maybe I was, Henry. After being with you I couldn't pretend
anymore. Not to myself and, I guess, not to him, either. He
accused me of cheating on him while he was away. I denied
it. He said he could smell another man on me, see it in my
eyes. I panicked and tried to distract him by accusing him
of cheating on me while he was out in the countryside. Which,
by the way, I knew was true. That was when he hit me. He
called me a whore, a faithless whore, and he hit me and hit
me till I blacked out or fainted, I'm not sure which.'

'The scum. The cowardly son of a bitch.' The anger flowed
through me so strongly that I began to feel light-headed, almost
out of body. I wanted to kill, to maim, to rip his head off with
my bare hands, and I felt I could.

Fannie went on. 'When I came around, he was still there.
He had picked me up and put me into bed. He raged at me
again. He said if he found out who I had been with, he'd
see my lover never intruded into his bed or any others ever
again. He went on for hours. It was more frightening than
being hit, Henry, because he wasn't talking about me
during that time, he was talking about you. He vowed to do
things I couldn't bear to think about happening to you, my
love.

'And then he stopped ranting. It was like he had exhausted
himself. He slumped into a chair, put his head in his hands,
and wept like a child. When he was finished, he came to the
side of the bed and knelt, and took my hands and kissed them
and begged me to forgive him. He said he would never lift
his hand against me again.'

I expected Fannie to cry but she didn't. I could see she had
steeled herself for this meeting with me. She was delicate and
injured and strong at the same time.

'Let's get away, Fannie. Let's leave Bauza, leave all of this
behind,' I said. 'I have a little money, very little, but maybe

we could get back to the States if you have some, too. We'll get by. I'll find a job. We can do it.'

'I can't. I can't go back, Henry. If I go back now, I've failed. I was washed up when I came here. My agent had dropped me. I couldn't get work in the States. The only reason they hired me here was because I was tall and blond, not for my voice. But it was the break I needed. And then Guillermo saw me perform one night and got me the job at Club Parisién. It's my last chance. I can't give it up.'

'Even if you have to take a beating to stay?'

She was silent for a long time and then said, 'Guillermo won't do it again, Henry. He has never done it before. As long as I don't cheat on him, I'll be fine.'

'As long as you don't cheat on him.' The words were bitter on my tongue.

'It's better this way, Henry. Better for both of us.' The thin trickle of a tear ran from beneath her sunglasses. 'We can't be together. It's too dangerous for you.'

I stood. She remained seated, crying without a sound. She seemed broken, broken like a child's doll. She took off her sunglasses. Her eyes were despondent, hopeless.

'I was falling in love with you, Fannie.'

'I know, Henry. I was falling in love with you. But it wouldn't work out. There are too many things we can't control.'

'That's it?' I said. She said nothing, turned her head away from me.

I walked slowly to the rear door of El Siboney, the weight of the world pressing down on me, hoping against hope that Fannie would speak, call out to me to stop, rush to my arms. With each step I could feel the chance of that slipping away, until I stood at the door I had so happily come through minutes before. I turned toward her. She still wasn't looking at me. She didn't seem to be looking at anything. She drained off the rum in her glass in one swig. Gustavo was already arriving with another when she finished.

I stepped out the door into the midday Havana sun. It felt like darkness.

TWENTY-SEVEN

'The day after tomorrow at four in the morning,' Marta said, nuzzling my ear as she whispered. She drew back and sipped her champagne. Every evening there was a bottle of champagne after her show. I was almost tapped out of money. A thousand doesn't last long when you live the false high life I was living, with a mistress who had to be wooed in an expensive, public manner, rent for an apartment and a house, and now a car to keep. The Tropicana was allowing me to run a tab, on account of I was keeping company with their most famous dancer. That wouldn't last forever, though.

'Where?' I asked.

'The Directorio will send someone to bring us to the place.'

'Benny again?'

'I don't know. They change the guide often. They were careful before and even more careful after what happened at La Finca. That is why they are alive.'

The next night we left the Tropicana immediately after the show, while the place was still hopping, Yankees on the floor dancing a rum-fueled rumba with tarts from Regla and Habana del Este, Cuban businessmen and politicos showing off their mistresses.

We went to the love nest and waited on the bed, as usual, for the knock. It came right on time. Benny was our guide, again.

'Hello, Genry. Hello, Señorita Marta,' he said cheerfully when I answered the door. 'We take your car.'

Of course we took my car, because you can't drag half a dozen rifles on your back through the streets, even at four in the morning. Benny directed us on a weaving course through the night, obviously trying to throw off any tail even though I could have seen one a mile behind us on the empty avenues. We finally ended up in the area of the harbor, surprisingly at the same warehouse where we'd been given the guns and the car several days before.

'Either the owner of this warehouse plays both sides of the fence or SIM is in cahoots with the Directorio,' I muttered to Marta after Benny left us waiting at the warehouse door.

'Flash your lights three times,' Marta said by way of answer. I did and the door slid open. I drove the Aero in, parked it in the same spot where I had first seen it, and got out. Two figures approached from a corner of the building, moving obliquely to the beam of the car's headlights. I saw one wore a skirt and the other was a tall man. As they drew near, I saw the man had a gun in his hand. Pointed at me. It was too late to drag the ungainly Woodsman out of the shoulder holster. I'd have to talk our way out of whatever situation this happened to be.

'Hey, friend, no need for the hardware. I'm a businessman here for a transaction. I'm not looking for any trouble,' I said.

'You will get no trouble if you make no trouble,' the tall man said in perfect English. 'Celia says you are a friend, or, at least, a merchant, but one cannot be too careful in Havana if one wishes to remain alive.'

The figure in the skirt stepped from the shadows along the wall. Celia. 'This is Freddy,' she said. 'Freddy, this is Mr Henry Gore, and you already know Marta.'

'No passwords tonight, Celia?' I asked. 'Can we please point the gun elsewhere, Freddy? Funny quirk of mine, I get nervous when I have to look right into the barrel like this. I'm worried that it looks like eternity and, if that's so, then eternity is a black hole with something very unpleasant at the end.'

'Celia did not tell me about your dark sense of humor, Señor Gore.' Freddy turned the pistol away from me but did not put it away. Still, just having the gun directed elsewhere allowed me to focus on Freddy rather than his deadly toy. He was not just tall, but massive, a huge slab of beef. The thought crossed my mind that I'd love to see him go toe-to-toe against Wingtip Larry back at the Capri. 'One can't be too careful,' he said.

'Yeah, Freddy, I understand.' I turned to Celia. 'Are your people going to inspect the goods here or are the four of us going elsewhere?'

'Here will do, Henry.' When she spoke I saw that Celia had a gun, too, holstered on her right hip. 'Freddy is the Directorio's armorer. He will inspect your wares.'

Thankful that the inspection would take place in the gloom of the unlit warehouse, I walked Freddy to the trunk and opened it to reveal the Tommy gun. Freddy expertly released the clip and pulled back the bolt handle. He took a penlight and showed it along the gun's receiver. He picked up one of the spare clips and inserted it, cocking the gun with the bolt handle. For a moment, I thought he was going to test-fire the weapon in the confined space of the warehouse. I had visions of blue-and-white police cars descending on the building.

Freddy didn't shoot, he just grumbled. 'This weapon is old. It is beaten to death. It looks like it would function but it has seen better days.'

Hoping to placate him and direct the conversation away from further discussion of product quality, I said, 'You know your way around military weapons.'

'I served in the Cuban Army for a decade during and after World War II. I worked with the Americans at the San Julian Air Base in Pinar del Rio during the war. That's where I learned English and where I learned about American guns. They are good guns, even if they have been abused like this one. Let's have a look at the Garands.'

'Yes, well, about the Garands . . .' I began.

'What about them?' Celia asked. She and Marta had moved in beside Freddy to stare into the Aero's trunk like there was something exceptionally fascinating inside. I suppose if you are trying to make a revolution, a trunkful of guns is fascinating.

'I ran into some supply problems. My source can't provide the Garands we talked about.' Actually refused to provide them, I wanted to say. 'But I do have some very good rifles available in their place.' I folded back the blanket like I was revealing a sought-after piece of art.

'What are these things?' Freddy's voice was tinged with disappointment.

'Ross rifles. Manufactured in Canada for their armed forces,' I said. 'Very high quality.'

'They are so long,' Freddy said. He lifted one of the rifles vertically and the bolt dropped off. Clean off, hitting the bottom of the trunk with a thud. 'Piece of shit,' he muttered, shining his penlight along the length of the weapon until he came to the information stamped on the receiver. 'French Foreign Legion. What the hell? This gun was made in 1905. We're not fighting the Boer War here, Señor Gore, though these rifles were made almost in time to fight it. They are worthless if they are all like this one. What kind of ammunition do they use?'

'.303 British.'

'Can you even supply it?'

'Yes,' I lied.

He tossed the first rifle back into the trunk. 'We won't take that one.' Freddy lifted and worked the bolts on each of the remaining Rosses. Luckily, none of them fell apart like the first. 'I guess they will do. They'll have to, although we won't pay the same price as what you wanted for the Garands.'

'I can let you have the Rosses for two hundred fifty each.'

'They are not worth fifty.'

'Two hundred each, then. In lots of ten.'

Freddy was not pleased. 'Celia, these guns might kill as many of us as they do the police and SIM.'

Celia placed a motherly hand on Freddy's arm. 'We need these weapons. If we don't act soon, there will be none of us left to fight. Who then will move the people to protect their own interests?'

Freddy nodded his grudging assent. 'Of course you are right, Celia.'

'All right,' I said. 'How many will you need?'

'Thirty of the Thompson guns,' Celia said. 'And one hundred fifty rifles.'

I did a quick mental calculation. 'Forty thousand five hundred for the guns. For the ammunition, another ten thousand. I'll make it an even number. Fifty thousand for the total package, delivered here to Havana. Payment in US dollars, not Cuban pesos.'

'How soon can you deliver?' Celia was all business now.

'My supplier needs time to move the guns to a port in the

States. From there, three days to get to Havana. Allowing another week for unknown delays, I'll say two weeks. Delivery will be at the waterfront, with your people offloading and handling all land transportation. Half the cash now, the other half on delivery.'

Celia acted surprised. 'I don't have the money now.' Good, just what I wanted.

'C'mon, Marta, let's get out of here,' I said. 'These people aren't serious. I can't believe it, after we risked our necks for them.'

'Do not be hasty, Señor Gore.' Celia spoke in her best soothing voice. 'You know as well as I that negotiations in matters of this sort are delicate. You will meet with the Council of Leaders of the Directorio Revolucionario in two days. Our supreme leader, El Fuerte, will be among them. After they speak to you, they will finalize the transaction and deliver the first installment of dollars. One-half of the total amount.'

'I don't know why I should put up with this. Those guns could go to Santo Domingo as easily as here.'

'Look into your heart, Henry Gore,' Celia said, her voice firm and strong. I saw for the first time with those words not only her persuasive ability but her charisma. She *did* make me look into my heart. What I saw there was clearly lacking. 'It is only two days. Two days to make as much money as a cane-cutter, no, an entire village of cane-cutters will make in their entire lifetimes. Two days to wait, to help all those around you who suffer under Batista's brutal hand.'

'OK. But any more delay and the guns go to Santo Domingo.'

'We shall be in touch,' Celia said. 'Come, Freddy.'

They disappeared into the darkness.

TWENTY-EIGHT

'Henry, my trusted partner, how are you?' Moncho Mercado's cheery voice blasted through the telephone receiver and the sleepy cobwebs in my brain. I glanced at the clock. Seven in the morning. Too-bright sun streamed in through the balcony window. The lilting call of the fishmonger wafted in with the breeze.

'How am I? I was sleeping peacefully until a minute ago.'

'How can you sleep on such a splendid day, my friend?'

'I'm sure I am about to learn why I should not indulge in such a slovenly habit as sleeping into the eighth hour of the day.'

'Ah, Henry, you have such a clever way of expressing yourself. That is one of the many reasons why I love you as a brother.'

'What's the scam, Moncho?'

'Scam? Oh, Henry, were it not such a perfect day, and were you not about to join me in such a manly recreation, I would be hurt.'

'Manly recreation? The chorus girls dance at night, Moncho. See you in twelve hours.' I leaned over to place the black receiver in its cradle.

'Not women, Henry. *Manly* recreation,' Moncho's voice cajoled from the phone, sounding tin-can hollow at arm's length.

Against my better judgment, I brought the phone back to my ear. 'OK, Moncho. You woke me up. I might as well listen.'

'We are going fishing, Henry.'

'Fishing?' The last time I had been fishing was with my buddy Roy Weltman on a lake in Maine. The water was so cold it turned the worms on our hooks white. 'I thought the fish in salt water waited until the afternoon to bite.'

'We have an invitation for now. To Cojimar.' Moncho was as excited as he ever got. 'With the renowned captain and guide, Gregorio Fuentes. Hemingway's captain. Hemingway has gone off to New York to meet with his publisher, you see, and Fuentes can take out a charter while he is gone. So we shall fish like Hemingway. What recreation could be more manly?'

I had to admit that a day away from Havana sounded enticing. Now that I was awake. 'We're not going on the *Pilar*, are we?' The last thing I wanted was an illicit trip on Papa Hemingway's boat.

'No, alas, the boat is not for hire.'

'That's OK, Moncho. I just wanted to avoid a charge of piracy, that's all. I guess I'm in.'

'Wonderful, Henry! You have a car. Come pick me up in half an hour.' Moncho hung up. Nothing like volunteering yourself a ride before one is offered, old partner.

I swung my legs out of bed and heard Benny's trademark 'tap, tap' sound on the door. 'Come in, Benny,' I said, and was greeted by my sometime factotum, carrying a *cafecito* and a plate of *buñuelos*. The coffee, bracing black, smelled of loamy richness; the pastry, of hot oil and anise. After wolfing the meal, Benny and I spirited the Thompson and the rifles, still blanket-wrapped, up to the apartment and stashed them under the bed. It didn't make sense to be driving around with an arsenal in my trunk.

Moncho met me at his door looking like an advertisement for what a fisherman should look like, in sandals, wide straw hat, linen shirt, and khakis that belonged in a Bogart movie.

The port town of Cojimar was close, a drive of an easy few miles from downtown. Approached through virgin jungle and forests of coconut palms, the sleepy fishing village seemed a thousand miles and a century away from sordid Havana in attitude. I was a fan of Hemingway from grade school, starting with his stories of Nick Adams in Michigan's north woods, so I persuaded Moncho to direct our route past the great writer's home in Cojimar. Finca Vigía, Hemingway's yellow-painted palace atop a forested hill, met my idea of where my macho hero should live. A group of kids, in new uniforms, played baseball on a worn diamond at the base of the hill.

'Hemingway, he buys the kids uniforms, bats, and gloves,

and lets them play there,' Moncho said, pleased to be able to convey this piece of Hemingway insider knowledge.

The docks at Cojimar's port appeared to date back to the village's founding in 1554. A turreted fort guarded the stone pier where a single, sharp-hulled fishing boat, decked in teak and fitted in burnished brass, was tied up. *La Gloria* – Glory – was painted in gold lettering across her stern. A barefoot mate in a ripped T-shirt and shorts helped us board.

Colonel Ernesto Blanco Rico emerged from *La Gloria*'s cabin like a slant-eyed cobra. As he stepped out, I caught sight of Sergeant Alvarez seated at a small table inside. I wondered if Lieutenant Trujillo was aboard somewhere as well, so that the trio of usual suspects would be complete.

'Henry, my friend, so good to see you.' Blanco Rico was all white teeth and good cheer. 'I feared that with us losing one member of our party already, your absence would further dampen the mood. But you have come! We shall catch large fish today, you will see. I swear Fuentes is a *palero*, a sorcerer, so able is he to call the mighty marlin to the hook. He must cast a spell before each trip. And Moncho, too! It is good for those of us who toil so diligently for the good of the nation to take a day to relax and enjoy the beauty it offers. Come, come, we'll have a drink before we get underway.'

With the colonel so effusive, there was no turning down the glasses of dark rum that Sergeant Alvarez, playing at steward for the day, served up to Moncho and me. Moncho drank his off with gusto, the mark of years of practice. I, already intoxicated by the short night I'd had and the dazzling sun off the harbor waters, sipped.

Gregorio Fuentes appeared just then, striding along the dock like a head of state about to review his troops. Except that he was dressed in clothing so raggedly poor I felt like giving him my shirt. The famed captain was a small man, and old, but not so old as the Hemingway character modeled on him, the fisherman Santiago in *The Old Man and the Sea*. He tossed a cigarette butt into the glass-green harbor water just before he came aboard, shook hands with Blanco Rico, said a curt word to the mate, and had us underway and out of the harbor in minutes.

'It is a fine day,' Moncho Mercado said, his mood made expansive by the morning tot of rum. 'A fine day to be a Cuban in Cuba.'

La Gloria rode the slight swell like a thoroughbred. Before long, Fuentes had two rods out, with a bonito on each as bait. The lines were clipped to outriggers and the baits ran wide in the foaming wake. The mate climbed to the cabin roof and scanned the horizon for the fins of a marlin or sailfish.

Colonel Blanco Rico lounged in the fighting chair bolted in the center of the cockpit.

'This is one righteous boat,' I said.

'She is new to the Caribbean this month,' Blanco Rico said. 'Guillermo Bauza had her made by the Chris-Craft Corporation in the United States. He has only had her out on the water a few times.'

'It is a pity the Senator could not join us today,' Moncho said.

Blanco Rico spat on the glossy varnish of the deck. 'Bauza is a good man but he is too sentimental. He should be out here in the fresh air and sun instead of hiding in his bedroom, mooning over that blond *coño*. A true man does not react to such things in this manner.'

Moncho must have noticed my questioning look. 'Oh, you do not know, Henry. Senator Bauza was to join us today but the Loring woman – you remember her, Bauza's mistress – she killed herself yesterday. He is quite broken up over it.'

'Yes, Henry. She cut her wrists. Bled all over the beautiful house he had bought for her, crazy *puta*.' Blanco Rico shook his head. 'She killed herself because he disciplined her, gave her a few deserved slaps when he thought she was cheating on him. The deceitful whore needed a first-class beating and she wouldn't have done this to him. I pity Bauza. Not for losing the whore but for his weakness with women.'

Moncho, Fuentes, and the mate listened to Colonel Blanco Rico, shaking their heads in disbelief as he spoke. None of them noticed as I moved unsteadily to the gunwale and leaned against it. Fannie, my Fannie, gone. Dear, sweet, fragile farm girl, oh, my Fannie! Only the gunwale prevented me from collapsing. I felt sick, sick with hurt, and rage, and a desire to kill or be killed, my very being dying here on this fancy boat among these heartless beasts who called themselves men. My legs went out from under me. My head swum in the strong light. It was like a kick in the gut, then, like being beaten in the alley behind the Capri. Only worse because now I didn't care to live. I vomited over the side, fouled the clear blue waters trying to retch out the cold awful black thing inside the pit of my chest, inside the core of my soul. I failed and it remained, a screaming pain inside me for which there was no relief, no alleviation, no hope of cure.

Moncho noticed me and spoke. 'Hey, look! Henry, *mi viejo*, are you having the seasickness?'

I remained where I was, head hung over the side, and retched again and again, trying to push out the pain. The others assumed the roll of the sea to be the reason for my illness and, in the manner of most on boats in those circumstances, moved away and left me to myself, occasionally casting a wary eye in my direction to make sure I didn't fall overboard.

The trolling for billfish continued. An hour out of port, a giant marlin struck and slashed across the oily surface of the sea from horizon to horizon, hacking at the wire leader with her sword as she attempted to dislodge the painful hook from her jaw, the agony of the fish not one iota of the hurt in my being.

My retching subsided. I half-leaned, half-lay against the gunwale at the intersection of the boat's cockpit and cabin, away from the action at the stern. The others grouped around the fighting chair where Blanco Rico wrestled with the marlin, giving him rum and encouragement. They ignored me. I hung my head and cried for Fannie, the tears dripping to the deck where they mingled with the seawater in the scuppers, flowing from me and away to oblivion, joined with the endless oceans.

An hour passed, and then two, and the others paid me no mind, so focused were they on defeating the marlin. The fish neared the boat, swinging from side to side behind the stern. She still slashed futilely at the leader attached to the hook in her jaw, her fins lit a neon blue in fear or in anger.

'Now, Alvarez,' Blanco Rico said. The sergeant drew the .45 automatic from his shoulder holster and emptied the clip into the fish's head, turning it instantly from the queen of the seas to a bloody lump of meat. The mate and Captain Fuentes each grabbed a gaff and dragged the body to the stern roller. From there, all the men rolled the fish over *La Gloria*'s stern by pulling on the gaffs and on a line Fuentes had looped around the fish's bill. With the catch aboard, the men laughed and cheered at their victory, the death of a beautiful living thing. I stared at the fish laying along the length of the stern and thought, this is what success and triumph is to these men and their kind. Domination and death. Taking without a thought of the harm the taking engendered.

Moncho, a glass of rum in hand, broke away from the celebration. 'How are you feeling, Henry?'

'Like shit, Moncho.'

He chuckled. 'Standing with both feet on land will cure that.'

I doubted that but I didn't dissuade Moncho from the thought. 'What will be done with the fish?' I asked.

'Fuentes says he will sell it for lobster trap bait.'

I wanted to kill them all then, these evil men who turned beautiful creatures, human and animal, into sordid decaying flesh for the pleasure of it. I wanted to rip Bauza's throat out, to bludgeon Blanco Rico, to turn Alvarez's pistol against him. I resolved that my time in Cuba would be devoted to this. I would have my revenge. I would purge these bastards from the face of the earth.

TWENTY-NINE

Captain Fuentes steered *La Gloria* in a great looping turn to the south. The mate settled onto a dry spot on the deck for a nap. Moncho peeled off his shirt and sandals and climbed to the cabin roof to tan, taking a pint of Havana Club for sustenance.

Colonel Blanco Rico leaned against the fighting chair, surveying his kill. 'Man is meant to conquer nature, Henry, and turn it to his own uses. Just as the elite, the leaders of men, are destined to turn lesser men to the elite's own uses. It is the law of the world, survival of those most fit.'

My shattered mood allowed me to take a risk I would not have only hours before. 'Is that what you and Senator Bauza do, Colonel? Turn lesser men to your own uses?'

Blanco Rico suppressed any surprise he felt at being spoken to in a manner that would get the average Cuban a tour of the Comandancia General's interrogation rooms. 'To a degree, Henry, to a degree. But we also provide them with that which they are not capable of providing for themselves – a vision for the nation and the strong and skilled leadership to carry it into action. Also, safety, security, and protection from those who would harm our great country. And a fruitful relationship with the United States, our big brother and ally to the north. All of these things we provide to the people at great personal sacrifice. So there must be some small recompense to us for our efforts. And do not forget, Henry, that you honorably share in our efforts. And in the recompense we allow ourselves for it.'

When Blanco Rico said the last part, I felt dirty. Dirty like I'd just swum through a sewer. Dirty sitting on that spanking-new boat, cutting a crisp swath through the glass-smooth sea on a pristine day. He was right. I was a participant. Maybe not as significant as he or Bauza or Batista or Lansky but I was a participant nonetheless, culpable to some degree in all their acts, the money-laundering, the prostitution, the graft. Even the beating that drove Fannie Knutsen to take her own life.

The colonel drew a cigar from his shirt pocket and clipped the end with a pink gold cutter. Sergeant Alvarez stepped forward and fired the stogie with a lighter of the same pink gold.

'Thank you, Sergeant,' Blanco Rico said. 'You may go below and take a short rest before we dock in Cojimar.' When Alvarez left, Blanco Rico said, 'A good man. Absolutely loyal. A quality that has become most rare these days. On your mission, for instance.'

For all his wiles, I knew Colonel Blanco Rico could not read my thoughts. I also knew that I had been performing my mission, if not flawlessly, at least in a manner which betrayed no disloyalty. 'There is an issue of loyalty on my mission?' I asked.

'Unfortunately, yes, Henry. Do not worry, my friend. The traitor has already disclosed to us that you have no involvement in her treachery. But I wish for you to speak to her, to determine if more information than she has already divulged can be obtained. We shall leave directly for the Comandancia General when we reach Cojimar.'

It didn't sound as if there was a choice for me in the matter. I rode the rest of the voyage staring out to sea, wondering how Fannie had passed her last minutes and why she had felt so desperate and helpless as to take her own life. And cursing myself for not seeing it and doing something to prevent it.

At the dock at Cojimar, the colonel pressed a one-hundred-peso note and two cigars into Gregorio Fuentes's hand while Sergeant Alvarez went off to retrieve the olive-drab SIM Pontiac that served as Blanco Rico's personal car. Moncho volunteered to drive the Willys Aero back to my apartment without prompting. It seemed my old partner had known from the start that the day was more than a simple fishing trip. The SIM car had blackout curtains which screened the rear passengers from prying eyes. I glanced back to *La Gloria* just before Alvarez pulled the curtains closed. The mate was already hacking at the noble marlin with a machete, cutting it into pieces suitable to bait lobster traps.

Colonel Blanco Rico did not speak during our ride to the Comandancia General and neither did I. When we arrived, Sergeant Alvarez pulled the Pontiac close to the entrance door for the SIM offices, and shooed the guards there away. Then he hustled me inside. After a minute, Blanco Rico joined us in a walk along the hallway in the opposite direction from his office to the area where I'd heard screams the first time I had been brought in. On this day, though, there was only silence.

Blanco Rico stopped before a door sheathed in metal. Sergeant Alvarez produced a key and swung it open.

I recognized the back of Marta's head as soon as Alvarez stepped out of the way to allow the colonel and me to enter. She was seated on a wooden chair. There was a puddle of liquid under the chair; the pungent smell of urine permeated the room. Marta's hands were tied to the arms of the chair, her legs to its legs.

Lieutenant Trujillo stood at one side of the dark chamber. He had traded his ill-fitting suit for a pair of khaki pants, no shirt, and a strange leather apron. He was sweating profusely in the close heat of the place. He smiled when he saw me.

A second man, in coveralls like those worn by street cleaners, was standing next to a table covered with a rubber mat, fiddling with a box with wires extending to a car battery on the tabletop. He looked up briefly when we entered, then went back to his fiddling.

'You know Lieutenant Trujillo, Henry. And this gentleman is . . . well, we call him the Electrician,' Blanco Rico said. The man in the coveralls dipped his head and smiled ever so briefly, never taking his eyes from the battery and his tinkering. 'He is one of our more successful interrogators. His methods are particularly useful where it is necessary to avoid bruising or scarring.'

My eyes followed the wires from the battery to Marta, where they disappeared, screened by her torso from where I stood behind her. Her head hung down, as if she had fallen asleep. I felt the bile rise in the back of my throat.

'This is, of course, a most unpleasant business.' The colonel spoke as if someone had spilled milk that needed to be cleaned up. 'But it is necessary when dealing with bandits and traitors. Come, Henry. Step around beside me.'

I did as told, now facing Marta. Her eyes were closed. A strand of spittle hung from her chin down onto her chest. Her blouse had been torn open. I could see then that the wires from the Electrician's box had been attached to her nipples with an alligator clip. I wanted to run screaming from the room but I stood rooted at the colonel's side.

'Wake her,' Blanco Rico said.

Lieutenant Trujillo approached Marta, broke apart a vial he held in his hand, and waved it under Marta's nose. Her head snapped up, her eyes wide with terror. She screamed. Not a woman's scream, a horrible primal scream, like a wounded animal, that went on and on, her mouth wide and her throat red and swollen.

After an eternal thirty seconds, Blanco Rico commanded: 'Silence!' Marta stopped screaming with her mouth but her eyes still screamed with fear, flashing from Blanco Rico's face to the Electrician, to Trujillo, then back to the colonel, and finally settling on me. The terror left her eyes then. There was no life in them at all when she stared at me. She tried to speak. Her first words were unintelligible, her tongue thick and uncoordinated. With more effort she spoke clearly.

'*Viva Cuba libre.*'

Blanco Rico signaled to the Electrician with a single finger. The torturer chuckled and turned a knob on a box connected to the wires between the car battery and Marta. Marta clenched her teeth in an ugly grimace. Her body convulsed until the Electrician twisted the knob back. Marta slumped like a rag doll.

'Very nice,' Blanco Rico said to the Electrician. He meant it to sound businesslike, a supervisor complimenting a subordinate on a job well done, but there was more in the words, a hint of sadistic thrill.

Marta stirred slightly and worked to form words. '*Viva Cuba libre.*'

Blanco Rico flicked a glance toward the Electrician like a

bidder who had captured the eye of an auctioneer. The knob was spun again. Marta convulsed and twisted in her bindings. The smell of shit filled the room.

The Electrician turned the knob off. Marta was panting as if she had run ten miles, sweating in the confined space. The Electrician switched on a bank of bright lights. Marta flinched in the glare.

'I hope you are proud of yourself, mercenary,' she said in my direction.

'Who are the members of the Council of Leaders of the Directorio Revolucionario?' Blanco Rico said, his voice barely a whisper.

'*Viva Cuba libre.*'

'Who are your contacts in the Directorio Revolucionario besides Celia Nunez?'

'*Viva Cuba libre.*'

Blanco Rico crooked his finger. The Electrician applied the power again. Marta ricked and clenched her teeth so hard an incisor splintered. The Electrician cut the power.

I couldn't help myself. 'Marta, tell them. They will do this to you until you do tell them.'

'*Viva Cuba libre.*'

'Marta, please. They will kill you,' I pled.

'Don't you think they will kill you, too, mercenary, when it suits their purposes?' The sights, and the sounds, and the smell in that room told me that Marta was right, that they would.

'Continue with her,' Colonel Blanco Rico ordered. 'And remember, we need her broken, not dead.'

'*Si, mi coronel,*' the Electrician said, speaking for the first time. His voice squeaked like a mouse.

'I had hoped Marta had formed an attachment to you,' Blanco Rico said, after we left the room. 'Something that would have allowed her to be persuaded.'

'What will happen to her now?' I asked.

'Lieutenant Trujillo and the Electrician will work on her for a few days. She will most likely break. Most do if their hearts do not give out first. The names she tells us will be false names given to her by the Directorio. They will be useless to us and she will not know the actual names we seek. Then she will be sent to prison for the rest of her life. If she were a man she would be executed as a traitor but the government of Fulgencio Batista is enlightened and humane. We do not execute women, no matter how heinous their crimes and how deserving they are of such punishment.'

Colonel Blanco Rico said it like he actually believed it.

THIRTY

A fly walked along the yellowed wall of my apartment and stopped at the coffee stain that extended from eye level to the floor. Earlier, after I had thrown the *cafecito* that Benny had brought in against the wall, the stain had been wet, a slick brown manifestation of my mood. Now, as the fly approached it, the stain was merely damp, hovering on the brink of dryness. Was there still enough there to allow for a fly-sized morning cup of coffee? When the fly drank to wash down its breakfast of my puke obtained from the floor beside my bed, did it relish the robust blackness of the coffee, as I had once done? Did it linger, as I had once done, savoring the morning quiet and dreaming daydreams of a fly-wife and fly-children, a well-kept fly-home with laughter ringing through the halls?

Or was the fly like me now, filled with thoughts of his fly-lover, dead by her own hand but killed by others, all hope gone. All gone. Had the fly attempted to wash away the preceding day of horror with rum, as I had tried to do with the now-empty bottle of Matusalem sitting on my bureau, the fly hoping to die as I had hoped to die, only to be disappointed by the rising of the sun and the knowledge that the quart of alcohol had only made it sick and added to its fly-misery?

Benny had retreated when I'd thrown the cup of coffee against the wall. Now he returned with a mop and a bucket borrowed from Señor Rojas downstairs.

'I clean up,' he said, splashing water onto the floor beside where I lay.

'Leave the place alone, kid,' I said.

'You need to clean up, Genry. I clean up.' Benny had assumed the household cleaning duties one day a week earlier, without any discussion or request from me. The place was better for it; before then, my bachelor-style efforts were haphazard at best.

'Not now, Benny.'

'I clean.'

'Get the hell out!' I bellowed at Benny, and rewarded myself with a wincing headache to go with my alcohol-ravaged stomach and general malaise.

Benny stared back at me for a second, realized I was in worse physical shape from my bout with Matusalem than I had been when he tried to pick my pocket in the alley behind the Capri so many weeks before, and continued to mop.

'I said, get lost, kid.' I sat up, angry enough to give Benny the back of my hand. The room whirled and I fell back onto the bed.

'You need a drink of water and some *menudo*,' Benny said.

'I need hair of the dog,' I groaned from atop my pitching pillow.

'What dog?'

'Never mind, Benny. There's a five-peso note in the top dresser drawer. Go out and get a bottle of Havana Club.' If I was going to drink myself to death I might as well use the good stuff.

Benny went to the dresser, got the money, and without looking me in the eye, finished mopping the floor I had fouled. He was gone before I could growl at him.

I closed my eyes, embracing the toss and spin of the mattress and room, and Fannie appeared to me. She was crying and begging me to do something but I couldn't make out what she was saying. This went on until I was shaken awake. Benny was back.

'Gimme the bottle, Benny.'

'I sorry, Genry. No bottle. I have *menudo* from Restaurante El Pollo Rico and Señor Rojas is brewing another *cafecito* for you.'

'You little shit, where's my booze?'

'No booze. *Cafecito* and *menudo*.'

'I'll throw the *cafecito* against the wall like the last one. I'll throw you against the wall after that, if you don't get me rum.'

Benny stared evenly at me, his old-gnome visage unmoved by my threat. 'You will eat *menudo* and drink *cafecito* and

water.' He said it with the finality of a mother addressing a
petulant child. Too broken to bicker with him, I accepted the
sentence and sat up. Benny put a bowl into my hands, and I
began to spoon the mystery soup into my mouth. The first
spoonful awakened my gag reflex. It was highly seasoned, not
typical of Cuban food. I bit back the gag and swallowed several
more spoonfuls. It was good, or as good as anything could be
with a churning gut and a half-drunk hangover.

'This ain't Cuban.'

'No, Genry. Señora Lopez at El Pollo Rico makes it. She
is Mexican.'

'What's in it?'

'The pig's foot, the cow's stomach . . .'

The soup in my stomach started to come up. 'OK, Benny.
Enough of the soup recipe. How about some water to wash
this down?'

I drank about a gallon of water, glad that Benny had ignored
my instruction to get more rum. I choked down more soup. I
knew then that I would live, even if I wanted to die.

Benny continued to fuss around me like a disapproving
mamacita, tut-tutting when I stopped eating, stripping the sheets
from the bed to be washed. When I'd finally downed a river
of water and two bowls of pig-foot-cow-stomach-and-other-
unmentionable-ingredient soup, he said, 'We go now.'

'Kid, I ain't going nowhere.'

'You must, Genry. I take you to the leaders of the Directorio
Revolucionario. Now.'

The US government-trained Henry Gore would never go to
meet with the Directorio honchos on the spur of the moment.
That Henry Gore would know that because Marta had been
compromised as a – what? a double-double agent? – he had
to have been exposed as well. That Henry Gore would know
that deliberation and caution made for operational success.
That Henry Gore would remember that men who took chances
in counterintelligence operations were the type of men who
had short careers and died glorious, useless deaths. But this
was a morning when I didn't care if I wound up dead.

'OK, Benny. Where is this meeting with the Directorio
leaders?'

'I don't know, Genry. I take you to the Victor Hugo Park.
A car will meet us there.'

'When?'

'At ten-thirty.'

I looked at my watch. It was ten already. 'I'll need to make
some calls, Benny. I'll meet you downstairs in fifteen minutes.'

'No, Genry. No calls. They order me, once I tell you about
the meeting, that I am not to leave you and you are not to
make calls. If you make a call, I am not to take you to the
meeting.'

So there it was. No calls to Colonel Blanco Rico or even
Moncho Mercado to let them know what was going on. No
backup tail of SIM goons following the car picking us up. It
was go-it-alone or no-go.

'All right, Benny. No calls. Just let me get dressed.'

I pulled on some pants and a shirt that was only two wear-
ings removed from its last laundering, and grabbed a linen
jacket. I was about to complete my outfit with the Woodsman
in its shoulder holster when Benny said, 'No gun, Genry.'

'Great, Benny. Anything else I should know about this
invitation?'

'They will blindfold you when you get in the car,' Benny
said.

'Wonderful. I might as well go naked,' I said. And if I had
given it any serious thought, I would have realized that I was
doing just that.

THIRTY-ONE

A canary-yellow Buick drifted to the curb in front of where Benny and I sat on a shaded bench in Victor Hugo Park. A man in dark glasses in the passenger seat faced us and took off his straw hat. On that signal, Benny stood and led me to the car.

The passenger put his hat back on and said to me in English, 'Please get in back.'

I did. The passenger slid in after me and the driver maneuvered the car gently into the flow of traffic. 'I will blindfold you and you will need to get on the floor,' he said.

I'd spent about as much time riding on the floors of cars since coming to Cuba as I had in their seats. I submitted to the blindfold and knelt on the floor. A few moments later, the car stopped and the passenger got out, leaving me alone with the silent driver. For ten minutes, the Buick followed a meandering path through the sparse midday traffic before halting. I heard the door open and strong hands picked me up from the floor and led me up a flight of stairs. Then I was pushed down into a chair.

The blindfold was removed from my eyes. Celia Nunez stood before me. Blinds or curtains covered all the windows in the room. A single light bulb hung from the ceiling. The whole set-up was very cliché, direct from the interrogation handbook of every police and intelligence agency on the planet. And when you had something to hide like I did, the set-up was terrifying despite being cliché.

'Welcome, Mr Gore,' Celia said, her voice cool and unreadable.

'You have an interesting way of making a fellow welcome, Señorita Nunez,' I said. I smiled at her, trying to show I was at ease. I hoped the smile didn't appear as false as it felt.

'As you know, Mr Gore, we must be cautious in our

dealings with others. Especially now that Marta has been . . . compromised.'

'Do you know how or by whom?' I figured I might as well get a little interrogation in before they started on me.

'The stooges of the regime are everywhere. One of them exposed her. We are uncertain as yet who it was but we shall learn.'

I thought only Celia was in the room but then there was a shuffling of feet behind me. I resisted the urge to turn around. Better not to see those who wished to remain unseen. Celia, though, had other ideas.

'Come, *patriotas*, and let me introduce you to Mr Henry Gore,' she said. Four men shuffled around until all were arrayed behind Celia. She spoke. 'Henry Gore, meet One.'

A thick-waisted man with arms of ropey muscle inclined his head.

'And Two.' Two was dressed in a tailored suit, polished shoes with spats, and had a diamond pin in his tie. He looked like one of the floor bosses at the Riveria or the Sans Souci. Two gave me a tight smile.

'Henry, meet Three.' Three had a rare-for-Cuba goatee, deep-set black eyes, and a tweed get-up like somebody's idea of a professor. 'Pleased to become acquainted, Mr Gore,' Three said, in accent-free English.

'And, finally, Four,' Celia said, with shining eyes. She was obviously smitten. Four stepped forward and offered his hand, which I shook. He had the matinee-idol looks of a Cesar Romero but he carried himself without any arrogance, such that his silent handshake, which might have been considered aloof, seemed friendly.

'These gentlemen make up four-fifths of the Council of Leaders of the Directorio Revolucionario,' Celia said.

'And the fifth? Is that the famous El Fuerte, the strong one? Or does one of these gentlemen have that name as well as a number?' I decided I'd better take the offensive if I wanted to come out of this room alive. I could see the bulge of a holstered gun beneath Two's and Four's jackets. I was sure the others were armed as well.

Three addressed my question. 'No, Mr Gore, none of these

gentlemen, including myself, are El Fuerte. But you are correct that the fifth member of the Council of Leaders is El Fuerte. She presides over the Council and stands before you now.'

'Celia? You are the leader of the Directorio?' The words came out in a tone reflecting the surprise I felt. If the dead El Máximo had heard himself spoken of in that tone, his pride would have been wounded. Celia Nunez took it in stride.

'I am one of the leaders of the Directorio Revolucionario and, like the other four, I am no higher or better than the cane-cutter who joins us bringing with him only his cane knife and his pure heart. But the five of us are not here to speak of me, we are here to see you. Or, should I say, the four other than me are here to hear from you and determine whether to go ahead with a purchase from you.'

'We are also concerned that you may have been the one who betrayed Marta,' Three said, in his best you-are-in-the-principal's-office-and-you-might-as-well-tell-us-the-truth voice.

'I didn't rat Marta out,' I said. A flashback of Marta convulsing as the Electrician turned the knob on his machine almost made the words stick in my throat.

'We know you work for the regime, Mr Gore,' Two said. 'Marta told us. You had to suspect she had done so, once you knew she had been compromised.'

'What if I do?' I asked the question for myself as much as posing it to Two. 'If you know I work for the regime, why are you talking to me? Why didn't you just have some patriot knock on my door and croak me?'

'We should have,' One said, his accent heavy.

Three spoke. 'We know they let you see what they did to Marta. We thought it might change your thoughts about who is on the side of the angels here.'

'I haven't seen an angel since I've been in Cuba,' I said. But I had. She had been taken away by the people I was working for.

Celia spoke up. 'You have seen what is done to the people. You have seen our children begging and our sisters turned to whores so that Batista and his cronies can line their pockets. You have seen the American gangsters who come to our island

and steal the very bread from the mouths of our fathers and mothers. Are you not moved by this?'

'It's none of my business.'

'I told you we waste our time with this *gringo*,' One said.

Three assumed a professorial air. 'Mr Gore, you served with honor in the Air Force of your country, from what we have been able to learn.'

So they had been checking. I nodded.

'Not only did you serve,' Three continued. 'You served in a capacity that shows your government's special trust and confidence in you.'

'I never really thought of it that way but I suppose you could say that. What of it?'

'Do you love your country, the United States of America?'

'I'm here. What does that tell you?' I said.

'I do not think that tells the entire story, Henry Gore,' Celia interjected. 'I think you, like all of us in this room, are a patriot, a believer in the freedom of men and women, a hater of oppression and tyranny.'

'What if I believe that? It doesn't mean I'm going to stick my neck out for you. Why would I do that?'

It was Three's turn again. 'You have already "stuck your neck out" for us, Señor Gore. When you defended Marta and Celia in the shootout with the police in the Bar La Finca. It would have been a simple matter for you then to raise your hands and let the police have Celia. You did not and there was a reason you did not.'

'Yeah, there was a reason,' I said. The reason was to keep from getting plugged by that nervous kid cop, I thought. I didn't say it, though. What I said was, 'Look here, I'm an American citizen and you all have a choice. You can let me walk, and get on with your plotting of revolution, or regime change, or liberation of the oppressed, or whatever you choose to call it. Or you can put one in the back of my head and dump me in the harbor. But if you kill me, you won't have to contend with just the police and SIM. Uncle Sam will send some folks down here who will make SIM and the cops look like amateurs and they and SIM and the police will hunt you all down. Killing an American isn't like knocking off a local cop or two. So let's cut to the chase.' Pretty brash, and, I don't mind telling you, I was scared shitless while I was saying it. I waited for the ride to the harbor and the bullet that I'd all but demanded.

One seethed with anger. Two, who hadn't said a word, looked from me to Celia.

'Help us get guns,' she said. 'We will pay you. And you will have the eternal gratitude of the Cuban people.'

I stick my neck out for nobody. The words were on my lips, ready to be spoken. The world-weary response I'd rehearsed dozens of times since I had seen Bogart say it in the movies at the Centennial Theater when I was a teenager. When I'd received my honorable discharge from the Air Force, I had decided those would be the words I would live by, my philosophy of life. But I couldn't say them to Celia Nunez.

You see, I used to think of myself as good. While I was growing up, while I was in the service, even when I first came to Cuba. Maybe the private-dick business, the way I had been conducting it, was not the most savory occupation but I was still able to tell myself that I'd done an honest day's work at the end of each day.

Somewhere along the way, though, I had become something less than good. Not truly bad. No, I couldn't consider myself to be bad in the way that men like Senator Bauza and Colonel Blanco Rico and Meyer Lansky and Santo Trafficante were bad. But in doing the bidding of men who were bad, I had fallen, become less. Become dirty by being bought by their dirty money. And what had it gotten me? The loss of someone who I had begun to love. The blood of persons, certainly not innocent but no more blameworthy than myself, on my hands. Complicity with the torturers and the pimps and the thugs who ran Cuba at the expense of the Bennys and the Celia Nunezes of the world.

'OK,' I said to Celia, and to her numbers One, Two, Three, and Four. OK. That was all. So simple and so monumental. Monumental to me. Maybe monumental to them and their revolution. With any luck, monumental, too, to Batista, Blanco Rico, Bauza, and the American mobsters who owned them, in the most negative sense. 'OK.'

'We will be able to pay you . . .' Three began.

'I . . . I don't need to be paid.' I heard myself say the words and expected to curse myself for a fool, a patsy. Instead, a weight lifted from my shoulders. No, from my soul. I was free. The grimy shame fell away. For a moment I felt like I was with Fannie Knutsen, felt her blond hair brush across my cheek, heard her whisper unintelligible endearments in my ear.

I felt something I hadn't felt in a long time. I felt clean.

THIRTY-TWO

'He cannot be trusted.'

I could tell One wanted to shout the words. He fought to keep his voice at a conversational level, knowing that it was only by seeming collected and reasonable that he might possibly persuade his fellows.

'We have been over this, One,' Celia said. She looked squarely at me. 'We all knew we would be taking a risk with him. A majority of the Council voted to take the chance.'

One was bitter. 'I hope we are satisfied with our exercise in democracy when SIM cuts all of our throats.'

'You know we must take risks if we are to succeed,' Celia said. 'I think Señor Gore is a worthwhile risk.'

'I hope your championship of this *norteamericano* does not result in the death of the revolution.'

'It won't,' I said. Watching the back-and-forth between Celia and One had me feeling like merchandise at a slave auction. It was good to cap their debate with my assurance, even if One didn't believe me. 'Now, how do you plan to get the guns you need?'

'You will sell them to us, as we discussed,' Celia said.

'This may come as a surprise to you, Celia, but I really don't have any guns to sell to you. Well, just a few; those six Ross rifles and the one Thompson. Those certainly aren't enough weapons to take on Batista's army.'

Celia smiled. 'No, Henry, I don't mean just those few. I am talking about a hundred fifty rifles and thirty Thompsons, just as we discussed. You are going to get SIM to provide them to us.'

'How?'

'The plan is simple but the best plans always are. You will go back to your handlers . . .'

'Handler,' I said. 'Just one. Colonel Blanco Rico of SIM.'

'Ah, Henry, the man at the very top. They must have great confidence in you.'

'Misplaced confidence. OK, I go to Blanco Rico . . .'

'And you tell him that the Council of Leaders are prepared to buy one hundred fifty Rosses and thirty Thompsons. Tell him that it is so important to the Directorio that the Council are willing to meet you themselves to pay the money and take delivery of the arms.'

'How is he going to believe that?'

'Your condition of sale was half the money as a down-payment, was it not?'

'It was before tonight,' I said. 'Any legit arms seller wouldn't chance bringing a shipment to a delivery meeting without half the purchase money paid up front.'

'And it still is a condition,' Celia said. 'We will give you half of the purchase price we discussed for the guns and ammunition, twenty-five thousand American dollars, now. Two, please show him.'

Two stepped into a shadowed recess of the room and came out with a canvas messenger bag, passed it into my hands, and pushed open the bag's flap to reveal its contents. Five banded stacks of one-hundred-dollar bills, fifty bills to a stack. I drew out a stack and riffled through the greenbacks. New notes. Maybe counterfeits but probably not. It appeared to be new money like you would get from a US bank. The Directorio Revolucionario had some moneyed supporters in the States, I decided.

'You were pretty sure I was going to fall for this scheme, weren't you?'

'I consider myself a good judge of character, Henry Gore,' Celia said, a spark of amusement in her dark eyes.

'OK, so you've got all this money.'

'No, you have it, Henry. We are delivering it to you. Here. Today.'

The thought crossed my mind that I had been on the wrong side of this deal from the start. The ten thousand pesos Senator Bauza had tossed in front of me looked mighty paltry compared to the two hundred fifty C-notes now in my hand, let alone the twenty-five thousand yet to come. The thought also crossed my mind that I could take the canvas messenger bag, leave Havana on the first flight out for anywhere, and start over.

Twenty-five Gs was six or seven years' wages for a working man in the States. If the plane I took landed in Mexico, it was two decades of wages. In Guatemala or Nicaragua, it was a lifetime's worth. And the Directorio couldn't very well run to the police and report that I had made off with the money that they'd hoped to use to purchase arms to overthrow the government. All I had to do was walk out the door and go to the airport.

By the time I completed the thought, I knew I wouldn't do it. I silently cursed myself for being a damned fool.

'Say I take the money right now, Celia,' I said. 'What do you want me to do with it?'

'Show Colonel Blanco Rico that you are a loyal employee. Take ten thousand dollars and give it to him.'

'Only ten thousand? What about the other fifteen?'

'You are a loyal employee but an opportunist as well,' Celia said. 'Keep the extra money in your apartment. The colonel will know to search for it. He would expect you to act as he would act. He will find the money and know then that there is no question as to your loyalties. Your only loyalty will be shown to be to yourself.'

'You don't think he'll be a little pissed off that I'm trying to steal fifteen thousand dollars?'

'He will chide you for the attempt but it will actually reassure him. And remember, he needs you to carry out his plan.'

'OK, then what?'

'Tell Colonel Blanco Rico that the Directorio will not deliver the balance until it sees all the merchandise.'

'That doesn't do you much good, Celia,' I said. 'He will just have me tell you the guns are in some warehouse or alley. The guns won't be there, but SIM will swoop in as soon as you and Señors One through Four show up to inspect the goods. You'll be facing half of SIM before you can buy the first rifle.'

'We have a plan that puts neither the money nor the Directorio Revolucionario at risk, other than one brave volunteer,' Celia said. 'You see, you must bring the guns into the country as a true arms dealer would, by sea or by air. You will bring them in by sea. We will insist that we inspect the rifles and submachine guns on the water, before they are brought into the port. Freddy – you remember Freddy – will take a small boat out to the vessel bringing in the arms, and make certain the guns and ammunition are on board. He will signal to shore if the arms are present. No signal, no deal. So we will not be lured to an empty warehouse and shot for our troubles.'

'That takes care of making sure the guns are there, Celia,' I said. 'How are you planning to deal with the ambush that will be waiting for you when you take possession of the guns when they come ashore?'

'We will ambush the ambush, Henry. We will insist that the guns be offloaded at the quay directly in front of the warehouse where Freddy and I met with you to be shown your samples.'

'You do realize that the same warehouse was used by SIM to deliver the samples, as you put it, to Marta and me,' I said.

'Yes, Henry, we are aware of that. We knew you were being given a car and weapons at that warehouse before you did. The owner allows SIM to use the building frequently, in return for which SIM reduces the amount of money the owner must pay to the government for "business licenses" and "protection from bandit elements". Fortunately for us, the owner, a man who worked his way up from being a stevedore on the docks, begrudges paying the license fees and protection money, even at the reduced rates. He may be a businessman and property owner now but he still has his stevedore's sense of fairness and resents paying money to those who provide him no benefit and simply line their pockets. He calls them "government pirates".'

Three chimed in. 'The buccaneers of the seventeenth century were not a tenth as greedy as Batista and his flunkies.'

Celia continued. 'We believe Colonel Blanco Rico will use the warehouse to hide a mixed force of army and police to strike us as the weapons are being loaded from the boat into trucks on the dock in front of the warehouse. He will not expect us to be present in force. It is prudent for us to be inconspicuous, to use only one or two small trucks, a couple of drivers, and a man or two, as well as the five of us, to load.

He will not know that twenty men will be concealed inside the trucks. He will not know that the warehouse owner will tell us how many police and soldiers are inside the warehouse. He will not know that we will have men hidden in the rafters of the warehouse who will, at a signal, fire down on his men below. He will not know that we will have an armed force of a hundred hidden in other buildings in the neighborhood, ready to mount a coordinated attack. We will kill the SIM men in the warehouse and take their weapons. With the guns on the boat and the weapons we already possess, we shall be able to field three hundred well-armed fighters. The same night, we will attack the Comandancia General, the presidential residence, and the Capitolio. The people will rise up to join us in revolt throughout the country.'

'That's an ambitious plan,' I said. It wouldn't have a snowball's chance in hell in a place like the US but in Cuba, it might. The rot ran deep here and the military and police just might lay down their arms or switch sides when confronted with a determined, well-armed foe.

'We will succeed if we act swiftly and forcefully,' One said. 'We will try our utmost. If we fail, we shall all become martyrs for the revolution.'

I wondered if he was including me in that category.

THIRTY-THREE

'Isn't the blindfold unnecessary, now that we are all up to our necks in the same pot of boiling water?' I asked, as Two led me, eyes covered by a rag, from the building where we had just met.

'One can never be too careful,' Two said. 'Besides, now if SIM starts to sweat you about the location of the meeting, you can honestly say you have no idea.'

'I'll remember that when they attach the wires to my nipples,' I said, trying to keep the conversation light.

'Don't worry about them doing that to you,' Two replied, as amiably as if we were having a couple of beers and discussing whether the Dodgers ought to be moved from Brooklyn. 'They only do that to women. For *hombres* like us they put the current through the *cajones*. They make you a soprano. Now, duck down to the back seat floor.'

I assumed the usual position. After half an hour on the road the rag was whisked from my eyes. Two said, 'You can get home easily from here,' shook my hand, and drove off.

Two had dropped me at a familiar spot, the post office, and I took the opportunity to check my mail before setting off on foot for the corner of Calle J and Calle 21. I had the messenger bag with the five stacks of dead presidents in it on my shoulder and I made sure to keep my right arm over the bag. Explaining to the Directorio Council of Leaders or SIM how I'd lost twenty-five grand to a pickpocket or snatch-and-grab artist was not an experience I wanted to have.

At first it appeared that my post-office box held only dust and an errant paper clip, until I saw two letters in the far corner. The first was from the agency in Chicago which had referred the wronged Annabel from Dubuque to me, explaining that she refused to pay my full fee as I had not provided the requisite photograph of her beloved and his loyal secretary *in flagrante delicto*. The check for fifty bucks enclosed with the letter would about cover my expenses on the case, including the sticking plasters for the places where Larry broke the skin when he beat me, and the Matusalem rum used to kill the pain. The other letter was from Janet. I pocketed it to read when I reached my apartment.

I left the post office and started the walk home, enjoying the sunshine after all my recent blindfold and dark-room time. I had only three blocks to go when Benny fell in step beside me.

'You are with us now, Genry.' Not a question, a statement.

'You mean you knew I wasn't before?'

'Everybody knew.'

'Everybody? Even you?'

Benny gave a grave nod.

'How?'

'We knew. But I tell the others, "Genry is a good man. Do not kill him. He will be with us."'

'Jesus, kid. I must be losing my touch.'

'When the revolution comes, we get Marta out of prison. We get everybody out of prison. *Mi mamá*, we get her out.'

'I thought you told me you didn't have any people, Benny.'

'I say that because when people go to prison, it is like they die.' He was matter of fact when he said this.

'Where is she?'

'Cienfuegos.'

'Have you seen her since she went in?'

'No. Nobody is allowed to see the people who make revolution when they go to prison.'

'How long has it been?'

'Four years. I was eleven.'

'What about your old man?' I asked. I got a quizzical look in response. 'Your old man. Your *papá*.'

'He died making the revolution.'

I didn't know what to say, so I marched on. How can a kid live like this?

We reached the steps to my apartment. Benny said, 'I have to go. I be back later. I am glad you are with us, Genry.'

Upstairs, my apartment was the same but seemed different

to me. I wondered if the condemned felt the same way about their cell on the night before their dawn appointment with Ol' Sparky. Hoping a few words from Janet would help to break my cheery mood, I tore open her letter. Jan was a bubbly writer, using short sentences, some phrases that weren't even sentences, and lots of punctuation, like she'd just had a class that day on exclamation points, semi-colons, and ellipses and wanted to try them all out in one writing. She was sometimes hard to follow but it was a pleasant hard to follow. This letter was different, though. There was a maturity appearing in her writing, even when she covered the same topics she usually had, writing of school, friends, teen diversions, and snippets about Aunt Ruth and Uncle Pete. The giveaway was her hand-writing. It was less looping and child-like, more adult. And at the end she wrote for the first time on a topic we had both taken pains to avoid.

I miss Mom and Dad, Henry. I was thinking about them today and how happy the four of us were back when we were kids. About how happy and safe and ordinary and good it was. Now they're gone and it's only us, Henry. We only have each other.

I glanced from the letter to where the messenger bag, stuffed with cash, sat on my bed. Twenty-five thousand would get me home in style. It would get Jan a college education, if she wanted it, or a real start on adult life. It would make a safe and happy and ordinary and good life possible for her again. Then I thought about Benny's mother in prison, and about the girls Janet's age turning tricks on the Malecón each night, and the evil that had taken Fannie Knutsen from me. Hang on, Janet, I thought. Your big brother is coming home to you soon. He just has some unfinished business here to take care of first.

THIRTY-FOUR

I signed for the telegram and gave the boy a ten-centavo piece. He brightened at his good fortune, tossing the coin as he bounded down the steps to his bike. I tore open the envelope and read the flimsy inside.

PLAZA DE LA CATEDRAL. 6 PM. OLD MAN ON BENCH.

No sender was listed. I almost laughed. Here I was, home for four days after my very impromptu meeting with El Fuerte and Numbers One through Four, and there had been no word from either the Directorio Revolucionario or Colonel Blanco Rico and the cheerful folks at SIM. I was starting to have daydreams of both sides forgetting about the entire arms transaction, leaving me with the messenger bag of c-notes and a way out of the push-pull between them. But a telegram? If the Directorio wanted to reach me, there was the ever-reliable and ever-present Benny to communicate the message. And, ever since Marta was sent to prison, if Blanco Rico wanted me he could have his two mutts, Trujillo and Alvarez, kidnap me off the streets as they had done in the past. Or just call me on the telephone. I couldn't believe we had to go through all this cloak-and-dagger but I played along with whoever had sent the missive, curious as to who would show up.

The Plaza de la Catedral is the front doorstep of the Cathedral of the Virgin Mary of the Immaculate Conception, in the cobblestoned heart of Old Havana. The entire common was already engulfed in shadow when I arrived shortly before six. Some of the nearby residents were enjoying a turn around the plaza in the evening coolness before returning to their homes for dinner. It wasn't hard to locate my contact; there were only two benches in the square. One was occupied by a pair of the city's ubiquitous lovers-who-ought-to-get-a-room. A geezer, hands propped on a cane and appearing to doze, sat at the end of the other.

I dropped onto the end of the bench farthest from the old man and said, '*Buenos tardes*,' in my best high-school Spanish.

'I remember when this place would be filled with beautiful young women and handsome men marching in the *paseo* of love at this time of the evening in the old days,' the ancient said, in passable English.

'It must have been different then,' I said, opting for idle chit-chat until my contact decided to get down to business.

'It was,' the old man said. 'Oh, it was, Henry.'

The man's voice changed when he uttered the last sentence, the English clearer and without accent. He had the appearance of being elderly but on closer inspection I could tell his age was the result of powders and dyes. I was sitting on the bench with Colonel Ernesto Blanco Rico.

The colonel noted my recognition of him by my change of expression. 'The disguise and the meeting place away from my office were necessary, Henry. I suspect the Comandancia General is being more closely watched than usual, so it was too risky to meet you there. Or, for that matter, in any public place where I might be recognized with you.'

'And no telephone for the same reason?' I asked.

'The operators at the Aquila Telephone Exchange have been suspect for many years. We have avoided arresting them because they are an effective way for us to spread useful rumors and misinformation to the bandits. On the other hand, the telegraph office is secure and sending the occasional telegram is a minor inconvenience. But I have not brought you here to speak about telephones and telegraphs. You met several days ago with the leaders of the Directorio?'

'Yes. All five of them.'

'Who are they?'

'They did not use names,' I said. 'They referred to each other by numbers, One through Five. Celia Nunez is Number Five. I did not recognize any of the others.'

'Describe them to me, then,' Blanco Rico said. I did.

The colonel thought for a moment and said, 'The one you

call Three is Pablo Chavez, a member of the faculty at the university. He is known for his radical ideas about democracy. We have had our eyes on him for years but he has never been caught in any anti-government activity and is too well-connected to simply bring in to the Comandancia General for interrogation without any cause. The others you describe are not familiar. This is extremely valuable information, Henry.'

'There's more,' I said. 'They are ready to do an arms deal. A deal that will put all of them in one place, together with others involved in the Directorio, at a time when they can be apprehended in the act of purchasing weapons and ammunition.'

'That is excellent, Henry. When and where?'

'In one week, at midnight, on the dock outside the warehouse where Marta and I were given the sample guns and the car.'

Blanco Rico smiled a rapacious smile beneath his old man disguise. 'The location is perfect.'

'I selected it with your needs in mind. They agreed without considering the exposed nature of the place.' I paused. 'There are just a couple things.'

'Yes?'

'We will need a boat. And we will need to have guns.'

'We have given you guns already, Henry.'

'Not just the samples. They want to see all the guns. One hundred fifty rifles and thirty Thompson sub-machine guns, plus ammunition.'

'That is ridiculous. We cannot put that number of weapons at risk of falling into the bandits' hands. Even allowing you the six rifles and the single Thompson we provided as samples was opposed by some in the government.'

'They won't show if they haven't seen the guns.'

Blanco Rico shook his head. 'They are not serious.'

'Oh, they're serious. They gave me a down-payment. Ten thousand dollars.' I took a fat envelope of cash from my jacket pocket and slid it toward my elderly companion along the seat of the bench. He pocketed it without looking inside.

'Your honesty is commendable, Henry,' the colonel said. 'A lesser man might have been tempted to not turn over the money.'

'That's not how we do things in the United States Air Force.' I put on my best eagle scout's expression to help along the words I'd uttered. If I were in Blanco Rico's shoes, I wouldn't have bought that for a second. I could see that he didn't, either. I wondered how long it would take him to have someone ransack my apartment.

'So the Directorio leadership is serious. But you still have not explained why we must assemble an arsenal for them.'

'They asked me if the guns were in Cuba, Colonel. I told them that they were not, and that they would arrive by boat from the North once they provided their down-payment. When they learned this, they insisted that one of their men, an arms expert, view and inspect the guns a short distance from Havana, while still at sea. If the guns and ammo are on the boat and in operable condition, their man will signal his approval to shore. The Directorio men on shore will then meet the boat with two trucks and a few men besides the five leaders, pay me, and offload the guns from the boat. If there is no signal from their man on the boat, they won't even go to the dock and the deal is off.'

'I give the *bastardos* credit,' Blanco Rico said. 'They make it impossible to set the trap without bringing a boatload of guns to the dock. Well, we shall be ready for them. How many men do they plan to have at the docks and in the trucks?'

'They said they would have one driver and one other man in each truck. With the four men in the Council of Leaders, Celia Nunez, and their arms expert on the boat, I figure a total of ten to contend with at the dock.'

'They will be met by two elite SIM platoons and the police flying squad. We will set up machine guns in the nearest warehouse and wipe out the scourge of the Directorio Revolucionario once and for all.' The colonel's eyes glittered with bloodlust at the prospect.

'Wait a minute, Colonel,' I said. 'I didn't sign up to get shot at. Can't you make this happen after I'm out of the way?' The prospect of being within range of the SIM machine guns was daunting enough, let alone what was sure to happen once the hidden Directorio fighters were unleashed on the ambushers.

'I will, of course, instruct my men not to fire on the boat

and will specifically tell them to avoid you, Henry. I will be there to personally lead the operation, and will hold off springing the ambush as long as possible to allow you and the boat to get out of the way. Understand, though, that once the last case of guns is taken off the boat, you will only have the time until it is put in one of the bandit trucks to make your escape. Do not linger.'

'Believe me, Colonel, I don't plan to.' I figured Blanco Rico would start the shooting well before then and, contrary to what he told me, I wouldn't be an exempt target. After all, if I was 'accidentally' killed in the operation, he could keep the nine thousand pesos he had committed to pay me. He probably intended to keep the money the Directorio was bringing to the party as well. It, like Henry Gore, would be regrettably lost in the confusion of battle.

'You have done good work, Henry.' Colonel Blanco Rico stood creakily and patted my shoulder in a very old-man way. 'The people of Cuba are most appreciative of your efforts.' Funny how the unidentified people of Cuba were involved on both sides of this tussle. If you could see in their true heart of hearts, I wondered, would they even care?

'All that's needed in the way of appreciation is the nine thousand pesos I've got coming, Colonel, and the good people of Cuba can call it even. What's the next step?'

'Lieutenant Trujillo will be in touch with your instructions,' Blanco Rico said, before hobbling off, just another lame old man, leaning on his cane.

THIRTY-FIVE

The next couple of days after my encounter with the old-man alter ego of Colonel Blanco Rico passed quietly. Benny made himself scarce, for operational security, I assumed. Instead of hanging around my door all day and all night, he only appeared once each morning, bringing my *cafecito* and *pastelitos*, and disappearing for the rest of the day.

That left me with plenty of time to myself. Time to contemplate the entire span of my life because, you see, I was certain that I was going to die when it came time for the delivery of guns to the Directorio Revolucionario. I was sure the crossfire from the machine guns would get me. Or the Directorio fighters would shoot down anyone they did not recognize. Or, more likely, Senator Bauza and Colonel Blanco Rico would give an instruction to the loyal Sergeant Alvarez, or his equivalent, to make certain I didn't come out of the fight alive to collect my nine thousand pesos.

It was liberating, really, to know that I would soon be dead. Funny, you always see the movies with the hero on his death bed in the clean white of a hospital, surrounded by comrades in arms, a wife or a girlfriend. Or a mother. The hero is stoic, almost noble in the face of death. But there is also a sadness about him and a tragedy in his demise. For me there was no sadness or sense of tragedy, only freedom from all that my life had become. Freedom from the loss of Fannie Knutsen. Freedom from the moral ambiguity that marked the decisions which had brought me to this point. Freedom from the degeneracy and debasement that is life in Havana.

How do you spend your last days when you know the end is coming? I had occasionally wondered what it would be like, as I'm sure we've all done on those nights when love, and work, and friends, and a happy future all fall by the wayside and we are left with only the darkness and the knowledge that the end must come sometime. In the past, in the blackness of those wee hours, I'd told myself that there would be high living, expensive drink, the finest food, and women, beautiful and compliant. That I would make sure that I had those fine things in my last days, when money was no object and time was on a short leash.

But how did I actually spend those days, liberated from the worst that life had sent my way? I wandered, in search of something to which I could not put a name. It wasn't truth, or beauty, or meaning. The closest I could come to putting a label on it was . . . life. I searched for life. I walked through the streets and plazas of Havana and observed it – the warmth of an elderly woman's smile, the sound of children playing baseball in the street, the touch of the humid sun on my skin, the savory crunch of a skewer of grilled pork purchased from a street vendor. I say 'observed' because I was already gone, no longer a participant in life, a mere tourist among those actually living. It brought me something close to peace, those last rambles in the vibrant presence of life, done with a detachment and distance I had never known before.

On some of the days during that week of living death, I walked from dawn to dusk and into darkness, seeing in the lighted windows of the little houses and apartments the joy and happiness so often absent from Havana's streets and public places. A family eating dinner together. A pair of lovers slow-dancing to the music from a radio. A middle-aged couple passing a quiet evening with needlework and newspaper, serene in each other's company.

Each night when I returned to my apartment, I expected to find it tossed by SIM henchmen in search of the fifteen thousand dollars from the down-payment money that I had kept. After three days, it was such an expectation that I was disappointed when I came in at midnight and found nothing out of place. I had a premonition that the next day would be the day, so I took five thousand dollars of the money, stuffed it in a manila envelope, and addressed it to Janet. No note, I decided, just the money, because how could I even begin to explain? The next morning I took the envelope to Señor Rojas downstairs, told him I would be going away in a few days, and asked him to mail it for me in four days, on the morning after the Directorio operation was scheduled to take place. Of course, he knew nothing about the operation. I gave him a five-peso note for his trouble and he was more than pleased to help his good tenant.

It's hard to explain but giving Rojas the package for Janet made my lightness of being even lighter and that day I undertook my rambling with a destination for the first time. I walked slowly, still taking in life along the way, and it was noon before I arrived at my objective. Havana's Colón Cemetery was named after Cuba's discoverer. Since the late 1800s, it had been the resting place for all those who passed in Havana. It was now a city of the dead almost as populous as the city of the living surrounding it.

There was a crone selling flowers at the gate. I bought a sheaf of calla lilies from her, walked through the gate, and down the long central boulevard of mausoleums which housed the remains of Havana's rich and famous departed. Some of the structures were large enough to be houses for the living. A few narrow pathways led away from the boulevard, to where the mausoleums there were smaller, less ostentatious, older.

I wandered for an hour and finally despaired of finding the grave for which I searched. I came upon an elderly sexton raking leaves in front of a tomb shaded by a massive ceiba.

'Can you help me locate a grave?' I asked in my broken Spanish.

'We have no graves here,' the man said, in English, recognizing a *gringo* when he heard one. 'All those who reside here are entombed above ground. Who is it you are seeking?'

'An American woman. Fannie Knutsen,' I said. 'She may be buried as Lola Loring. She sometimes went by that name.'

'I am not familiar with either of those names,' the sexton said. 'Was she buried long ago, in the area of the old tombs? I am not so familiar with the residents in that part of the cemetery.'

'She should have been buried in the last few days. She died about a week ago.'

The sexton looked skeptical. 'Are you certain, señor? There

was no one entombed by either of those names in the last week.'

'She died in Havana. Would there be a place besides this in the city where she could be?'

'No, señor. All those in the city who go to meet Our Savior are brought here. Might her remains have been returned to the United States?'

For some reason, I had not thought of that but something told me that she was somewhere in Colón Cemetery. 'I don't believe so. Can you check your records?'

Accustomed to dealing with fragile mourners, the sexton shrugged and said, 'I can, señor. Come this way.'

We walked in the midday sun along the avenues of stone, the chitter of birds the only sound besides our footfalls, until we reached a plain mausoleum which contained no dead and served as a record storage and tool shed for the cemetery. Inside, the sexton pulled down a thick canvas-backed ledger, newest in a line of two dozen on a shelf, and ran his finger along a page near the back of the book. After repeating the motion a second and a third time, he said, 'I am sorry, señor.'

My look of disappointment caused him to consider further. '*Perdón*, señor. How did this lady you search for die?'

'By her own hand, I'm told.'

The old man made the sign of the cross. 'I am sorry, señor. This explains why I could not direct you. We have a . . . special place for the suicides. This way.'

He led me across many avenues of the dead, to a walled ground in the farthest corner of the cemetery.

'The suicides are buried here, in unconsecrated ground,' he said. 'We buried three of the poor unfortunates last week. All were brought in wrapped in shrouds, as is the custom. I myself made simple pine coffins for each of them. The parish priest, though suicide is a grave offense in the eyes of the Church, takes pity and collects money to pay for the wood.' He pointed to three fresh mounds of earth, side by side. 'My younger helpers do the digging; they buried the three there. I was not present when they did. *Pobre de mí*, the headstones carry no names and we keep no record of them.'

'She – Señorita Knutsen – was a young woman, in her

twenties, blond, pale, tall and thin.' I could see Fannie sitting in the sun-drenched courtyard at El Siboney as I said this. 'Was she one of the three?'

'In the usual instance, señor, I do not see the faces of those who are brought here but I remember the shroud fell away from the face of one of the three last week. *Sí*, a young blond woman.' The sexton paused and bowed his head in thought for a moment, as if considering. 'I do not wish to visit more disquiet upon you, señor, but I must tell you that her face was very bruised, as if she had been beaten. She is not the first to come to me in this condition. It hurts my heart to see one so young depart life in this way, but if this damage was evidence of how the señorita's life was going, I can understand why she chose not to continue on.'

'Was she really a suicide or had she been beaten to death?' Saying the words felt like my heart was being torn from my chest.

'I do not know, señor. The remains were brought in *el coach mortuorio* of the police coroner, and the men who brought them said they were to be buried with the suicides. In Cuba these days, one does not question. I am sorry for your loss.'

The sexton left me standing before the three fresh mounds of earth, latest in a legion of graves – of suicides or the regime's victims made to look like suicides – that extended along a low rise. The bastards. The bastards had not only taken her, they hadn't even given her the dignity of a marked grave. I divided the lilies between the three fresh graves, the tears falling as I did. Fannie, oh my dear Fannie. My only solace was that I would soon join her.

THIRTY-SIX

When I returned home the sun was already dipping toward the horizon. My door was open. Not much, just a crack but enough to let me know that my apartment wasn't as I'd left it in the morning. Pushing inside, I saw that the place had been tossed. Very professionally tossed. By that I mean every drawer had been dumped, the bedclothes and mattress were off the bed frame, and the few paper files I had from my failed private-dick business were scattered everywhere for effect. And in the middle of the darkening room sat Lieutenant Trujillo in his cheap suit, drinking a glass of my Matusalem.

'I am here to give you your instructions for Tuesday night,' Trujillo said, by way of greeting.

I scanned the room and said nothing. What was I supposed to do, invite him in? He was already in. Offer him a drink? He'd drained most of the third of a bottle I had left from my latest binge. Offer him a bribe? I guessed he had already taken what I might have to offer.

'While you were out I made myself at home,' he said.

'If this is how your home looks, the kids must be pretty rambunctious.'

Trujillo ignored the remark. 'You are a thief,' he said.

'Oh? I thought I was the one with the ransacked apartment.'

'You know what I found.' A statement, not a question.

'My cash, I'm guessing,' I said.

'I found cash but it is not yours, Señor Gore.'

'It is not yours, either.'

Lieutenant Trujillo straightened upright in his seat. 'It rightly belongs to the duly elected government of the Republic of Cuba and its president, Batista, since it is the ill-gotten funds of the bandits who plague our people,' he said.

'You've got it wrong, Lieutenant,' I said. 'I already turned in the money the Directorio gave me. To Colonel Blanco Rico.'

'Except for the ten thousand dollars I found in your mattress.'

'The mattress was too soft. It needed some firming up.'

'And the five thousand you gave to the baker Rojas downstairs to send to your sister in the United States.'

'Damn. I should have known.'

'He is a "thirty-three". It was well worth the thirty-three pesos and thirty-three centavos we pay him each month to learn where your true loyalties lie.'

'You mean to my family?'

'And to yourself, Señor Gore.'

'Ah, well, Lieutenant, I'm sure Colonel Blanco Rico will be most impressed with your performance when you turn over those fifteen thousand greenbacks to him. Maybe you'll even get a nice commendation in your file, signed by the colonel himself. Of course, you can't eat a commendation. Or drink it. Or buy a little *coño* with it. Now if, on the other hand, some of those greenbacks blew out the window of your SIM car on the way to the Comandancia General to turn them in . . .'

'That might happen,' the lieutenant sneered. 'And it's none of your business if it does. Be certain you understand that.'

'I just might have to mention to the colonel how diligent you were in your search,' I said. 'And how scrupulous you were in counting out the entire fifteen thousand when you found it.'

Trujillo ran the back of his hand along the inside of his jacket to show me the butt of a .45 in a shoulder holster. 'You could come in and find me in the middle of my search,' he said. 'And become combative. Try to disarm me. You might be killed in the struggle over my gun.'

'I might be. But I suspect that would be disappointing to Colonel Blanco Rico, losing the key man for the trap he's setting just two days before the operation. All that work down the drain. And, of course, that could cause some special scrutiny, so much special scrutiny that you couldn't afford to have any of those greenbacks, not one, blow out the car window on the way to the Comandancia General.'

Trujillo narrowed his eyes at me. Up to then, I hadn't noticed what small, piggy eyes he had. He looked like his pig-slop was about to be removed from right beneath his piggy nose. 'What is it you are saying, Señor Gore?'

'I'm a practical man, Lieutenant Trujillo. You are a practical man. Fifteen thousand frogskins is a lot of money. Enough for everyone to have some and neither of us gets accidentally shot or court-martialed. We will all live our lives a little richer, but not greedy-rich.'

'How much?'

'Ten thousand was already turned over to Colonel Blanco Rico. That's a nice round number, and if I were going to short – excuse me, if funds were going to be accidentally lost in transit – there's a logic to it being half of the total amount already given. So say you reported to the colonel that you found five thousand in my mattress. That, plus the five Gs in the envelope from the baker downstairs is ten grand. That leaves five thousand to be divided equally between us.'

Trujillo went red-faced. 'Equally!'

'That's right,' I said. 'You see, whether I lifted ten grand from the original amount or fifteen makes no difference. I'm a thief, either way. The punishment for me will be the same, either way. And I don't expect the punishment to be too severe, given the services I'm providing to Senator Bauza and the colonel.

'You, though, Lieutenant, are currently above reproach. You have only stolen from the appropriate people up to this point in your illustrious career, and never from the boss. Or at least you haven't been caught. I would hate to call Colonel Blanco Rico's attention to any breach in your stellar service record.'

Trujillo seethed. 'I will kill you!'

'No, you won't, Lieutenant. We've already covered that ground and the very practical reasons why you will not,' I said. 'Half of five thousand dollars is a lot of months of soldier's pay. Take it and be happy. It's found money.'

Trujillo's hand went to the butt of the automatic inside his jacket. For a second I thought I'd made a terrible error in judgment. Then his hand fell away from the gun and he said, 'All right,' through gritted teeth. He counted out twenty-five one-hundred-dollar bills from the messenger bag which had been hidden from view beside his chair and handed them to me.

'A wise choice,' I said. 'Thank you, Lieutenant.'

Trujillo rose from his seat, clipped me in the jaw with a left jab, and said, 'Tuesday at sunset on the dock at Mariel. Don't use the car to get there. Take the bus. Be ready for a boat ride.' He spit out a few other necessary details and left, slamming the door.

I sat on the floor where the punch had dropped me, surrounded by crisp bills scattered around me like new-fallen green snow.

THIRTY-SEVEN

T he sun was setting when I arrived at Mariel, an industrial port about twenty-five miles west of Havana. The weather promised a smooth sea passage. I'd left my apartment in the late afternoon and made the trip aboard a diesel-belching bus jam-packed with locals and their purchases from their outing to the big city. It was hot and close during the ride but the air cooled in the evening on the wings of a light northerly breeze.

I came in alone. The SIM boys wanted it that way, I guess to avoid the off chance that someone might see me traveling with them and queer the operation. The guns and ammo had been brought in from the west in two trucks earlier in the day. I wasn't told where they had come from. It wasn't something I needed to know.

The plan was fairly simple, the best way for plans to be since even the simplest ones generate screw-ups and glitches, and the fewer moving parts there are, the better. The guns, the boat to transport them, and I would all assemble at the harbor. The theory was that Mariel was far enough away that any Directorio Revolucionario spies wouldn't put the loading of crates from two trucks there together with the arms purchase to take place at midnight on the docks in Havana. The boat would leave Mariel harbor as soon as full darkness set in and run to the northeast for a couple of hours until it was due north of Havana, about thirty miles out to sea. From there it would turn south and make a beeline toward the city, appearing to come from the States rather than from down the coast at Mariel. A rendezvous with a Directorio boat would take place ten miles out of Havana harbor, where Freddy, the Directorio arms expert, would come aboard to inspect the weapons. From there, we would go to the docks and the fun would begin in earnest.

My direction from Lieutenant Trujillo was to go to the

Mariel docks and that I would understand where I needed to be once I arrived. I was a little baffled – it seemed like a pretty slipshod way to run a military operation – until I walked out onto Mariel's stone quay and saw *La Gloria* moored in a far corner. It heartened me to see the boat there because it meant that I might make it alive after all, as long as I stayed aboard. I knew that while I might be considered expendable, there was no way Senator Bauza was going to allow his expensive new fishing boat to be shot up in the SIM ambush. I just hoped the word that *La Gloria* and those aboard her were to be spared had traveled all the way down the chain of command to the machine-gunners.

As I walked down the gangway to *La Gloria*, two stevedores, accompanied by two plainclothes SIM mongrels, loaded the last case of rifles into the stern cockpit of the boat. The SIM boys were just about to hustle me away from *La Gloria* and her clandestine cargo when Lieutenant Trujillo emerged from the cabin and called them off with a casual wave of his hand.

'So, Señor Gore, the day of reckoning has arrived,' Trujillo greeted me. I wasn't sure I liked the sound of that. But, again, the lieutenant's presence on *La Gloria* reinforced my hope that she wasn't supposed to be shot up. That meant I only had to worry about Trujillo pumping a slug into the back of my head once the ruse was over and the guns began to blaze. Oh, joy.

I stepped aboard. I wore a tropical-weight suit. It was not exactly boating wear but the jacket did conceal the Woodsman in its shoulder holster and provided convenient pockets to carry the two extra clips. I saw Trujillo had done a better job dressing for the sea, barefooted in khakis and a grimy T-shirt, the perfect imitation of a first mate on a sport-fishing boat.

The emergence of another man from the cabin answered the question of whether Hemingway's man, Gregorio Fuentes, captained gun-running trips in addition to fishing outings. Tall and authoritative, this man looked nothing like Fuentes. 'Captain Armondo Hernandez, Cuban navy, at your service,' he said, by way of introduction. Like Lieutenant Trujillo, Captain Hernandez was in civilian boating attire – weathered gray pants, a short-sleeved cotton shirt, and deck shoes, the latter the primary way to distinguish captain from crew on most Cuban vessels.

The sun was low but it was still too early to leave. Hernandez and Trujillo covered the crates in the cockpit with canvas to protect them from prying eyes while in the harbor and salt spray once we got underway. There were five long crates in the cockpit – fifty rifles – and another ten in the cabin, together with three crates of Thompsons and dozens of boxes of ammunition. In short, things were very crowded in the cabin, with the captain's chair the only place to sit on something other than a crate. We all moved inside so as not to attract attention. Lieutenant Trujillo, certain of his ultimate role in the night's events, field-stripped and cleaned a Tommy gun that hadn't come from one of the crates. It was in almost-new condition. Trujillo handled it the way a good tennis player handles a racket or a skilled lumberjack handles a saw; it was more than a tool, it was an extension of the man himself, albeit a most deadly efficient extension. Hernandez, too, readied for action, cleaning and checking a semi-auto pistol that had a familiar look.

'Browning Hi-Power,' I said, trying to make small talk, thinking it might make Captain Hernandez hesitate for a moment before plugging me, if that was his assignment. 'A good, reliable pistol.'

'Actually, it is a Rosario Hi-Power. Nine-millimeter, made in Argentina,' Hernandez said. 'But you are correct, it is a fine weapon.' He sounded as if he spoke from experience.

After the two men finished their preparations, Hernandez brought out three Coca-Colas from a small cooler and we sat atop the gun crates, drinking in silence, until the sun went down. Personally, I could have used something stronger than a Coke for my nerves but at least the sugar and caffeine would help me keep my edge. I had a feeling I would need it.

The last shred of light had disappeared in the west when Captain Hernandez told Lieutenant Trujillo and me to loose the lines from the dock. He then idled *La Gloria* through the dark channel and out to sea. Once clear of the harbor by half a mile, he pushed the throttle forward. The boat seemed sluggish at first, given all the extra weight of guns and ammunition aboard, but soon we were slicing across the flat sea at twelve knots.

We ran without lights. No one spoke, either, though conversation would have been difficult anyway over the roar of the engine. I stepped out into the cockpit and sat in the gimbaled fighting chair. There was no moon. A north breeze had cleared all the clouds away and then dropped to nothingness. The sky was awash with stars from horizon to horizon, the same stars I remembered from warm summer evenings as a kid in Indiana and crisp winter nights from my Air Force time in Maine. The same stars Fannie Knutsen had dreamed beneath on her family's farm in North Dakota, longing for fame and escape from drudgery. The stars contained a promise of the hereafter, just a hint that it might actually exist, and I saw in their ice-brightness a flicker of hope that Fannie and I might be united among them.

My reveries ended when the sound of the engines dropped to a low thrum and the boat's speed fell off. The sea was smooth on the surface, with a lazy swell beneath, making the roof of starlight oscillate slowly back and forth overhead. Then Hernandez cut the engine completely and all was silent save for the slop of water against the hull.

'Where are they?' Lieutenant Trujillo said. He smoked a small cigar made from tobacco seconds, rolled rough, turning the air in the cockpit acrid.

'They'll be here,' I said, with a confidence I didn't feel in my bones. The whole set-up was worrisome. The primary characteristic I'd observed among the Directorio's leaders was paranoia; if it got the better of them now, they might not show at all. Then I thought about Celia Nunez, hard, whip-smart *El Fuerte*, and I knew they would arrive.

We all scanned the water.

At the edge of the horizon to the north, an irregularity appeared. It made no discernible movement. It was not in the direction from which the Directorio boat was expected. I pointed it out to Trujillo and Hernandez.

'It is the *Baracoa*,' Trujillo said. 'She is a Cuban navy corvette, stationed there to protect us. She will approach if we fire a flare or if we call her on the radio.'

'What makes you think the other side won't spot her and hightail it back to Havana?' I asked.

'They will not,' Hernandez said. 'They are bandits, not experienced seamen.' I decided that pointing out that I had seen the *Baracoa* and I wasn't an experienced seaman would not be productive and sat back to wait.

The wait was not long. In ten minutes a darkened vessel cut through the sea from the south, with only her white bow wave making her visible. When the boat neared to within a half mile, its engine was cut, leaving both *La Gloria* and the mystery boat drifting in silence.

A red light, probably a flashlight covered with a red bandana, blinked twice on the boat, then once, then twice again, the signal I had agreed upon with Celia. I flashed a light with a green filter in response – one blink, then two, then one. The darkened boat idled forward to within one hundred feet and shut down its engine again.

'Do not let them tie up to us,' Lieutenant Trujillo said, pulling back the bolt handle on his Thompson to emphasize the point. 'They cannot board us with overwhelming force if they have to come to us in a small boat.'

That had not been part of the plan but I had no choice. '*Viva Cuba libre!*' I called through cupped hands.

'*Libre y soberana!*' came the response. 'Are you prepared for us to raft up together?'

Trujillo caught my eye and shook his head in the negative.

'No,' I called across the water. 'Have the man who is to inspect the goods swim over. Alone.'

Unintelligible discussion could be heard among those on the other boat, followed by a splash and the white wake of a swimmer headed to *La Gloria*. In three minutes, Freddy was at the gunwale. Hernandez and I reached out to him with a boathook and levered him over the stern.

'I would have dressed differently had I known I was going to be swimming,' Freddy, clothed in long black pants and a black T-shirt, said when he stepped aboard.

'I can't afford to be too careless,' I replied, adopting my gunrunner persona, despite the fact that all present knew I was not. Pretty funny when you think about it but I wasn't laughing. I spoke to Trujillo. 'José, pat this man down for weapons.'

The lieutenant did. 'Clean,' he said.

'All right, Freddy, what do you want to see?' I said.

'Open each crate. I need to count the merchandise. I will select several to examine their condition.'

'Get to it, José.'

Trujillo began pulling the lid from each crate. They were nailed shut and he had to work with a claw hammer to get them open. By the time he had done four, he was panting with exertion.

'C'mon, José, speed it up. We're sitting ducks out here,' I said. I enjoyed seeing Trujillo sweat and I knew that taking orders from me grated on his SIM I-take-no-shit-from-anyone attitude. Good – I might as well have some fun before the shooting started. As the lids came off, Freddy lifted a rifle from each crate, working the action and dry-firing the gun. I had not been given a chance to look in the crates before we left Mariel but what I saw now in the dim light of Freddy's flash-light appeared to be used arms in moderately good shape, much better than the ratty samples provided earlier. And when we came to the Thompsons, Freddy exhaled a satisfied murmur. The sub-machine guns were in almost-new condition, with stick magazines and even a couple of fifty-round drum magazines in each of the three crates containing them. Perhaps Colonel Blanco Rico had been forced to raid one of the army's armories to come up with enough Thompsons for the deal.

'I will need to test-fire the weapons,' Freddy said.

'What?' My response was tinged with disbelief. 'Do you want to tip off the authorities with a bunch of shooting?'

'Just a couple rounds each for the rifles and the Thompsons.'

'OK,' I said. 'But keep it to a minimum. José, break open a box of rifle ammo and bring out a full stick magazine for a Thompson.'

Lieutenant Trujillo disappeared into the cabin and emerged seconds later with the ammunition. Freddy picked a random rifle from one of the crates in the cockpit, loaded a round, and fired into the night sky. The muzzle flash was blindingly bright but ten miles away on the mainland it would be barely visible. He then snapped the stick magazine into one of the Thompsons, moved the selector to single fire, and shot once.

'These will do,' Freddy said, replacing the Tommy gun into its crate. He turned to the Directorio boat still drifting nearby and waved his flashlight in a circle. A moment later the boat's engine coughed to life and it moved in a wide arc to the southeast.

La Gloria, with her cargo of spies, revolutionaries, guns, and my fate, took a heading toward the lights of Havana on the southern horizon.

THIRTY-EIGHT

'Hit the running lights, Hernandez,' I said. 'We want to look like we belong here, not like we're sneaking in. And stow those guns.'

Captain Hernandez quickly unstrapped his Rosario and placed it in the console beneath the binnacle. Lieutenant Trujillo hesitated, then remembered that I was supposed to be the one in command and dropped his Thompson into a locker in the gunwale.

Freddy stared anxiously up at Morro Castle on the headland guarding the mouth of Havana harbor. A soldier on guard on one of its parapets watched as we passed below. I waved to the man and he presented his gun in mock salute. At least we wouldn't have any trouble from the garrison in the ancient castle; the structure was on the opposite side of the harbor from where we would dock.

We passed the ferry terminal and approached the dock, almost exactly opposite Cayo Cruz in the center of the harbor. Though the night was cool, beads of sweat popped out on my forehead. In the harbor lights, I could see similar beads of sweat on the brows of Freddy and Trujillo. Only Captain Hernandez seemed collected, his task of bringing *La Gloria* in safely consuming his attention and preventing him from wondering, like the rest of us, if he would see the next morning's sunrise.

As we turned toward the shore, I saw two trucks waiting on the roadway that ran along the dock's base. They were delivery trucks like you see used for bread or groceries, the most innocuous instruments of revolution I could imagine. If the plan was being carried out as Celia had told me, they were each crammed with ten fighters and their weapons, and a hundred or more others waited in ambush in buildings surrounding the warehouse behind the trucks. The warehouse where dozens of police and SIM troops waited, also in ambush.

Two planned ambushes, both with us at the center. I tilted my head up to the sky, hoping to see the myriad stars one last time before I died but the harbor lights blotted out those astronomic pinpoints, man's meager nearby handiwork overwhelming God's distant creation.

'Get the lines,' Hernandez said. Trujillo did a passable imitation of a mate, jumping onto the stone dock and looping first the bow line and then its stern counterpart around the dock bollards. *La Gloria*'s engine rumbled to a stop. The midnight silence enveloped us, broken only by the ring of a line slapping against a sailboat mast somewhere off in the darkness.

The rear door of one of the trucks opened and Celia Nunez emerged, dressed in olive drab with a fatigue cap containing her unruly hair. She had a double-barreled shotgun in her hands, an old bird-hunting piece. She looked every bit the revolutionary. I must confess that, at that second, she inspired me as much as anyone or anything had in my to-that-time-uninspired existence.

Her comrade known as One fell in beside her, a street-fighter rather than a revolutionary, with a revolver tucked into his belt. Three, the man Colonel Blanco Rico had identified to me as university professor Pablo Chavez, stepped out of the cab of the other truck, dressed for a faculty meeting in a tie and linen jacket, carrying no weapon that I could discern. It was he who spoke. 'Freddy, is all satisfactory?'

'*Sí*,' Freddy said quietly, as if afraid to disturb the soft silence that enveloped the harbor.

The affirmative answer brought a driver and another helper out from each truck. Two and Four stepped from the shadow of a shed at the end of the dock, each with a scoped bolt-action rifle in their hands. They looked like they were off to a dawn deer hunt in Pennsylvania, not starting a revolution in a Caribbean city of a million souls at midnight.

The appearance of so many guns ashore made *La Gloria*'s crew justifiably uneasy. Trujillo brought out his Thompson from its locker and Hernandez strapped the Rosario Hi-Power to his waist. I thought about telling them to stow the guns again, but a true gunrunner wouldn't do that. A true gunrunner would meet firepower with firepower, so I joined them by taking off my jacket to allow the Woodsman in its shoulder holster to show.

A true gunrunner would also be concerned about payment. 'Have you got the money?' I said, directing my question to Professor Chavez since he was the one who had spoken.

'Right here.' Celia walked toward *La Gloria*, patting an ammunition bag on her hip. Her intelligent eyes moved from Trujillo, to Freddy, and then focused on me. 'Twenty-five thousand American dollars, as we agreed. If the guns are right.'

Freddy stepped ashore. 'The guns are right.'

Celia, her shotgun cradled like a quail-hunter, handed the bag of cash across the gunwale to me and then waved to the men standing beside the trucks. One and Three, together with the two drivers and their helpers, marched onto the dock and began to offload the crates of guns. Each heavy crate required two men to handle it. The going was slow, the men sweating in the night air. I noticed the first three crates to come off *La Gloria* were stacked on the dock instead of being carried to the trucks.

It was then that the shooting began.

THIRTY-NINE

The first shot was muffled, like the gun had been fired inside a box. In a way, I guess it had been, since the shot was discharged inside the darkened warehouse at the foot of the dock. We should have expected it but everyone seemed surprised, almost as if we had all deluded ourselves into believing that the ambushes both sides had planned were not really going to happen. During four or five seconds that seemed like an hour in the slowed time of life-and-death events, nobody moved.

'*Viva Cuba libre!*' Celia Nunez shouted, her voice sounding louder than the muffled gunshot that had preceded it. The frozen scene on *La Gloria* and on the dock was set in horrific motion by her call. Celia swung the long blued barrels of her shotgun toward Hernandez, intent on preventing him from moving the boat, with the remaining part of its cargo of weapons, away from the rebels. The captain was drawing the Rosario from its holster when the buckshot hit him, slicing away most of his face and neck. His already-dead body flopped once or twice like a boated bonito after he dropped to the deck.

The shotgun blast spurred me to action of the most sensible type – I dove and rolled to the threshold of the cabin, making myself as small a target as I could in the process. I fumbled the Woodsman out of its shoulder holster, then lost my grip on the gun when I cowered as the first shots from Lieutenant Trujillo's Thompson, on full auto, cracked out. The Woodsman skittered out of reach on the deck already wet with the blood that had pumped from Hernandez's dying corpse. I stayed right where I was, deciding that crawling six feet to recover the Woodsman was not worth the risk, given the duel of Tommy gun versus shotgun about to take place.

The unarmed Freddy saw opportunity in the quick confusion of shooting and dove for the Rosario still clutched in

Hernandez's dead hand. Once he had it, he rolled aft, racking the slide as he did. He began to lift the pistol in Trujillo's direction as he stopped rolling but he wasn't quick enough. Trujillo's Thompson sounded a tearing snarl and a stitch-line of bloody wounds bloomed on Freddy's chest. Trujillo started to swing the Thompson toward the men near the crates on the dock. He never made it. A roar from the second barrel of Celia's shotgun lifted him off his feet like a heavyweight's uppercut, tossing him over the gunwale and into Havana harbor.

The thunder of the shotgun died away and for a ringing ten seconds the gunfire stopped. I caught Celia's eye, received a nod from her, and stood. She reached into the ammunition bag that she'd said held the twenty-five thousand for the guns and drew out two shells, cracking the shotgun's breech to reload. Apparently she intended to pay the regime for the arms with a pound of buckshot.

I needed a gun. Fast. The Thompson had gone overboard with Lieutenant Trujillo. I took a step toward the Woodsman sitting in Hernandez's pooling blood and then remembered the Rosario Hi-Power in Freddy's hand. With its thirteen-round magazine and greater stopping power, it would be much more useful in this firefight than the .22 Woodsman. And it was of no use to poor dead Freddy. I pulled the Rosario from his still-grasping fingers just as all hell broke loose.

A series of bright flashes lit the line of high windows in the warehouse at the end of the dock, accompanied by muffled explosions. A clamor of voices shouting, '*Viva Cuba libre!*' rose into the night as masses of Directorio Revolucionario fighters took to the streets from inside a number of buildings where they had been hiding. It was a ragtag army of men and women, in street clothes and fatigue uniforms, all wearing the Directorio's signature green armband. In their hands they carried all manner of weapons – hunting rifles, shotguns, revolvers, cane knives, machetes, even lengths of pipe and wooden clubs. One old mossback charged ahead in his Spanish-American War rebel get-up, carrying a Mauser that he had probably last used in support of Teddy Roosevelt's Roughriders when he was a teen.

Part of the rebel horde made for the doors of the warehouse, to envelop the police and troops inside, while the rest ran for the crates of arms on the dock and still aboard *La Gloria*. Celia Nunez rallied her fighters, shouting orders and waving her shotgun. She bounded to the gunwale of the boat, directing four men with claw hammers to tear the lids from the crates.

'Where is the ammunition?' she asked.

'In the cabin,' I said. 'Come with me.'

Celia followed, flanked by more fighters with hammers. I showed them where the ammo was and they ripped the boxes apart. In seconds a relay line of men was formed to hand out guns, pouches of rifle rounds, and sticks of .45 ammunition for the Thompsons.

As soon as a gun was loaded one of the men ran off with it, another replacing the first in the line waiting for weapons. While this was going on, sporadic firing could be heard from inside the warehouse but not nearly as much as I would have expected. It appeared that the day would be won by the Directorio as the newly armed fighters took up positions surrounding the warehouse. The twenty men in the trucks armed themselves as well and dispersed around the building.

Finally, the last of the crates was emptied and all the guns distributed. Celia stepped up on the gunwale to climb onto the dock. The firing inside the warehouse stopped, the midnight silence broken only by the heavy breathing of the rebels as they waited in their positions behind walls, boxes, and piles of netting. Waited for the signal to storm the warehouse.

The Directorio leader known as One, a Tommy gun in his hands, jumped to the hood of one of the trucks and was about to give the order to attack when the sound of vehicles could be heard coming from all points of the compass. Celia, frozen by the sound on the edge of the gunwale, gave me a questioning look.

'I don't know,' I said, just as a jeep mounted with a recoilless rifle rounded the corner of a building two hundred yards from where the Directorio trucks stood on the quay. The jeep halted and the gun crew took hasty aim and fired. The 105-millimeter projectile from the gun tore One in half where he stood on the truck's hood and continued through the windshield, exploding in the vehicle's interior. The gun crew was quick at their task. A second round from the recoilless rifle shredded the second truck, setting it aflame.

A deuce-and-a-half army truck slammed to a stop behind the jeep, soldiers disgorging from it like angry hornets from a disturbed nest. I expected to see the troops cut down by fire from the rifles and the Thompsons as they emerged but only a handful of shots rang out, with just a single soldier falling as his fellows took up positions of cover.

The recoilless rifle sounded again, striking the door of a store next to the warehouse. A woman fell across the shattered doorframe into the street, a rifle still in her hands, her skirt and blouse on fire.

More army trucks appeared at the opposite end of the street from the jeep-mounted gun. The soldiers from those trucks also dispersed largely unchallenged by any gunfire from the rebels. Shouts of anger and dismay arose among the Directorio fighters caught between the two groups of soldiers. Everywhere I saw rebels working the bolts of the rifles and Thompsons they had just been given, trying to clear rounds that had misfired and jammed. Some stared blankly at their guns, baffled as to why they wouldn't fire.

The SIM troops wasted no time, taking up protected positions and pouring murderous fire into the rebels caught between the two main groups of soldiers. Hundreds more soldiers began to appear, taking positions in every nook and cranny up and down the waterfront.

Two and Four worked their bolt-action hunting rifles as fast as they could, with deadly results, until the soldiers realized the two men were the source of effective fire and cut them down in a hail of bullets.

The other rebel fighters still tried to clear their newly acquired weapons, to no avail. I realized then that Colonel Blanco Rico, forced by the Directorio's insistence of an at-sea inspection to ensure delivery of the correct number of guns, had made certain that those guns would be useless by giving us defective ammunition. Lieutenant Trujillo must have given Freddy the only sound ammunition in the crates for his test-firings at sea.

I grabbed Celia's arm. 'Celia, we've been tricked. The ammunition is no good,' I said.

She turned away from the carnage ashore toward me, her eyes wide and intense.

'I didn't know,' I said.

For a split second, I thought she might swing her shotgun in my direction, believing I was in on the ruse. Instead, she weighed my words, then turned toward shore. 'The bullets for the new guns are defective! Use your other weapons, my brothers and sisters!' she yelled. '*Viva Cuba libre!*'

The rebels tossed down their new rifles and Thompsons, the guns as useless as sticks against the modern firepower of the SIM soldiers. Reverting to the weapons they had brought, they filled the air with revolver shots and scattergun pellets. The troops stayed back, out of the effective range of the pistols and shotguns, slowly picking off the rebels with their rifles. A .30 caliber machine gun was set up by a squad of soldiers on the roof of a house to the north. Its staccato bursts and the periodic slams of the recoilless rifle punctuated the unrelenting small-arms fire from the soldiers and police. One by one, the Directorio fighters fell, until only a handful remained.

FORTY

Celia Nunez crouched, preparing to leap from her perch on *La Gloria*'s gunwale to the dock. I pulled her down into the cockpit. 'If you go ashore now, you'll just die with the rest of them.'

'Then I will die with the rest of them,' she said, moving back to the gunwale. As she did, a single shot cracked out from behind us and Celia was thrown to the deck. I spun to face the source and found myself confronting Lieutenant Trujillo. Soaking wet, his right arm shredded and bloody from the entry wounds of half a dozen buckshot pellets, Trujillo had his Thompson slung across his body, using his good arm to try and clear a misfire. His face was pale with shock and anger, and then surprise as I put three rounds from the Rosario into his chest. As I fired the last round, Celia's double-barrel roared from behind me. Trujillo's face disintegrated into a pink mist, his lifeless torso collapsing to the deck.

I turned and knelt beside Celia where she had fallen and propped herself against the fighting chair. She held her right arm tightly, with blood oozing between her fingers. 'I am fine,' she said, her contorted face telling a different story. 'It is not serious.'

'Let me see.' I rolled her torn sleeve back. She was right, the injury was not serious, a through-and-through wound to the upper arm that had managed to miss any large blood vessels. The bullet had tumbled only slightly, the exit wound just a bit more elongated than the entry. I found a towel and Celia held it to her arm while I searched the binnacle console for a first-aid kit.

'Just bind it so I can get in the fight,' Celia said as I rolled gauze around her arm.

'You can't get into the fight now,' I said, just as the firing ended. I stopped wrapping and duck-walked to peer over the gunwale toward the rebel position in front of the warehouse. Celia slid across the deck and popped up beside me.

At the Directorio position, backlit by the burning trucks, less than ten fighters, men and women, remained unwounded. Only half of that number held a pistol or a long gun; the rest, out of ammunition, had discarded their guns and crouched behind rifle crates and piles of fishing nets with cane knives and machetes in their hands. The professorial Three, still alive and unwounded, was central among them. He spoke rapidly to three other men and two women close to him. There seemed to be a consensus reached. Three drew out a white handkerchief and waved it above the barrier which shielded him from the government forces.

'We surrender. There are women and many wounded among us,' Three called out. 'Do not shoot. We will put down our arms.'

I recognized the voice of Colonel Blanco Rico shouting from behind the recoilless rifle. 'We accept your surrender. Put down your weapons and walk toward us with your hands above your heads. You will have safe passage if you do not try anything.'

Three stood in full view and dropped his pistol. 'There are wounded who are not able to walk,' he said.

'Have those who cannot walk throw their weapons out where we can see them. The rest of you raise your hands and walk toward me. Now,' Blanco Rico said.

Three motioned with his hands for those around him to arise, like a priest bringing his congregation from their knees. 'Do as he says,' he said. The remaining fighters tossed away their weapons and stood.

'Walk toward us,' Blanco Rico called.

With Three in the lead, the tiny group of rebels walked slowly forward, arms raised. The only sounds were the crackling of fire from the burning trucks and the groans of dozens of wounded, some soldiers and policemen but mostly Directorio fighters, scattered along the harbor-front road. The night air smelled of acrid gunpowder and iron-sweet blood.

When Three and his little group reached the midpoint of their transit, Colonel Blanco Rico rose and screamed: 'Treasonous dogs! Fire!' The recoilless rifle thundered a final time, its report almost drowned in a chorus of machine-gun and small-arms fire. In seconds, Three and his band were reduced to tattered lumps of meat by shrapnel and bullet.

'Bastards,' Celia hissed. 'I will kill every last one of the bastards to avenge you, my comrades. *Viva Cuba libre!*' There was firm resolve in her voice.

'We'd better get the hell out of here or we will end up just like your comrades,' I said. I hurriedly tied the end of the gauze strip I'd wrapped around Celia's wound. As I did, there were sporadic gunshots heard from the dock road. I looked back to see the SIM troops moving among the Directorio wounded, executing them where they lay.

I caught sight of Celia in the firelight. The resolve was gone from her face, replaced by tears streaming down her cheeks.

FORTY-ONE

'm not much of a swimmer. A few dips in muddy Indiana farm ponds as a kid and a plunge or two into icy August Maine lakes during the time I was in Presque Isle were the sum total of my voluntary encounters with the wet stuff outside of bathtubs and showers. One of the reasons I joined the Air Force instead of the Navy was to avoid the possibility that I might end up in the drink and need to make it from point A to point B. True, I'd splashed in the waves on the golden beach at Vedado but even there I had taken particular care to not get in more than knee deep. Now I was confronted with the unhappy prospect of plunging into Havana harbor, with its inky waters much greater in depth than my comfort zone. The only redeeming feature of the swim was that it was better than the prospect of the bullets I was certain awaited Celia and me if we tried to make our escape on land.

Mind you, I considered throwing up my hands and shouting out to Colonel Blanco Rico to let him know it was me. My consideration of that course of action lasted for only a second; I'd seen how well Three and the last-stand Directorio fighters had fared in choosing surrender. I guessed that Blanco Rico would see my utility at an end, now that the Directorio Revolucionario had been wiped out, and my death would allow him to keep the unpaid balance of my ten-thousand-peso fee. A simple explanation of my inadvertent killing in the crossfire would probably satisfy the US embassy. Shoot, maybe the colonel would embellish the story by sending Janet, Uncle Pete, and Aunt Ruth a nice medal along with my bullet-riddled body, for my exemplary service to the grateful people of the Republic of Cuba.

So when Celia said, 'We have to swim. Strip down to your underwear,' I didn't hesitate. Celia emptied the shotgun shells from her ammo bag and stuffed in our clothes, after first wrapping them around the Rosario Hi-Power and the Woodsman.

'We will need two life vests,' she said. I opened the locker where the vests were stored and pulled out two. On shore, a man could be heard pleading, 'Spare me, I have four children and a wife,' followed by a single shot and no more pleading. We had only seconds to escape.

'Slip into the water,' Celia said. 'Try not to splash. Push the life vest in front of you and kick with your feet underwater.'

The night air was a cool contrast to the blood-warm waters of the harbor as I slid from *La Gloria*'s rail. Celia tossed me a vest and immediately followed, balancing the bundle of clothing and guns on her vest as if she did it every day. The boots of SIM troopers pounded along the quay toward the boat as we began to swim.

We headed directly out from shore, away from the light of the burning trucks and the flashlights of soldiers and police that crisscrossed the area by the warehouse and the land end of the dock. When we were several hundred yards offshore, Celia wordlessly turned east so our path ran parallel to shore and away from where the jeeps and trucks of SIM had now collected. We kicked along slowly, only our heads above water, to avoid the attention-getting noise and white wake that paddling on the surface would cause. The moon had set before we entered the water. I felt like we were moving along silently and almost invisibly. I began to think that both Celia and I would see another dawn.

'Patrol boat,' Celia whispered. At first, I didn't see or hear it but soon enough the rumble of the boat's diesels could be heard from across the harbor. Its two searchlights suddenly illuminated, sending stabbing fingers of light in all directions across the still water. The boat moved toward the site of the action at a rapid clip. Then it slowed near the dock where *La Gloria* remained tied up, its lights probing the underside of the dock and the seawall along the shoreline in search of rebels who might be trying to escape by sea. Rebels like Celia and me. I could see Colonel Blanco Rico, backlit against the fire on shore, directing the crews manning the searchlights where to look. On both sides of him, soldiers and cops peered along the seawall and the wharfs.

Given my limited experience, the swim had been tiring for me. The efforts of the patrol boat and the searchers on land gave me a shot of adrenaline and I frog-kicked as hard as I dared without splashing. Celia glided alongside me with no apparent difficulty, pushing the life vest and clothing before her.

'We must go ashore before the patrol boat widens its search,' she said. 'Over there, at the rail yard.' She inclined her head to the yard where a yellow switch engine, rusted from years in the harbor's salt air, moved a string of boxcars along a siding.

'Kick,' Celia said. 'Kick hard.' She abandoned all pretense of stealth, splashing noisily with her legs. I followed suit, wondering when the gunfire would blaze in our direction.

But it didn't. Five minutes of hard paddling found us on a mudflat that stunk of rotting fish and diesel oil, hunkered in the shadow of a seawall. On the other side lay the cobblestones of the old harbor road and, beyond that, the rail yard. Celia broke open the bundle and we dressed quickly, jamming the pistols into our belts. Edging my eyes above the seawall, I could see the soldiers at their clean-up work a half mile down the road, checking the bodies of dead rebels and bearing away the few injured SIM troops. The good news was that none of them seemed to be facing in our direction.

The bad news was that the same could not be said of the patrol boat. Its searchlights and, presumably, the eyes of its crew, worked from where *La Gloria* remained docked along the seawall toward where we crouched. If Celia and I stayed where we were, duck meat would be a more apt description for our situation than sitting ducks when the boat brought its fore and aft .50 caliber machine guns to bear.

I made a stirrup with my hands. 'Over the top now, Celia.' She placed a bare foot in the stirrup and I boosted her over the wall. I hoisted myself up behind her, folding flat against the land-side curb of the seawall just as a searchlight swept the mud bank below. Celia had already crossed the street and disappeared into the rail yard.

I assumed we had not been seen because no shots rang out and the patrol boat continued on, playing its lights along the

water and the shore. I made a cowering dash into the center
of the rail yard, stopping in the shadow of a guard shack that
was, fortunately, empty. Away from the searchlights of the
patrol boat, it was pitch dark. My eyes had not fully adjusted
when I felt a hand grab my left arm. I swung with my right
and barely stopped in time to avoid punching Celia.

'Don't you announce your presence when you sneak up
on a man?' My hoarse whisper was louder than it should
have been, fueled by the rush of adrenaline that coursed
through me.

'Just what am I supposed to announce?' Celia shot back,
too loudly as well. I guess the sight of a fist headed for your
kisser provokes an adrenaline rush, too.

'*Viva Cuba libre?*' I said. Hardly the time for that but the
sarcastic side of me couldn't resist. 'We've got to get away
from here, Celia.'

'No,' she said. 'I have a friend in the rail yard. He will hide
us until morning, when there will be many workers on the streets
and it will be safe to leave. If we try to run now, we will stand
out and they are certain to capture us.'

I'm from the run, hide, fight school – run first, hide if you
can't, and fight only as a last resort. Celia's plan didn't fit my
philosophy but it was her home turf, so I deferred. 'OK. How
do we find your friend?'

Celia was about to speak when a car's headlights washed
along the rail-yard fence toward us. Just before the light hit,
Celia wrapped herself around me in a passionate kiss. A month
ago I might have been surprised by this. Now I'd learned that
it was chapter one in the female revolutionary's handbook of
evasive maneuvers. I joined in, hoping the intruding headlights
would continue on their way.

They didn't, coming to a stop focused on us two pretend
lovers. The driver's door opened. A typically slovenly Havana
cop got out with the ease of a man in charge of the
situation.

'Hey, *chica*, don't your *gringo* man know we have laws
against whoring in Havana?' the cop called to Celia, although
his speaking in English was for my benefit. He had the classic
tourist shakedown in mind, I figured, because he didn't have

a hand on or anywhere near the Smith and Wesson .38 riding low in the scuffed holster on his belt. Instead, he was picking his late dinner from between his teeth with a wooden toothpick. He didn't think we were a couple of revolutionaries escaped from the carnage a half mile down the road. He saw us as a chance to extract a few pesos or greenbacks. Even the fact that we were still damp from our harbor swim didn't clue him in.

The cop swaggered out from behind the open patrol car door. 'Hey, *gringo*, looks to me as though the señorita is a minor, a child. We don't like that here in Havana. You just might spend the next few years in prison for corrupting one of our delicate young ladies.' He folded his arms, flabby in his short-sleeved white police uniform shirt, across his chest.

I played for time. 'I didn't know I was doing anything illegal, officer. I swear. Isn't there some way to resolve this without it going further?'

He ignored my question and said, 'Hands up.' I raised 'em, hoping my shirt tail would hide the Woodsman in the waistband at the small of my back.

The cop shuffled forward to frisk me, probably just to throw an extra scare into the Yankee before putting the bite on for a bribe. He was casual, running his hands down my sides until his groping collided with the gun. He stiffened, gave a little grunt, and pulled the Woodsman from my belt.

'*Qué es esto?*' The cop spit the toothpick.

Celia, ignored up to now by the cop, reached for the Rosario she'd hidden in her belt. The policeman caught the motion in his peripheral vision. He had just begun to turn toward her when she put a round in his left eye, followed by two in the neck. The cop fell dead, his bright arterial blood splashing onto my shoes.

FORTY-TWO

'What the hell, Celia?' was all I could get out. She had executed the cop when we still might have talked or bribed our way out of the encounter. Not to mention that the three shots she had fired in the process might bring every SIM soldier and policeman within a half mile sprinting over to investigate.

'Get in the driver's seat,' Celia said, motioning to the police car. Then she bent over the dead cop to grab the Woodsman from the poor son of a bitch's hand and the Smith and Wesson from his holster. With no time to argue, I did as told, swinging the patrol car into a U-turn as she climbed in the passenger side. I wasn't sure of our destination but I was as sure as God made little green apples that it was in the opposite direction of the cops and soldiers running our way.

In addition to the guns, Celia had snatched up the dead policeman's hat and now she jammed it on my head. It was sticky with blood and bits of flesh but it made a believable silhouette for anyone passing in another car in the darkness.

I gunned the engine and looked in the rear-view mirror. The police and soldiers, seeing that the departing car was a cop car, stopped running and turned back. There had been enough gunfire that night that three more shots didn't rouse any suspicion, as long as the cop doing the shooting was driving away. I'm sure our pursuers thought it was just another of their compatriots dispensing more justice to the wounded.

I eased off the accelerator to confirm to Blanco Rico's boys that it was just that, and that the cop inside the car, his duty done with appropriate patriotism and viciousness, was now going back to leisurely patrol. I turned right at the first intersection to get out of the direct line of sight.

'Well, what do we do from here?' I said, glancing at Celia. She sat, composed, peering ahead and then into the side mirror, looking for the pursuit that didn't seem to be coming.

'Drive west,' she said. 'Toward the big hotels and the casinos. They will not be looking there. Yet.'

We passed some blocks in silence. The wee-hours-of-the-morning streets were mostly empty. We met few approaching vehicles and each time I saw lights in my rear-view mirror, I turned at the next corner. In minutes we were out of the harbor area and through Chinatown, cruising unobtrusively toward the Malecón.

'Turn here,' Celia said. In a few blocks, she pointed. 'Into that alley, behind the Hotel Inglaterra.'

I parked the cop car in a shadowy spot down the alley. 'I think we should ditch this car,' I said. 'It's only a matter of time before they find that dead cop and start to hunt for his patrol car.'

'I agree, Henry,' Celia said. 'And we should part company.'

I thought about that. Thought about asking to stick with Celia and the tattered shreds of the Directorio Revolucionario. Thought about doing something noble with my aimless life by joining the fight against the criminals and grifters who ran Cuba, and probably going down in a hail of bullets with that nobility worn like a crown on my brow, tomorrow or in a month or a year. But if I was that noble and that willing to die, whether for the Cuban people or just for the sake of dying, I'd have charged into that hail of bullets when Celia had wanted to go ashore at the dock. So, as I sat next to the idealistic Celia in the humid Havana night in that alley, I was forced to admit to myself that I wasn't that noble, or idealistic, or virtuous, or whatever it was that made a man or a woman attempt daunting tasks against impossible odds simply for the benefit of their fellow man. And I was forced to admit that I wanted to go on living, and not join my poor tormented Fannie in Havana's suicides' graveyard. I thought about all this in the space of a minute, and then I told Celia, 'Yes, we should part.'

We got out of the car. I wiped down the car door handles and steering wheel, hoping I got all our prints. I handed her the Woodsman. 'Here. There must be someone left in the Directorio Revolucionario who will need this.'

She looked down at the gun in her hand. 'Yes, there will be some of us left, I am sure, even after tonight's failure. We will fight on, and we will need this. Thank you, Henry.' Celia Nunez turned and walked into the night.

The sensible thing would have been for me to go to ground, to find a place to hunker down and hide until I could find a way to get out of Cuba. The sensible thing would have been to assess my available resources, formulate a plan, and begin its execution. The sensible thing, when you think you are a man wanted by the police and the military forces of a brutal dictatorship, would have been to do almost anything but what I did.

What I did was walk to the Floridita Bar. It was only a few blocks away, at the corner of Calle Obispo and Calle Montserrate. I strolled in, went to the far corner of the bar, ordered one of the daiquiris that Ernie Hemingway had made so famous, and drank it. Then I ordered another and drank it. And another. And so on. And when the *cantineros* hinted, as the first pale edge of dawn appeared at the apex of the bar's tall windows, that they wished to go home to their wives and children, I took out a few pesos still soggy with the water from Havana harbor and paid for my drinks.

Then I took a cab home to my apartment and went to bed. Isn't that what you do when you attempt to foment a revolution and it doesn't go as planned?

FORTY-THREE

I had hoped for a lingering morning in bed, watching the sunlight work its way up the gaps between the slats of the closed plantation shutters, and listening to the shuffle and step of patrons entering Señor Rojas's *panaderia*, the spring-bell on the shop door triggering Pavlovian salivation in them in anticipation of a morning *cafecito* and *pastelitos*, with the bell's message confirmed by the welcoming scent of the baked goods behind the glass counter. I had hoped for Benny's tentative tap on the door, and his agreeable smile and bonhomie, along with a tray of the selfsame *cafecito* and *pastelitos*, all confirming to me that the events of the prior night had been a horrible nightmare. I had hoped mightily for these things.

What I got was the business end of a Colt .45 jammed into my left nostril as I slept into the eighth hour of the morning, poor accompaniment to the headache that was just beginning to replace the numbing bliss of the Floridita's sugary daiquiris. Attached to the .45 was the monolinguistic Sergeant Alvarez, his mutt-mien dead serious, his only explanation a wave of the automatic toward my clothing on the floor and then the door. I took the hint and dressed, the damp and briny scent that clung to my clothes an affirmation, if one other than the sergeant's pistol was needed, that last night had not just been a bad dream.

The Comandancia General was as homey and inviting as ever in the golden morning sun. I wondered if it was the last morning sun I would ever see or, if not, whether the cell in which I was to be held for the few or many remaining days of my life might have the luxury of a high barred window to let in the rays.

Colonel Blanco Rico's face, when I was shown into his office, did not betray any satisfaction at his men's victory over the bandits of the Directorio Revolucionario. He was focused on a stack of paperwork when I entered, the picture of the diligent bureaucrat, rather than the murdering oppressor of his countrymen that I now knew him to be. When he brought his eyes up from his papers, he did not betray any surprise at my presence, although his words said otherwise.

'Señor Gore! We had believed you lost in last night's action against the bandits, just as we suffered the loss of the brave Lieutenant Trujillo and Captain Hernandez.' He gestured to the guest chair before his desk. 'Come, sit.'

'It is tragic to lose such men as the lieutenant and the captain,' I said. 'I am certain the people of Cuba will honor their service to their country with gratitude.' Best to shift the focal point of the conversation away from my whereabouts the prior evening, although I knew we would inevitably return to the topic.

'Indeed, all true Cubans are grateful to your two courageous companions in your difficult mission, as well as the equally valiant soldiers and police who fought and died last night defeating the criminals,' Blanco Rico said. 'A cigar for you, Henry?' The offer of a stogie showed what the dead really meant to the colonel – they were a necessary inconvenience but not so important that one should forgo the pleasure of a morning smoke.

'No, thank you, Colonel.'

Blanco Rico took a cigar from the humidor on his desk, rolled it between his fingers, and made a slow production of clipping its end with a cutter and lighting it. The ritual was designed to make me squirm in my seat. It had the desired effect.

Taking a long draw on the corona and exhaling, Blanco Rico said, 'I suppose you are here about the balance due for your services?'

No, I wanted to say, the reason I am here is because I was too stupid to hide, and because your goon Alvarez dragged me out of bed at gunpoint and brought me here. Of course, there were a number of reasons I couldn't say that, so I played along. 'That's correct, Colonel.'

Blanco Rico flicked a nub of gray ash into the onyx ashtray on his desk. 'Very well, Henry. Let us conduct the accounting.

The agreed total for your services was ten thousand pesos. Less the thousand-peso advance already paid takes us to nine thousand. Then there is the matter of the twenty-five hundred American dollars you stole from the bandit down-payment for the guns.'

I opened my mouth to speak but he waved me off. 'No, no, Henry. No explanation is necessary. We knew you were in this strictly for financial gain from the start. It was only reasonable that you would use every opportunity that you had to enhance the amount you would receive for your efforts. Although, I must tell you, there were those who took a very unfavorable view of what you had done when Lieutenant Trujillo, may he rest in peace, reported it to us. Senator Bauza, for example, suggested we quietly execute you for your theft of government funds, if you survived the completion of the operation. He was very adamant until I reminded him that you, unlike him and me, were not involved in the operation for love of country and the ardor of patriotic duty. That you are a mercenary. That such things are to be expected from a mercenary. That, indeed, the comfort, the very joy of dealing with a mercenary is the clarity of impetus – money – without all the murkiness and changeability of motivation arising from glory-seeking or career advancement or even altruism. When I explained to Senator Bauza that the mercenary must, as a matter of instinct, pursue financial gain as the lion must pursue the antelope, and that you, unlike the two of us, were not driven by nobler motives and therefore must be excused for your instincts, as we excuse the feline, he agreed. Reluctantly, though, and at least in part because he viewed the amount of the . . . misappropriation to be of small consequence. And also because of the availability of recoupment through set-off from your fee. I must tell you, though, it was a spirited discussion. You were lucky to have me as a champion for your cause, as well as your countryman, Señor Trafficante. He spoke very highly of you.'

The colonel paused and looked to me with grave eyes. I was reminded of when I was caught with a hand in the cookie jar or accidentally tossed a baseball through the neighbor's window as a youngster and my mother explained to me how she had dissuaded my father from more severe punishment than she was about to mete out to me.

'Thank you,' I said, waiting for the other shoe. It didn't drop.

'Nine thousand pesos, less twenty-five hundred American dollars,' Blanco Rico said. 'An exchange rate of one peso to the dollar. So, I calculate six thousand five hundred pesos remain unpaid and due pursuant to our agreement.'

He said it so matter-of-factly, just an accountant announcing the figure at the end of an added column, that I experienced a spark of hope. Maybe I would get out of this alive. Maybe I would get my sixty-five hundred pesos and walk out the front gate of the Comandancia General, catch a cab to the airport, and hop on the next airplane flying out of Cuba to anywhere before minds were changed.

'That's fine,' I said. 'I'd appreciate it if I could be paid now.'

'Of course, Henry. But before we get to that, tell me. How is it that you went from being aboard *La Gloria* yesterday to waking up in your bed this morning, while Lieutenant Trujillo and Captain Hernandez wake this morning in their coffins?'

So there would be no waltz out the door with cash in my pocket and a plane ticket out of this tropical hell. Maybe I should ask to call the US embassy, I thought. Maybe I should insist on it. But I remembered the wails of the prisoners echoing down the SIM hallway on my first visit to the Comandancia General and I knew there would be no call to the American embassy or anywhere else. I was on my own, with a man whose profession was making people disappear without a trace.

FORTY-FOUR

'I was lucky,' I said. Would Blanco Rico believe that? 'I was below deck in the cabin of *La Gloria* when the shooting started. Two of the men from the Directorio Revolucionario and I were bringing up the ammo boxes while others were carrying crates of rifles and Thompsons to the trucks on shore, in front of the warehouse. When the shots began, they weren't directed anywhere near the boat. They sounded like they were on the street outside the warehouse, and inside of it, maybe. So I stayed below, out of harm's way. After all, my work was done at that point. You weren't paying me to be in a gunfight, just to deliver the Directorio leadership into your hands. Which I did.'

'True,' the colonel said. 'But you did not stay on *La Gloria* or we would have found you there.'

'I was forced to leave the boat,' I said. 'The shooting on the street grew more intense, from what I could hear. Then there were shots much closer, up on deck. Shotgun blasts, some pistol shots, and a few rounds from one of the Thompsons. I hope you understand, Colonel, that I wasn't about to stick my head up out of the cabin right then to see who was winning, not with only that peashooter you gave me to defend myself.'

'That reminds me, Henry,' Blanco Rico said. 'We will need you to return your gun. We must keep very careful track to prevent lawless elements from obtaining weapons, as you know.'

'I'm sorry, Colonel,' I said. 'I don't have the Woodsman anymore.'

'Don't have it? Where is it?'

'It was lost in the confusion of the fighting.'

'Ah.' Blanco Rico steepled his slender fingers and nodded understanding. 'These things happen. Go on then. You were speaking about the gunfire on *La Gloria*'s deck while you were below.'

'Yes. As I said, I heard the shooting on deck and I didn't

think I had matching firepower with the Woodsman for anything that was going on above me, so I hid in the cabin. Under a bunk. Eventually the shooting on deck stopped. I waited for Lieutenant Trujillo or Captain Hernandez to come below and give the all-clear. But they didn't. There was still some shooting, far off, but none above, so after a few minutes of waiting I decided to stick my nose out of the cabin.

'I found Captain Hernandez on the deck just outside the cabin door when I opened it. He'd been shot in the chest and was dead. There was no one else around. I circled the deckhouse, hoping to find Lieutenant Trujillo, but he was nowhere to be seen. I was alone on *La Gloria*. I looked toward shore. I saw the recoilless rifle firing there and a machine gun being set up on a rooftop. I could tell then that the soldiers and police were beating the rebels . . . er, the bandits. Many of the bandits were already dead or injured. Some of them had thrown down their rifles. So I decided the best thing for me was to stay aboard the boat until it was all over and things had been mopped up.'

'A sensible course,' Blanco Rico said. 'A course obviously disrupted, as you were not found aboard *La Gloria* but asleep in your bed.'

'Yes. Well,' I stalled, spinning the tale in my mind only seconds before its telling. 'I was hunkered down below the gunwale closest to shore, watching the action. My back was to the dock. By then, both of the trucks in front of the warehouse were on fire, lighting up the whole area. The shooting had become pretty sporadic. Then I heard someone jump from the dock onto the deck behind me.

'I turned, reaching for the Woodsman in its shoulder holster at the same time. One of the bandits had jumped onto the boat. He had a shotgun and he was swinging the barrel in my direction. The Woodsman caught on one of the straps of the holster. It pulled out of my hand and dropped at my feet. There was no way I was going to be able to pick up the gun and get off a shot before the bandit fired. So I jumped over the gunwale just as the shotgun went off.'

'And you made it without so much as a scratch,' Blanco Rico said. 'You were very fortunate, Henry.'

'Yes. Yes, the buckshot tore into the rail right where I had been standing. As soon as I hit the water, I swam right up against the hull of the boat, treading water there in case he came for me. And it was a good thing, because he did, looking over the gunwale, searching the water for me. He looked out, away from the boat, expecting me to swim for shore but I kept treading water in the hull's shadow. After a couple of minutes, he left. He must have thought he got me with the shotgun blast and I'd sunk after I hit the water.

'I treaded water for a good fifteen minutes. I didn't want to take the chance that the gunsel was sitting on *La Gloria*'s deck waiting for me to come back aboard. I heard things go quiet on shore, then some shouting, and a minute later a big fusillade of fire. After that, there was only a single shot here and there.

'I figured it was all over and tried to haul myself up by one of the boat's lines that was dragging in the water but I wasn't strong enough. Too tired, I guess, after all that time treading water. So I swam around the bow, looking for a way out of the water. When I came around to the other side of the boat, there was a strong current from the incoming tide. It pushed me away from the boat and carried me further back into the harbor.

'At first I tried to fight the current but I'm not a strong swimmer and I realized that, as tired as I was, if I fought it much longer I'd drown. So I rode the tide along the harbor shoreline for maybe five hundred yards until it pushed me near a mudflat. I used what strength I had remaining to swim to the flat and climb over the seawall to shore.

'I stayed there a while, recovering. I could see along the road to where the soldiers moved among the dead and wounded bandits. I could see what the soldiers were doing to the wounded bandits.'

'Unfortunately, this murderous criminal element has to be dealt with severely,' Blanco Rico said, making a good show of his distaste at what he'd no doubt ordered his troops to do.

'I thought about walking down the road to the troops and police,' I continued. 'But, given what I was seeing, walking in soaking wet and out of uniform didn't seem to be the smartest move to make. So I walked in the opposite direction and then looped around north, looking for a taxi. There were none until I got all the way to Chinatown, where I found a cabbie asleep in his car in front of a dim sum place. I woke him up and he took me home. By the time I got in, it was four in the morning. I was exhausted and fell into bed. Next thing I know Sergeant Alvarez was knocking on my door.'

I waited to see my story's effect. I'm a pretty good liar. You can't do intelligence work if you're not but I hadn't really had much call for it when I was in the OSI. Presque Isle wasn't a hotbed of the type of counterintelligence activity that requires much lying. The situation I was in now, though, needed a master. And I knew, in Colonel Blanco Rico, that I was up against a master. The next few minutes would let me know if I belonged in the same category as him. Or if I was going to end up like Marta, or worse.

The colonel stood. 'A remarkable story, Henry. You are very lucky to be alive.'

I thought I might as well brass it out. 'I consider myself lucky but some say a man makes his own luck.'

'There are many in the casinos along the Malecón who say that luck is in the hands of the gods, or fate,' Blanco Rico said.

'Or the house,' I said. 'Whatever way it is, it's time for me to cash in my chips. I agree to the sixty-five hundred pesos. You can even take the cost of the lost gun out, if you wish. Either way, I'd like the money now, if possible.'

'Of course, Henry. Do not trouble yourself about the firearm. I am certain that one of the soldiers or policemen picked it up and the report simply has not reached me yet. There were so many guns to be accounted for, after all.' The colonel opened his desk drawer and counted out thirteen red-backed five-hundred-peso banknotes from a manila envelope there. Unlucky thirteen. I hoped it wasn't an omen. He pushed the money across the desk to me. 'With the gratitude of the Republic of Cuba.'

'Thanks,' I said. I riffled through the red and gray stack of bills and dropped them into my jacket pocket. 'I guess I'll be on my way, Colonel.'

'I will see you out, Henry.'

Something about the colonel's eyes told me I really did not want him walking me out. 'That's OK, Colonel. I can find my own way.'

'No, Henry, I insist. There is something I want to show you on your way.'

FORTY-FIVE

C olonel Blanco Rico's words felt like a punch in the gut with a pair of brass knuckles. I had already been down the long hall leading from his office. I had seen all I wanted to see of what went on in the dank rooms along that hallway and heard all I ever wanted to hear from the tormented souls closeted behind the black doors lining it.

The trouble was, it didn't seem as though I had a choice. The door to the colonel's office popped open. Instead of the clerk who had ushered me in and out in the past, Sergeant Alvarez waited there with two particularly muscular enlisted men, each of whom had a Thompson slung over his shoulder. And I had to believe that the ammunition in those Tommy guns' stick magazines was not defective.

Blanco Rico stared at me expectantly.

'Well, Colonel, I guess I have some time available to see whatever you have to show me,' I said.

'Good, Henry.' Blanco Rico gave an 'after you' gesture with his hand. 'I think you will be very interested.'

As I walked out the office door, Sergeant Alvarez fell in step in front of me. The clerk in the outer office glanced up for a moment as I passed, before returning to pecking at his typewriter. I guess people were escorted out of the colonel's inner office by armed men fairly often, given the clerk's bland response. Blanco Rico walked beside me, with the two big boys and their Tommy guns bringing up the rear. I hoped this little parade was not my escort to a permanent home in one of the Comandancia General's musty cells. I kept an outward appearance of calm that probably didn't fool any of my companions by telling myself that if Blanco Rico had intended to put me in a cell, or worse, he would not have gone through the charade of paying me in his office. I told myself that and I found it almost believable. Almost.

'You know, Henry, many brave soldiers and police officers

died fighting the bandits last night.' The colonel spoke in a familiar, easy tone, as if we were two old friends gossiping during a stroll along the Malecón on a sunny afternoon. 'One policeman was killed somewhat removed from the rest of the action, near the harbor rail yard. The bandits must have been scattered all over the area.'

'That so?'

'Yes. Tell me, Henry, the place where you came out of the water after the tide took you, was that near the rail yard?'

'Yes. Maybe two hundred yards away to the north.' Just like adding a pinch of salt to bread to make it palatable, it's best to include a bit of truth with one's lies. I hoped Blanco Rico would swallow what I said, wherever this was going.

'Did you see any police there, or nearby?'

'As I said, Colonel, I really wasn't seeking any encounters with the police. But, no, there were none in the area where I came ashore. None that I saw.'

'This officer, the one who was killed, had his patrol car taken by the killer. The car was found earlier this morning, near the Hotel Inglaterra. We searched the neighborhood for perpetrators but none were found. The officers who did the canvassing did not even turn up anyone who had seen anything. And the patrol car had been wiped clean of fingerprints. A very professional getaway. You did not see a police vehicle in the area near where you came ashore?'

'No, Colonel. Like I said, I came in maybe five or six hundred feet away from the rail yard. I didn't see a soul.'

'And you heard nothing?'

'There was still some shooting going on.' We walked by the first of the black cell doors along the hallway. The sound of a beating taking place behind the door, with labored breathing and the heavy thump of a truncheon on flesh, reached my ears. Apparently the recipient was too far gone to utter a sound, even to plead for mercy. 'But the gunfire wasn't close, more like down by the two trucks parked outside the warehouse. Nothing close by.'

'That is surprising, because the police officer died of multiple gunshot wounds. There had to have been loud reports when that occurred.'

It was not a question but the colonel paused like it was, so I answered. 'Maybe it took place before or after I was in the area. Or maybe the gun had a suppressor.'

'The bandits are not that sophisticated, Henry. And it was nine-millimeter ammunition which killed the officer, not a caliber the bandits usually use. They tend to stick to the more common loads that can be obtained from the United States – .45, .38 caliber, even .22.'

We passed a cell with its door ajar. A cleaning lady was inside, mopping a dark stain at the foot of the room's only furniture, a metal table with its legs bolted to the floor.

'Even most of our military forces use calibers common to the United States,' Blanco Rico continued. 'Except for the navy. It issues the Rosario Hi-Power pistol to its officers in nine-millimeter.'

'Yes,' I said. 'I saw that Captain Hernandez carried one.'

'It was not with his body when he was found.' I was beginning to feel as if Blanco Rico was toying with me in his perverse and sadistic way.

'One of the bandits must have taken it,' I said.

'Yes, I suppose,' the colonel said. 'Well, here we are.' He stopped before a wooden door like all the others, dark with age and reinforced with strap iron. There was a small barred window set in the door, with a cloth hung on the inside, almost like a curtain. Homey, except there was nothing remotely homey going on in the cell. I heard a muffled voice from interior, moaning and begging, followed by the buzz and snap of electrical current passing through the stale air. The smell of ozone and feces wafted into the hallway through the thin cloth covering the window.

Sergeant Alvarez drew a loop of keys from his pocket, fingered his way through several, and jammed the one he selected into the lock. He gave me a Cheshire cat smile as he stepped out of the way to reveal the horror inside.

FORTY-SIX

t was all there as I remembered it – the bulb dangling from the single cord providing the only light in the vault-like gloom; the chair in the center of the room; the smell of every human bodily fluid, all expelled involuntarily, commingling in a stench which made my gut twist and the gorge rise to the back of my teeth; the heaviness of the air with humidity, fear, and dread, a heaviness so palpable it felt like a weight on my skin; the silence, pregnant, ominous, magnified by the anticipation of the next discharge from the electrical apparatus on the small table and the attendant wail for mercy from the figure strapped upright in the chair. There, too, was the man Colonel Blanco Rico had called the Electrician, fiddling as before with his electrical control box and car battery, a craftsman whose aptitude was the infliction of pain to the point of his subject's mental and physical collapse, and the nick-of-time withdrawal of his victim from that precipice.

'Please, Henry, step in,' Blanco Rico said. 'This is what I wanted to show you.'

The hallway leading to the cell had hardly been well-lighted but it could have been a Broadway stage compared to the twilight gloom that greeted me when I entered. My eyes did not quickly adjust to allow me to see who was in the inter-rogation chair. I was able to see that the figure there was male – no long hair – and that he was small in stature. The shoulders were hunched, the product of unconsciousness, giving the body of the interrogatee a diminutive, almost elderly appearance. The man wore not a shred of clothing.

Sergeant Alvarez took hold of my upper arm and led me forward into the cell. I followed with zombie-like compliance, my mind numbed by abhorrence to what I knew occurred there, my psyche unable to resist in the face of such monstrosity. As Alvarez moved me to stand in front of the chair, the figure seated there became vaguely recognizable, and, as my eyes adjusted further, familiar.

It was Benny.

'The police picked him up last night as they rounded up stragglers from the gun battle with the bandits,' Blanco Rico said. 'He was not fighting and was not armed. At first, the officers who captured him thought he might not be involved, that he was probably just a street urchin who had been caught up in the dragnet. But they were not sure, so they turned him over to SIM. We have been attempting to converse with him since early this morning. He refuses to speak, despite the Electrician's efforts to . . . persuade him otherwise. You know him, do you not?'

Alvarez steered me to where I faced the pathetic figure in the chair full on. Benny's brown skin was slick with sweat. His head drooped against his chest, eyes closed. He was breathing, shallow rapid breaths that weren't quite gasps but were anything but normal. Two wires ran from the Electrician's control box to his genitals.

'Yes,' I said, swallowing back the shock of seeing my young friend this way, knowing that my responses might mean his life. 'He's just a street kid who hangs around my neighborhood. A little slow in the head. He's harmless.'

'He works for you?' Blanco Rico said. Damn, the local stool pigeon, the baker Rojas, must have told them.

'He occasionally runs errands for me. Gets me coffee, that kind of thing. I think everyone in the neighborhood has him do a little something for them once in a while.' They had connected Benny with me, so the best I could do was to make the connection seem commonplace.

'We have reason to believe he has an association with the bandit cadre which battled our forces last night.' The colonel's tone said he was not certain of this, said he invited comment and an explanation. Said that a reasonable explanation would get Benny released.

'I certainly didn't see any associating with bandits from him. He's just a poor kid. Let him go.'

'I'm afraid we cannot do that, Henry. Not until we are certain that he is not a member of the Directorio Revolucionario. You must understand that.'

Of course, Colonel Blanco Rico, I understand. Your hands are tied. You are required by a boy's, a mere child's, lack of cooperation to torture him into a sniveling shell of a human being.

'It's a shame that the boy is not more forthcoming,' the colonel said. Like, it's a shame the store is out of milk today. It's a shame you cut your finger. It's a shame the Cuban Sugar Kings lost the second game of the doubleheader.

'Maybe he would be more forthcoming if your man eased off a bit.' I nodded toward the Electrician. 'My OSI experience taught me that you catch more flies with honey than with vinegar.'

'Catch more flies?' The colonel looked puzzled.

'That you get better results, more information, by treating people with dignity and using persuasion, rather than torturing them.'

'But, Henry, torture, distasteful as it is to me, is persuasion,' Blanco Rico said. 'The ultimate persuasion.'

'It doesn't seem to have worked for you here, Colonel.'

Blanco Rico paused in thought for a moment and then said, 'No, it has not. Perhaps you are right, Henry. Perhaps you can show us how it is done.' He spoke some rapid words in Spanish to Sergeant Alvarez, who picked up a bucket of water from beside the Electrician's worktable and splashed it into Benny's face.

Benny's body reacted to the deluge with a drowning man's gasp and a struggle against the bindings holding him in the chair. His eyes suddenly sprang open, terror-filled and confused, searching the room for context, his brain seeking escape from what it hoped was merely a ghastly dream.

Benny's gaze settled on me. 'Genry,' he said, his affect flat, snot dribbling from a nostril.

'Benny, kid,' I said. I realized I had been thrust into the role of his interrogator and I had to think fast if he, and I, were going to get out of this chamber of misery alive.

'Genry.' Now Benny mustered a smile, the terror fading away, his mind telling him that maybe, just maybe, it *had* all been a nightmare.

I took out my handkerchief and wiped the water and snot from his face.

'Get those things off his balls,' I said, pointing to the two wires coiled around his testicles. Colonel Blanco Rico translated for the Electrician, who snapped on a pair of rubber gloves like he was going to wash the dinner dishes and clumsily unwound the wires. Benny gritted his teeth during the process and sighed with relief when the torturer had finished.

'Do you have a towel or something to cover him?' I asked. Blanco Rico motioned and Sergeant Alvarez went out the door in search of a towel.

'Untie his arms and legs,' I said.

'No, Henry. We will not do that,' the colonel said. 'He still needs to understand where he is.'

Deciding it was best not to argue with the man, I turned my attention to cleaning off Benny with the towels Sergeant Alvarez brought. When I was finished, I draped a towel across Benny's lap.

'Thank you, Genry,' Benny said, his dignity more important to him than the torture he had endured.

'You're welcome, Benny,' I said. I placed a hand on his shoulder and looked him square in the eyes. It was a moment of truth for both of us, where the next few answers to my questions might decide each of our fates. 'Benny, these men have been trying to talk to you, to get information about you. I've told them you're just a kid from the neighborhood but they want to hear it from you. You need to tell them and be honest and then we can both go home. Can you do that for me, Benny?'

I expected Benny to talk then. I expected him to lie, lie through his teeth, put on the Benny charm and sincerity, maybe even the grin, and tell us all he was just a kid who didn't know nuthin' 'bout nuthin'. And then, after a few more hours of me approaching him with the same questions from different angles, and him giving the same innocuous answers, maybe Benny and I would walk away from this dark hole free and easy.

Benny talked all right. He said three words. *'Viva Cuba libre!'* The same three words that were on the lips of the dying men and women of the Directorio Revolucionario during the gun battle the night before, the same three words called out

by assassins as they flung themselves at officials of the corrupt
Batista regime, the same three words that were spoken with
their last gasp by the tortured and the doomed in this very
room every day. Three words of rebellion, defiance, and death.
Three words of hope, triumph, and liberation. Three words
that I knew sealed Benny's fate. Three words that Benny had
chosen as his own epitaph.

Colonel Blanco Rico and Sergeant Alvarez looked on,
recognizing the words as confirmation of Benny's rebel status
but smart enough to stay silent in the hope that more information could be extracted now that Benny had chosen to speak.
And then, once as much intelligence as possible had been
gleaned from him, they would do to Benny what they did to
all rebels. They would kill him.

I racked my brain for a way out of the box Benny had put
himself in, a way to show that he had unknowingly parroted
the words of revolution, that he did not know what he was
saying, that he was a simpleton. I had to pose questions, I
decided, and fast, if the damage which had been done by the
speaking of those three words of defiance was to be mitigated.
I would proceed with a straight interrogation and hope that
Benny would backtrack.

'Who are the members of the Directorio Revolucionario
known to you, Benny?' I asked.

His answer was silence accompanied by the slightest of
twists at the corner of his mouth, a secret sign to me that he
knew the game I hoped to play and he had chosen not to
participate.

'How many cells does the Directorio Revolucionario
have in the greater Havana area, Benny? Just give me the
information and I am sure you will be released.'

Silence.

'You've got to trust me on this, Benny. Who gave orders to
the Directorio cell that you belonged to?'

More silence. Silence for hours. Silence in the face of
question after question, all during the morning and into the
afternoon. Silence and just the slight twist of a smile.

FORTY-SEVEN

'Enough of this,' Colonel Blanco Rico said from the darkness behind where Benny sat. Chairs had been brought in for the colonel, Alvarez, and the guards after the first hour of my interrogation. Only the Electrician had remained standing, waiting expectantly beside his control box and wires while I tried to get Benny to save his own life.

'Gadiel, prepare him.' I wondered to whom Blanco Rico spoke until I saw the Electrician begin working with his equipment. So he had a name, after all.

'Colonel, you don't need to do this,' I said. 'He is just a kid. He doesn't know anything except a meaningless saying he picked up on the street. He doesn't know anything except how to be stubborn.'

Electricity crackled in the room as Gadiel the Electrician tested his apparatus.

'Why do you have an interest in protecting this filth, Henry?' the colonel said. 'He is nothing to you. He is nothing at all.'

'I just don't think the kid knows anything, that's all.'

'We shall see.' Blanco Rico signaled. The Electrician pulled on his rubber gloves with a snap and applied his wires as Benny sat impassive. Then the screaming and convulsions, the twisting against the leather restraints until one broke in half. Benny slouched, spent and glassy-eyed, while the restraint was repaired.

The Electrician began another session, more intense than the last, if that was possible, until Benny evacuated all that was left in his bowels and his bladder. The Electrician cut the power.

Then, sitting in his own waste, Benny spoke, barely able to get out the whispered words.

'*Viva Cuba libre.*'

'This is a useless expenditure of my valuable time,' Colonel Blanco Rico spat, the disgust on his face either a reaction to

Benny's resolve or to the fouled air in the cell. 'Sergeant Alvarez, the pistol.'

Alvarez looked at me and smiled, then opened his uniform tunic and drew out a gun from a shoulder holster. A Colt Woodsman. *The* Woodsman.

'I see from your expression that you recognize your gun,' Blanco Rico said. 'The bandit Celia Nunez was seen tossing it into a trash barrel just before she was killed evading capture this morning. The serial number on the second gun she carried, a Rosario Hi-Power, matched that of the one issued to Captain Hernandez. It was the second gun that she used in the shoot-out which ended in her death.'

It was all I could do to keep my poker face. Or maybe I didn't. I don't know. I do know I said, 'She was one of the five on the Council of Leaders of the Directorio.'

'Yes,' the colonel said. 'All five are now dead. Only the one known as El Fuerte may still be at large. Or he may have been one of the five killed. That is why we worked so hard on this one, this Benny, in hope of learning who El Fuerte is, or was. It is important to know if El Fuerte is dead, and to publicize the death so that any followers who remain loyal to him abandon their hopes.'

'They never spoke of him by any other name,' I lied. 'How can this kid know? They didn't tell me and they trusted me with almost everything.'

'Possibly,' Blanco Rico said. 'Or possibly you know more than you admit. Possibly you have loyalties that you are not prepared to admit, either, Henry.'

'What do you mean, Colonel? My loyalty on this is to you, or rather, to the agreement we made. I fulfilled that agreement. End of transaction. In fact, I've gone above and beyond today, assisting in the interrogation of this prisoner.'

'I understand what you are saying, Henry. But, as you know, some among us had questions of your loyalty to the government of the republic even before yesterday's events. There was, of course, your transgression with the down-payment received from the bandits. And the events of last night, while successful, served only to raise new questions. How, for instance, did Celia Nunez manage to obtain your gun and that of Captain Hernandez? Why did you flee from the fighting rather than remain aboard *La Gloria* until found? I know, you have related your version of events and I want to believe you, I really do. But there are some who feel you are implicated in the deaths of Captain Hernandez, Lieutenant Trujillo, and the policeman killed near the rail yard. There are some who believe you had a hand in Celia Nunez's near-escape. There are some, like Senator Bauza, who believe you have taken the side of the bandits against the duly elected government of the nation.'

'Colonel, you know I didn't do those things. You know I've kept my end of the bargain.'

'What I know, Henry, is that some things point in a direction the opposite of what you suggest. What I also know is that a factual determination of your loyalty based upon the information we have been able to gather, and probably what we shall learn in the future, is impossible. This is problematic not just for me but for you, because those who suspect you would resolve all doubts by the expediency of putting a bullet in your brain.' He paused to let the threat sink in.

'I have pondered this question and come up with an alternative which should resolve the issue,' Blanco Rico continued. 'And spare *you* the bullet to the brain. We have here your acquaintance Benny, who has proven by his conduct and resistance that he is most certainly a bandit member of the Directorio Revolucionario. He deserves a sentence of death for his participation in the killing of the soldiers and police officers which took place last night, and on many occasions before that time, at the hands of the Directorio. So, with one bullet we can resolve two issues – Benny's punishment and your loyalty to the regime.'

Colonel Blanco Rico held out his hand to Sergeant Alvarez, who placed the Woodsman in it. Though there was no signal made to them, both enlisted men unshouldered their Thompsons, drew back the bolts, and stood at the ready. The colonel racked the slide on the Woodsman to put a round into the firing chamber, snapped on the safety, and handed the gun to me, butt first.

'Execute the traitor, Henry,' Blanco Rico said.

Benny looked up, then. His head had been lolling against
his chest but now he sat as upright as possible in the restraints
and gazed straight into my eyes.

'I'm no murderer, Colonel. And this isn't my fight,' I said.
There was no way I was going to pull the trigger. I decided
in that second that I was ready to die, ready to join Fannie
Knutsen in the suicides' graveyard, willing to end it all. I
considered turning the gun on the colonel but he had stepped
to one side and his two mutts had their Thompsons trained
low on me. If I so much as twitched the barrel of the
Woodsman in Blanco Rico's direction, they would cut me in
half before I could snap off a shot.

I stared down at the pistol in my hand, not moving, feeling
trickles of sweat run down from my armpits along my ribs and
the small of my back, the room stuffy and hot as a thousand
furnaces. And I did nothing.

'Come, Henry, you must decide. It is the criminal or
you. I would hate for it to be you,' Blanco Rico said.

I stood stock-still.

'Ah, I had hoped it would not come to this, Henry, that you
would not be prepared to die for this scum who will die
anyway.' The colonel gave a sad shake of his head. 'We had
plans for you, Henry.'

'I guess you'll have to scrap those plans.'

'So unfortunate, Henry.' Blanco Rico sighed as though in
his black heart he was genuinely chagrined. 'But there is still
hope for you. Sergeant Alvarez, go see about the call.'

FORTY-EIGHT

Sergeant Alvarez hustled out through the cell door. We who remained waited silently, except for Benny, who murmured the Catholic prayer of the dying:

> *Holy Mary, pray for me.*
> *Saint Joseph, pray for me.*
> *Jesus, Mary and Joseph,*
> *Comfort me in my last agony.*

In a quarter of an hour, Alvarez returned, carrying a black telephone with a short cord ending in a three-pronged plug. He inserted the plug into a jack I hadn't noticed in the wall, placed the device on the Electrician's table, lifted the receiver and listened. Then he said, '*Sí*,' and handed the telephone to me.

Not knowing what else to do, I put the receiver to my ear and said, 'Hello?' There was a whirring sound on the line, then static and a pop. Then an excited teen voice. 'Henry? Hello, Henry, are you there? Henry? It's me, Janet.'

My head spun. The incongruity of getting a call from my kid sister while in a torture chamber in a Cuban prison was more than my knees could handle. I sank into one of the chairs which had been vacated by one of the enlisted men.

'Janet?' It was all I could get out.

'Henry! Oh, Henry, I can't believe I'm talking to you all the way down in Cuba from New Jersey! And it's so clear, Henry. Oh, it's so good to hear your voice!'

'Janet . . . how?'

My kid sister giggled, her laughter like a dozen tiny glass bells, like she was standing next to me. 'Oh, it is a surprise! Your friend said you'd be surprised. Oh, he's so nice, Henry, bringing me a big bouquet of flowers and . . .'

'My friend?'

'Your friend Larry from down in Cuba. He wants to talk to you. Here, Larry.'

There was a rustling on the line and then, 'Hiya, sport, how ya doin'? I guess your old buddy pulled one over on you this time, hey, sport? How're things down sunny Havana way? Still chasin' the señoritas?'

Even across the miles and with the sometimes mediocre telephone connection, the voice of the man at the other end of the line was easily recognizable. I guess maybe when a man beats you up, your body and your brain remember everything about the experience. The sound of Santo Trafficante's errand boy's voice hit me as hard as one of his punches.

'Yeah, that's rich, Henry,' Larry laughed. He was carrying on the conversation whether I was going to participate or not. 'We really surprised you, Janet and me, didn't we?'

I gripped the phone as if Janet's life depended on it and said, 'If you harm a hair on her head . . .'

'What's that, Henry? What're you gonna do?' Larry carried on the imaginary conversation between us good friends. 'Oh, yeah, yeah, sure, they're treatin' me fine. Fine. Your sister's a peach, and your Uncle Pete and Aunt Ruth are swell. They've been acting just like I'm family once they heard how we's friends down in Havana. Shoot, your Aunt Ruth has asked me to stay to dinner. What a fine lady. She's makin' a big pot roast, says it's one of your favorites and bein' as I'm your bosom friend I ought to love it, too. An' your Uncle Pete even brought out the good hooch, poured me a big glass. Course, they were mighty happy to get the package I brought with me for them. They're treatin' me like I was more than just a buddy of yours making a delivery to them.'

'Package?' My blood was ice in my veins.

'Yeah, you know. Hey, your kid sister wants to thank you for it.'

Janet's voice came back on the line, filled with excitement. 'Henry, we couldn't believe the gift you sent along with Larry. Twenty-five hundred dollars! You must be doing great in Cuba to have that kind of money to spare for your little sister and your aunt and uncle.'

I got out a 'Yeah, great' before Janet bubbled along. 'Henry, the money is going to come in so handy for us. Uncle Pete's old Crosley station wagon is about on its last legs, so we're going to trade it in for a newer car. And we're going to get a television! Oh, Henry, I can't believe how lucky we are to have you helping us. And you're lucky to have a good friend like Larry helping you in Cuba. He says you and he are gonna be business partners, maybe open up a detective agency together. Is that right, Henry?'

'Yeah. Sure. Say, could you put Uncle Pete on the line?' I didn't know what I was going to say but I had to try to clue him in to the danger posed by Larry.

'Hiya, nephew. How's things down Havana way?' Uncle Pete's voice was cheery, not offering any hint that he knew the danger he, Janet, and Aunt Ruth faced. He slurred his words slightly, evidence that he and Larry had indeed been partaking of the good hooch.

'Things are fine, Uncle Pete. How's Aunt Ruth?'

'Ah, she's fine, boy. Says if it wasn't for me holding her back, she'd go off and find a younger man in Havana herself, since life must be so easy down there.' Uncle Pete gave a bluff guffaw. 'Say, Henry, things must be pretty good there, to send that kind of money up for us.'

'Yes. Yes, they are. Say, Uncle Pete . . .' I hesitated and knew in that moment that there was no way I could convey anything to my uncle that would result in something other than placing my entire family in more danger than they already were. 'Say . . . can you put Larry back on. I have some business to discuss with him.'

A rattle and scrape and Larry was back. 'Yeah, sport?'

'I swear to you, you bastard, touch any of them and I will hunt you down and there is no place where you can hide . . .' Then Colonel Blanco Rico jerked the phone from my hand.

'Stand by,' he said to Larry. 'And keep talking.'

'OK, sure,' I heard the faraway voice on the phone say and then begin an inane monologue of questions and answers that trailed off as the colonel wrapped the receiver in a towel and placed it next to the Electrician's torture machine.

Colonel Blanco Rico had me in a box. The presence of Santo Trafficante's muscle was to send a message to cooperate or my family would pay. The only way out of the box was for someone to die. If I chose myself as that person, it was possible that Janet, Uncle Pete, and Aunt Ruth would die, too. At least, that was the implication. And I was sure Benny would die as well. But what if I acceded and followed the colonel's instruction? What if I chose Benny to die?

'The traitor must die,' Blanco Rico said, seeming to read my thoughts.

I looked at Benny. He stared directly into my eyes and smiled his twisted, little-old-man smile. Then he said, 'It's all right, Genry. Do it. You have no choice.'

The Woodsman in my hand seemed to weigh a ton. My movement was clumsy with the weight of the gun, the weight of dread, the weight of hopelessness, as I swung the barrel to within inches of Benny's temple. I moved the safety open.

'Do it, Genry.' Benny gave an encouraging nod.

I pulled the trigger.

FORTY-NINE

The hollow snap of the firing pin into the Woodsman's chamber drove a jolt through my very being. In the split second between the snap and the realization that the gun was not loaded, something died inside me. I don't know what it was, exactly. Maybe it was my last shred of humanity. Maybe it was my immortal soul. Whatever it was, it felt like it was gone, and gone for good, never to return.

The dry firing of the pistol had sent a shudder through Benny, too, a massive reaction to the minuscule click of the trigger. As the shudder subsided, he began to weep, quietly at first, and then in great racking sobs, his head turned toward the wall. Part of me wanted to embrace and hold him, to comfort him as he tried to claw his way back to life after looking into the yawning maw of death, to tell him he was alive and it was going to be all right. But it wasn't going to be all right and I knew that it never would be again, not for him, if the thugs arrayed around us in the room allowed him to live. Not for me, ever.

I let the arm holding the Woodsman fall to my side, heard a chuckle, and turned to see Alvarez and the Electrician enjoying the moment. Sick bastards.

Colonel Blanco Rico was more restrained, his face severe as he said, 'Good, Henry. I had no doubts as to where your loyalties lay. I will be able to tell Senator Bauza, Señor Trafficante, and the others that their misgivings were without foundation.'

I stared down at the towel holding the telephone receiver from which Larry's muffled voice prattled on. The colonel nodded to me and picked up the phone. 'Larry, this is Colonel Blanco Rico. The situation here has been favorably resolved. Please bid farewell to Señor Gore's family for him and see that they come to no harm. I will be certain to mention your careful handling of your role in this matter to Señor Trafficante.' He hung up the phone and unplugged it from the wall.

I wanted out of the room, out of sight of Blanco Rico, out of Havana, out of the whole rancid, rotting country of Cuba. I stepped to the Electrician's table, dropped the Woodsman on it, and made for the door. The two enlisted men interposed themselves between me and the exit, their Thompsons at port arms.

'I've done all you've asked, Colonel,' I said.

'You have,' Blanco Rico said. 'You have even delivered El Fuerte to us. That is right, Henry. Celia Nunez admitted she was the leader of the Directorio Revolucionario with her dying breath. You have done much. But there is more to be done.'

'Not for me. I'm leaving Cuba. On this afternoon's flight to Miami. For good.'

'Henry, think about what you are doing. Have you not been well paid? And do you not have the satisfaction of aiding President Batista and the people of Cuba in their fight against the lawlessness which threatens our country? A reliable man with your background and capabilities is difficult to locate. We need you, Henry.'

'Some other time, Colonel.'

'Well, Henry, I had hoped it would not come to this, but I cannot allow you to leave the country. The senate has decided to hold hearings on the bandit menace. Your testimony will be needed. Senator Bauza has instructed me to hold your passport for safekeeping until the hearings are concluded.'

'When do the hearings begin?'

'They have not been scheduled as yet.'

'I see.'

'And there is the question of your family.'

'I see.' And I did see. I saw it all. Saw that they owned me. Saw that I would probably die in Cuba.

'The kid walks, then,' I said.

Colonel Blanco Rico made a great show of his insincere dismay. 'I am afraid that is not possible, Henry. The young man is an enemy of the people and must pay the price for his crimes.'

'No crimes have been proven, or admitted,' I said.

'A release from custody in the face of such damning evidence would be most irregular. We are, after all, a nation of laws.' When the colonel said this, I knew the door was open, only a crack, but open. Blanco Rico wanted something. Benny's life, maybe even his freedom, could be obtained if I could just deliver that something.

'What is it you want, Colonel Blanco Rico?' I asked. In 1957 Havana, where mothers and daughters plainly offer themselves on the street corners, where the police stage shakedowns of tourists on the Malecón in the broad tropical daylight, where gangsters like Santo Trafficante and Meyer Lansky pass bags of cash across lunch tables in the finest restaurants in town to politicians on the take, the oblique approach is not in vogue. 'Tell me what you want.'

'There is a minor bandit problem in the east, in the Sierra Maestra,' Blanco Rico said. 'A renegade lawyer named Fidel Castro, his brother Raúl, and a handful of others are hiding in the mountains, claiming to make a revolution. They have been desperately trying to acquire arms. We have an informant, a "thirty-three", who has made some peripheral contact with them, claiming he can get them guns from America. I believe an operation like the one you just completed will put an end to them. We need a *gringo* to masquerade as an arms dealer. You.'

'Only if Benny walks free.'

Blanco Rico did not hesitate. 'If that is what it takes, Henry, yes.'

'I'm your man, then,' I said.

ACKNOWLEDGMENTS

Thanks are due T.J. English for his book, *Havana Nocturne*, which provided valuable background information on pre-Castro Cuba and the involvement of American gangsters there.

Posthumous gratitude to my mentor and law partner, J.C. Wm. Tattersall, who shared his experiences as a US Air Force Office of Special Investigations agent in the early 1950s with me, providing the backstory for the protagonist in this work. I only wish he had lived to see this book.

Thanks to first reader Ed Duncan for his always-cogent input on this story.

My appreciation and sincere thanks to my editor, Rachel Slatter, for her gentle editorial manner and reasoned insights. Thanks as well to Nicholas Blake for his exacting copyediting; to Martin Brown for his crackerjack marketing and publicity efforts; to Natasha Bell for putting this book together; and to the rest of the team at Severn House for all you do.

And to Irene – least-critical critic, most enthusiastic reader, tolerator of the intolerable – my thanks and love.